BANK

BANK

a novel

david bledin

Back Bay Books
Little, Brown and Company
New York • Boston • London

For my family

Little, Brown and Company
Hachette Book Group USA
237 Park Avenue, New York, NY 10169
Visit our Web site at www.HachetteBookGroupUSA.com

First Edition: May 2007

The characters and events in this book are fictitious. Any similarity to real persons, living or dead, is coincidental and not intended by the author.

Library of Congress Cataloging-in-Publication Data

Bledin, David.
Bank : a novel / David Bledin.—1st ed.
p. cm.
ISBN 978-0-316-01673-5
1. Investment bankers—Fiction. 2. Success in business—Fiction. 3. Self-realization—Fiction. I. Title.
PS3602. L45B35 2007
813'.6—dc22
2006023021

9 8 7 6 5 4 3 2 1

Text design by Meryl Sussman Levavi
Q-MART

Printed in the United States of America

BANK

#REF!

You know that random idea, this one: If you shove an infinite number of monkeys before an infinite number of typewriters, in a couple of days they're bound to type up every literary masterpiece conceived by their more evolved brethren, albeit with a smattering of typos? Can't you see their furry brown heads bobbing up and down, a few of the more pretentious sporting spectacles and blunt pencils behind their ears, hands pushing keys with a furious sense of purpose, of fulfilling this rhetorical whimsy?

It's an allegory for the Street, sort of. Not that there's an infinite number of us, only a couple thousand confined to our steel-and-concrete spires, and we're not all so hirsute. I'm a bit hairy (my dad's side of the family), have ears that stick out from the sides of my head, and tend to chew on my lower lip, so physically I'm about as close as it gets.

And I'm not typing up the next Great American Novel perched on this wobbly IKEA swivel chair at two in the morning at the end of another non-weekend weekend, meaning I've worked the entire two days. It's a Mergers & Acquisitions spreadsheet calculating what would happen if a huge trucking conglomerate operating out of the Midwest decided to buy seventy-three derelict grain silos down the coastline of California. The spreadsheet's 226 pages. Version 63b. A veritable beast. It's taken four months (off and on) to put together. It's beautiful in its own lunacy, the way raving homeless people can sometimes trick you into believing they're prophets. There's toggles for everything: what would happen if tornadoes wreaked havoc in Missouri, if competitors purchased the silos, if a random terrorist attack resulted in the silos being blown to smithereens, erupting in gales of sulfur and the blackened feathers of pigeons roosting in the rafters. Because that's extremely likely: Al-Qaeda plotting away, twirling their beards—*The silos, we get the silos and victory is ours!*—and throwing their heads back with the inevitable sinister cackling.

I'm almost done, though. Just have to figure out why this balance sheet doesn't balance, pretty sure it's a tax thing, and—

The monitor goes black.

Oh dear.

Oh frickin' dear.

Heart palpitations. I'm breathing funny. Heat rushing up my neck, through my trachea or esophagus, whichever the tube, then spreading downward, so that my fingers and toes tingle. Is this what it feels like to get a heart attack at the tender age of twenty-three? What ever happened to being virile, to being in my physical *prime,* for god's sake? (It's all gone. The last saved version is from eight o'clock, six hours ago.)

I scream. I'm hoping for a thunderous barbarian roar, a bellow to clatter the windows, at the very least some sound that will tear the Star—one of the other analysts who sit in my neck of the woods—away from his spreadsheet, but it comes out as more of a whimper, the sound a small animal like a ferret would make if it was accidentally kicked down the basement stairs.

The phone rings: blocked number. Those weird heart palpitations start up again. It could be the Sycophant, my VP, having tossed and turned in his twin bed (he's recently separated) until he derived a completely revamped approach to the merger.

"Why didn't you call me?"

A flood of relief. It's not the Sycophant.

"This really isn't a good time."

"When is a good time? There hasn't been a good time in the last three weeks."

"Out of all the not-so-good times, this one is probably the worst."

Silence on the other end. I feel an eerily familiar nagging sensation. Yes, it was there at lunch, again at dinner, only for a few seconds before the onslaught of work fizzled it out.

"It's past midnight. You officially missed my birthday."

Of course it was her birthday.

"Look, I . . ."

"It was my goddamn birthday."

There's not much I can say to that. I should have called. Without a doubt, I should have called. Yet the injustice of it, that here I am at two in the morning on a Sunday (technically Monday), and it's not like I'm cavorting around the streets, chugging beer after beer, groping her best friend's breast while I thumb-type groggy birthday wishes into my BlackBerry.

"You're such a bastard."

"Wait, it's not what you— "

Brusquely interrupting, the Girlfriend says, her tone imperious, "You do realize this is the end, right?"

"The end of what?"

"Our relationship. No, scratch that, our anti-relationship."

"But we have an agreement."

I interpret the agreement as follows: She's a fiercely independent redhead in her final year of a master's degree in art history, studying to become a museum curator or a gallery owner, who once confessed she likes the idea of having a boyfriend without really having a boyfriend. I'm a banker, horribly lonely, and I need a focal point for my wealth accumulation, a raison d'être for this bout of slavery, and I enjoy the occasional hand job (you're not exactly a Don Juan when you're consistently pulling one-hundred-hour weeks). To put it bluntly, it's a relationship of convenience for twenty-somethings.

"The agreement's off. My hand is tired."

"That's a low blow."

"Hey, it's the truth."

"We'll go for dinner next week. That Italian place in the Village."

I sound defeated. The Tenuous Girlfriend chuckles wearily.

"You really don't get it, huh?"

"No, I really don't."

Her voice is softer, with not a hint of self-righteousness anymore: "I don't know how it happened, I've been thinking about it and none of it makes any sense, but somehow or other I did the stupid thing and fell in love with you. God forbid genuine feelings should ever creep into this clinical business arrangement we have going, but that's how it is: I really do love you. And I know it's selfish of me to expect you to just stop, to become a vegan farmer or a bassist in an indie band, I'm not asking that of you, but god, couldn't you at least call me on my birthday? I mean, is that such a crazy thing, to want you to pick up the phone for two full minutes and talk to me?"

Silence slips out the pores of the receiver, engulfing the room. I know she's granting me this window of opportunity to backtrack with just a few syllables: I'm truly sorry. I love you, too. I'll be better next time. Then gaining momentum: We can take a trip somewhere; let's head to the Cape next weekend.

But I just can't do it. This is why I cannot do it:

> From: TheSycophant@aol.com
>
> To: Me@theBank.com
>
> Hope you're still at the office. I've been thinking about the model for the trucking deal, the revenue-optimizing correlation in particular. Decided we should do the inverse. Remember Client coming in 8 am, so want to see this by 6 at the latest. If there's an emergency, get my BlackBerry. Don't call—you'll wake my son.

"Fuck."

Blurted out reflexively, the receiver still at my ear.

"I can't believe you—"

"Wait. An e-mail. VP wants the model changed around completely. Cussing is not relevant to anything you just said."

I try to gush it all out before she can hang up on me.

"Hello?"

No answer. There's no dial tone, though, so she might still be on the other end.

"Are you still there?"

An awkward pause, then a barely audible "Yes."

I put my head in my hands, rubbing at my forehead, an exaggerated gesture for nobody's benefit.

"Look, I'm just so tired."

For a second I think I'm going to add to this, spew words worthy of a Shakespearean sonnet, soft, billowy metaphors that somehow don't seem contrived, but no—my head is throbbing, my body is chewing up its own tissue in a foolhardy effort to stay awake, and I have no fucking clue what this revenue-optimizing correlation is all about. So I repeat:

"I'm just so tired. I'm sorry, I know I should say something else. But I've got this terrible headache and I can't think straight and I've still got to put through this change to the model."

She's sobbing now. Nothing overly dramatic; muffled heaving racing along the phone wires. One of the sobs gets lodged in her throat, then breaks free in a wretched hiccup.

"I can't hate you. You said it would be exactly like this right at the beginning. You weren't trying to sugarcoat it or anything. I guess I just didn't believe you. Or maybe I never considered we'd get to the point where I'd actually care how much time we spend together."

I kind of know what she's expecting from me. If I'd just woken up fresh from an eight-hour sleep, if we were sitting outside on a beautiful terrace drinking really good coffee, I feel I'd know exactly what to do. The Girlfriend's not a drama queen—she's smart and genuine and wouldn't want me to say things just for the sake of hearing them. It would have to be more subtle: This is all so comfortable, the coffee, sitting here like this. Or maybe not saying anything at all, just reaching out and touching her cheek, or the back of her neck or something.

But right now it's just not going to happen. It's as if this super-empathetic version of me is goofing around on another planet, trapped under impenetrable layers of fog. And this current me is only a dried-up husk barely capable of forming understandable syntax, let alone trying to navigate a situation as delicate as this one.

"I just can't deal with this right now."

"I'm not going to call again. And please don't call me."

"Look—"

"No, I'm really serious about this. I'm not upset with you, I don't blame you for any of it. I feel bad for myself, sure, but I feel worse for you. Anyway, nothing good is going to come out of me being confrontational right now. Well, good luck."

"I—"

Click.

A moment passes when I know I should be feeling a poetic sense of loss and desertion, but in my current predicament it comes out as more of a relief. Oh shucks. So be it. It's probably for the better anyway; I had no idea what was going to follow that "I—."

I slip into zombie mode. It's official when I'm scrolling down my spreadsheet without doing anything, staring listlessly at the screen while my fingers go *click! clack! click!* against the keyboard. Delete a number. Carry a formula across. Delete a sheet. Should I have deleted that sheet? Probably not. Close the file without saving. Reopen file.

I shrug off my fugue to grab a Coke from the fridge. The first sip is glorious, that slightly acrid taste on my tongue. My body loves this Coke, has triumphantly declared Coke the nectar of the gods. It has to be some near-perfect formula; how else could it be so popular in the West, coveted by little children in Africa, guzzled down by misplaced pygmy tribes? I've got thirty minutes of a sugar rush before I'm going to crash and burn; I need to make sense of the revenue-optimizing correlation in that time frame, and hopefully the rest can be finished up while I'm semicomatose.

There it is, right at the bottom of the second-to-last tab, the work a summer student put together two months back because I couldn't cancel dinner plans with the (now Ex) Girlfriend for the fourth time in a week. It feels funny to dwell on saving a relationship that just ended earlier tonight. Funny to dwell on summer students, these young whippersnappers (look at me calling them whippersnappers when I'm, what, one, at most two, years older) who come to the Bank for a few weeks of kissing ass, hoping to get an offer by the end of their term. Everybody paints the industry in rosy colors because they're as innocent as little lambs. So let them make their own decisions. Don't tell them your dirty little secrets: how you seriously consider doing a flying leap out the window at least once every ten minutes; how you look at hot-dog vendors and homeless people and the guy who scrapes gum off park benches and think, Hey, at least they're not shackled to a computer for twenty hours at a stretch. Instead, there's the nauseating enthusiasm: Look at me, look at me, I was destined for this stuff, I popped out of the womb with a receding hairline and a holster for my BlackBerry.

Calculating the inverse of the revenue-optimizing correlation involves changing E56, one measly cell. It's frustrating to consider I could have changed E56 two hours ago and called it a night, but, thank the lord, it could have been worse. Switch a 1 to a 0. Easy-peasy. I'm about to save the file, flipping through a few of the worksheets, when I spot it:

#REF!

Farther down: #REF! #REF! #REF! #REF! #REF! #REF!

The third sheet is an entire field of #REF!s, those malevolent little imps clamoring for my attention. The source is a circular reference, which means you have a cell referencing another cell that's referencing the original cell—heh, don't worry about it. Take my word that it's a messy situation. A recently dumped, dead-tired investment banker just doesn't stand a chance.

An hour passes with minimal progress. It's always at this point of unbearable bleakness, the overhead lighting in the musty corridors of your brain flickering off bulb by bulb, when you have your brief flash of lucidity. Here it comes, right on schedule:

Nobody cares. Not the Star (who still sits across the room, mirthfully plunking away at his keyboard), not the Sycophant, nor anybody else at the Bank. Nobody gives a damn. And why should they care? You're but one of a few hundred monkeys drooling all over yourself, pumping your bloodstream full of sugar and caffeine, slaving away for a few decades so you can eventually have a long shot at a soft pink creature with shapely legs who'll bear your hairy countenance and stick-out ears for a couple of years while your yacht is moored off the Italian Riviera.

There's a flip side, though: This moment of heightened awareness is also when the monkey transcends its monkeyness. It sees an infinite array of paths looming on the horizon. It can do anything, be anything. See the hole in the mesh cage by the pile of rotten banana peels? That, my fellow monkeys, is freedom. Enough with scratching our butts and licking our fingers in public, swinging endlessly from branch to branch only to elicit a few nervous laughs from otherwise sullen tourists. Come, my brothers and sisters, let us truly live up to our anthropological status as proto-men.

I turn off the monitor and place my head on the desk. It's an awkward position—I'm going to have a sore back in the morning, paper-clip imprints on my cheek—but right now it's pure bliss. The only sounds are the soothing drone of the ventilation unit, the clicking of the Star's fingers racing across the keyboard. The Star, who does not sleep. The Star, who, defying all logical constructs I have developed about this world, is somehow able to love this job. Passionately. You'll be talking to him about this movie you managed to squeeze into your weekend, and all of a sudden he'll have this eerie smile, rock back and forth on his heels, and blurt out, "How great is this? I mean, can you really see yourself doing anything else?"

Try sleeping, buddy.

I nod off. Truly horrible dreams. Not the nightmares of my youth, where old men with wizened faces and rusty box cutters popped up between the cracks of shuttered windows. Not even visions, really. I'm dreaming of Excel functions: tabulating columns, inserting rows, vanquishing the circular references and thereby eliminating the evil #REF!s. Even with the body pleading for release, for just a meager half hour of uninterrupted REM sleep, the mind plays its most sinister trick: It will not shut itself off.

I wake to slivers of glaring August sunlight pouring in through the window across the hall. I feel terrible—tongue caked in halitosis, neck stiff. I'm still exhausted, though my head is no longer pounding as much. Aside from the wrinkles, my shirt has a mysterious brown swath across the front that I don't remember from last night. I turn on my monitor and check the time: 8:15. I won't have time to go home and change before the client meeting.

Client meeting. Fifteen minutes ago.

The zookeeper cracks his whip. The monkey loses its glimmer of transcendence and curls up in a fetal position by the pile of rotten bananas.

That's it.

I'm finished.

One

An axiom of investment banking: It always comes together in the end. Despite impossible deadlines, printer malfunctions, incompetent assistants, carpal tunnel syndrome, network crashes, and wild dashes to the copy room to bind booklets five minutes before a pitch, somehow or other, ninety-nine percent of the work that goes in front of a Client is flawless. Or at the very least, the Client doesn't know any better. It's as if the Bank has little pockets of space that defy conventional physics, wormholes opening up seconds before utter damnation that allow for number crunching surpassing the speed of light.

Or else there's the Star. He wanted to go on a coffee run at four in the morning, whipped an eraser at me, noticed I didn't flinch as it bounced off my forehead, switched on my monitor and read the Sycophant's e-mail, spotted all the #REF!s in the model, promptly slid my swivel chair aside, plunked himself down in front of my computer, and had everything in tip-top shape, delivered in a company car to the Sycophant's bachelor pad by six. My savior is now sitting exactly as I left him, upright in front of his spreadsheet, though he's somehow found the time to change into a freshly pressed shirt.

"Thanks."

I really struggle to make it sound genuine; I can't even begin to fathom what would have happened if the Star hadn't stepped in and saved my ass this morning. Still, there's a poorly concealed reality behind it—the dogged truth that I find him utterly despicable. I'm well aware this is an evil thought, up there in the same league as those dark secrets muffled by a screen during confession. The Star is hands-down the nicest guy in the entire analyst class at the Bank. He's interminably pleasant and modest, chugging along with the disposition of a Buddha, though I've never seen him sleep a wink.

"Don't worry about it. I'm sure you would have done the same."

Would I have? Like hell.

"Yes, of course."

So where does this despicability spring from? Perhaps it's because he can't be entirely human. He just can't. He's like this investment banking superhero, capable of constructing seven discounted cash-flow models while rescuing pregnant ladies from burning buildings. A cyborg, maybe. Or he suffers from a mild case of autism: a bit of a dweeb but with awesome analytical powers. Who knows. Either way, he's setting impossibly high standards.

I hear the Sycophant's voice from just outside the doorway.

"That was a brilliant recommendation. Brilliant! We'll definitely incorporate that into our future models."

Cringe worthy; he has to be talking to the Client.

"It was really a pleasure to meet with you this morning. If you come up with any more suggestions about the competitive environment, you have my card."

The Client mutters something and then he's off. I pull up a spreadsheet, one with lots of numbers, and scatter a few papers across my desk. The Sycophant has this eerie way of sneaking up on you. No footsteps, no friction from the carpet, just this sudden prickling on the back of your neck.

"We could have used you at the meeting. The Client didn't understand the change you made to the revenue-optimizing correlation."

The Sycophant's voice is high and shrill now that he's no longer sucking the lifeblood from some Client's sphincter. He has a rodentlike physicality, so it suits him well. Thin nose, pointed ears pressed flat against the sides of his skull, aerodynamic bone structure. Beady little eyes. There's something unnerving about those eyes being so close, boring into my skin. They're gray and watery and filled with the bitterness of a geeky kid who couldn't get the girls and couldn't play any sports and couldn't even do what's expected of geeky kids like that, mainly cashing in on the late-nineties tech-bubble bonanza and retiring in the Caymans at the age of thirty-something with some washed-up supermodel.

"The package was also fifteen minutes late this morning. When I say six in the morning, I mean six in the morning. Not six-fifteen. You've got to manage your time better from now on."

Those beady little eyes study every twitch of my body. We've all picked up on the fact that the Sycophant's becoming even more of a bastard lately, which is somewhat understandable with his wife running off with the cable guy (a rumor, uncorroborated but highly probable).

"I'm sorry," I mumble.

That's all I'm going to give him, not much to work with. I know it seems like a lack of integrity. What am I saying?—it *is* a lack of integrity.

"And I don't know why you inversed the revenue-optimizing

correlation. It was fine in the previous version. Fix the correlation, then put through these other changes. The Client wants to see the revisions first thing tomorrow."

By handing me his markup he effectively dismisses me. No thank-you for pulling an all-nighter, no acknowledging I'm barely awake, hanging on to reality by only the merest of threads. I look over the markup. His handwriting is barely legible, though this sort of thing is endemic at the Bank. You get accustomed to the omission of vowels, the plethora of code words that are often made up on the fly: STET. Up arrow. Arrow to the right. An omega symbol. Hmm, that's a new one. Surprisingly, it's not too brutal—only a few hours of minor modifications. I can work off a previous version and have the inverse of the inverse of the revenue-optimizing correlation already calculated. Meaning, back to where I started.

♦

"The Star really saved your ass this morning, huh? You look like shit, by the way."

This is from the Defeated One, the other analyst who shares our office. He is the Star's antithesis. He would be the Star's archnemesis if the Star gave us any opportunity to hate him. But no, the Star's just too damn nice. The Defeated One despises investment banking, though he's never going to leave. It's not that he's sadomasochistic. It's the high-maintenance girlfriend. It's the presents that must be lavished on the high-maintenance girlfriend after he's cancelled their dinner plans for the fifth time that week. And also a fledgling coke habit.

He rocks back and forth in his swivel chair and eyes me critically. The Defeated One has a full year of seniority on me, which apparently gives him the right to act the seasoned veteran, while I remain the perpetual newbie.

"Come on, Mumbles. Let's round up Postal Boy and Clyde and get some coffee."

Mumbles is what I go by, a nickname derived from a propensity for mumbling, I guess. The caliber of wit at the Bank is truly staggering. Postal Boy and Clyde are two of the other analysts in the Mergers & Acquisitions group. There's six of us in total: three in this office, three just down the hall.

It's easy to persuade Clyde to join us. Clyde is always up for coffee; he's reliable that way. It's because he does the least amount of work aside from the Prodigal Son, blessed progeny of some executive at the Bank, and the sixth analyst in the M&A group.

Postal Boy is hunched before his monitor, making grunting noises under his breath. There is a possibility he looks even worse than I do. Big bags droop under his eyes, and his glasses are askew on the bridge of his nose. His hair is matted down unsuccessfully, so little strands poke up in a myriad of directions. Postal Boy is the second-hardest-working analyst in our M&A sextet, just below the Star. Yet unlike the Star, who makes everything look so easy, Postal Boy shows the strain of his effort: pimples induced by an endless stream of sugar between four and six in the morning, a nervous twitch of his left eye, and the tendency to curl his hands into fists for no apparent reason.

The Defeated One is convinced Postal Boy's going to lose it one day, a Columbine of the banking world. I disagree. He works too hard, no doubt about that, and there is definitely some serious repression going on, but *postal?* The eye twitch is pretty creepy, though, I'll give him that.

"Postal, get your shit together. We're heading down for some coffee."

Postal Boy speaks in a slow, monotonous drone. "Can't. Have to finish these comps."

"They can wait."

"No. They have to be finished up by ten."

The Defeated One kicks the back of Postal Boy's chair hard. Postal Boy lurches forward, knocking a Diet Coke off the desk, which spills onto a stack of papers left on the floor. Postal Boy frowns at the wet papers and the growing splotch on the carpet and readjusts his glasses.

"Fine," he sighs with resignation, "but we have to make it quick."

On the way to the elevators, walking slightly ahead with the Defeated One, I say, "You shouldn't have done that."

"Done what?"

"Kicked his chair like that."

"Why not?"

"Hey, you're the one who called it. It's going to be on your shoulders if we're all riddled with bullets one day."

The Defeated One chuckles, shaking his head. He's not really an asshole, just very, very bitter.

"Think about it. It's brilliant. Get him all riled up and who does he take out first? Prodigal Son—bon voyage. Clyde—that's a bit of a bummer. Sycophant—gone. The Philandering Managing Director—gone. By the time he's through with them all, we'll have barricaded the door to our office. Maybe used the Star as bait or something. It would be a beautiful thing. Can you imagine never having to deal with the Sycophant again? For that, we sacrifice Clyde."

"I don't know. He might come looking for you first. I go second based on geographic proximity."

"Nah, Postal's eruption will be so atomic that logic won't play a factor. He'll take out the first things moving."

The Defeated One is designated the scout. He pokes his head out into the reception area, ensuring there is no senior employee waiting for the elevators, and we make a scramble for it. Dammit—all the elevators are on the ground floor. Bad scenario: The elevator pings open and somebody superimportant steps out and cracks some smart-aleck remark ("Hey, you fellas are all taking the elevator down together? Has the M&A department bought out some insurance policy for that?"), and we chuckle politely, blush a bit, and the superimportant person shuffles off, thinking, Man, those analysts don't work as hard as they did back in the day. Worse scenario: Superimportant person steps into the elevator with us, and during the awkward descent of thirty-two floors, we have to scrounge up some basketball statistic or enlightened commentary on inflation when all the while the superimportant person is thinking about the six-over-par round he shot that morning.

The elevator opens. It's empty. First sigh of relief. The elevator closes without anybody karate-chopping the doors at the last instant. Second sigh of relief. A cardinal rule of elevators: Unless there's a superimportant person in there with us, somebody worthy of foolish chatter in a futile attempt to impress, the elevator is a temple of silence. As with a urinal. Chattering away while using a urinal is deserving of ancient forms of torture.

The little screen that displays ads and bits of trivia and SAT words we're never going to use once in our lives, not ever, is filled with static. A buzzing noise. Not the static. Clyde is singing something. It's mostly under his breath, but I think I hear the Spice Girls, the chorus of "Wannabe."

Clyde is an odd one. Not that we aren't all a little odd, especially in this industry, but Clyde is a little odder than most. It's a difficult sort of odd to pinpoint. The Defeated One and I have played this game many times before: What is it about Clyde that's not quite right? Physically he is fairly nondescript: reddish hair, pale skin, an unassuming mouth and nose. He looks a bit like Archie from the comics, the sucking-up-to-Mr.-Weatherbee Archie, not the suave incarnation who has those two babes lusting after him.

Maybe it's because we don't really know him. Sure, he laughs at our jokes, makes a few half-hearted attempts of his own, but it always comes across so detached, like he's trying to seem relatively normal when there is something else churning around that head of his. God knows what. Flying monkeys. Promiscuous cowgirls. We know this: He's kind of lazy, but then, he doesn't really need the money; his dad is a construction magnate or something like that. He frequently does crazy shit just for the sake of doing it: smoking pot in the drug-testing bathroom tucked away behind the trading floor, trying to figure out which porn sites escape the filters, in the middle of the day, when the assistants are still roaming about. We're pretty certain he's a nice guy, but then, maybe he isn't. Maybe he goes home to wherever he lives and sticks pins into little effigies of us. Or plays ultra-violent video games. Maybe he's the real postal potential.

Make it last forever, friendship never ends.

At the twenty-first floor, the Defeated One breaks the cardinal rule of not speaking in elevators.

"Clyde, are you singing the Spice Girls?"

"Yeah, I am."

"Why?"

"Because it's catchy."

"But it's the Spice Girls."

"Who cares?"

The Defeated One shakes his head, but there's not much he can say to that. Such is the Way of Clyde: He just doesn't give a damn.

A line of Cole Haan loafers and Prada heels snakes out from the perpetually packed Starbucks in the lobby of our office tower. Starbucks—last refuge of the investment banker, the only place you have some modicum of privacy, and even then you're never entirely certain a Managing Director isn't breathing down the back of your neck. There is a quartet of ridiculously hot twenty-somethings a little ahead in the line. Based on the manner of their dress—oversized tinted sunglasses, weird frilly handbags, cleavage-enhancing blouses—they have to be in Public Relations. The Defeated One tries to make eye contact and fails miserably.

Clyde mutters behind me, "Crap. Philandering Managing Director at three o'clock."

I look over my shoulder as discreetly as possible. If we stay facing forward, there is a chance he may pass by without distinguishing the back of our suits from the rest of this crowd. The Philandering Managing Director is a bulky ex-linebacker alpha-male type whose previous four assistants resigned abruptly over the past six months. He stops at the other end of the lobby to chat up a blond woman in a librarian's skirt. She looks vaguely familiar; I think she works in Technical Support.

Postal Boy is getting fidgety. He's mopping sweat off his forehead and his left eye is twitching all over the place.

"I can't wait any longer. I've got to get back upstairs."

The Defeated One eyes him sternly. "No. You look like shit. Mumbles looks like shit. You have my word that I feel like absolute shit. Postal, we are entitled to our coffee."

The Philandering Managing Director and his latest conquest cross the lobby and exit through the revolving doors.

"See, they won't even notice."

Clyde has the best vantage point; he can see them through the window.

"Nah, she's just having a smoke while the Philanderer chats her up. There's no movement toward the parking garage; this doesn't look like it's gonna turn into a quickie. He'll drop in on the way back."

There are three people in front of us in the line now and three cash registers. The odds are pretty good we'll have our coffees before the cigarette is out.

"No fancy drinks," the Defeated One instructs. "Just black. We don't have time for any namby-pamby cappuccinos."

I like my namby-pamby cappuccinos, especially when the Asian barista with the Coke-bottle glasses is at the drinks station. She's one of the rare Starbucks employees who's mastered the art of the foam: She ensures it stays in the cup all the way down and doesn't dissipate after the first few sips, leaving you with a run-of-the-mill latte.

Clyde says, "She's ashing her cigarette pretty intently. I'd say she's getting close to the filter."

"Fine," I concede, "black it is."

Then the cash register manned by the tall, pasty guy who makes possibly the world's worst cappuccino, not worth the sweat and toil of the Guatemalan or Ethiopian farmer picking the beans for the latest international blend, makes a clunking noise and the screen at front fades out. A collective groan from the line. One of the other registers opens up, and the old man standing two places in front shuffles over. Now there is only one further barrier between us and our coffee, a woman with an Hermès scarf tied taut around her neck. She's young and polished, and everything about her screams type A personality. The Italian hand-crafted flat heels, the severe cut of her suit, the way she clutches her handbag possessively, hugging it close to her chest. She is pretty in a strange way. Big brown eyes, a nose that is slightly too large, thin pursed lips. Not bodacious like the foursome from Public Relations—she wouldn't stand a chance strutting around in a California bikini contest—but she pulls off the whole corporate image well.

"The smoke is tossed," Clyde observes. "There's no movement toward the parking garage. Philanderer's expected arrival time is T-minus thirty seconds."

"Let's just go," Postal Boy croaks.

He's really nervous, his eye twitching like crazy.

"No," orders the Defeated One, "we are staying for our coffee. Look, we're next."

The Woman With The Scarf heads to the open register.

"Watch this. You can tell from the shoes. Superefficient coffee order coming right up. Ten seconds tops," I wager.

The man at the other working register doesn't look as promising. He's ancient and confused, and he gesticulates wildly at the case of pastries. Every time the barista reaches in to grab a muffin or a danish, he gets all flustered, curses in a foreign language, and points to something else.

"Christ," the Defeated One mutters, looking over his shoulder.

I discreetly follow his gaze to the back of the line: The Philandering Managing Director is charming the pants off a sixty-year-old secretary in front of him. What the hell is taking the Woman With The Scarf so long? Oh lord, a piece of paper in her hand; she has a fucking list.

She speaks in a rapid-fire monotone; that's good, but god, listen to the complexity. One percent wet (absolutely NO foam, she emphasizes) caramel cinnamon latte with the ultra-low decaf blend, double cup sleeves. The barista's marker flies across the cup. Next: low-fat two percent extra-hot cappuccino. The barista stops her marking.

"Huh? That doesn't make any sense."

The Woman With The Scarf looks up from her list.

"What's the problem?"

"Low-fat two percent. It contradicts itself."

The Woman With The Scarf visibly tenses.

"I don't have time for this," she snaps. "Just make it."

From the frown of the barista, the hands lowered to her hips, I know what's coming next. She's not backing down.

"You tell me how to make it, then."

"Oh god," the Woman With The Scarf snarls. "I just can't deal with this right now."

"Miss," the barista states coolly, "you're holding up the line. Please explain how I should go about making your low-fat two percent cappuccino."

The Woman With The Scarf won't back down either.

"Look, I have seven very agitated lawyers upstairs, and if I don't bring them their precious coffees soon— "

"Not my business."

"Philanderer is looking our way," Clyde mutters. "I think he's spotted us."

Postal Boy begins to whimper.

"Visual contact is now confirmed," Clyde says.

The Woman With The Scarf is *still* feuding with the barista: "Where do you get off giving me this attitude? Who exactly do you think you are? Last time I checked, you're getting paid to make my insanely overpriced coffees."

Postal Boy's whimpering escalates into a full-fledged moan.

And suddenly the situation becomes unbearable: Postal Boy is about to wet himself, the Woman With The Scarf is losing it, and the Philanderer is now furrowing his forehead as if recollecting us from some distant dream. Do I know you guys? Yes indeed, you work in the office right next to mine!

"Just order seven goddamn regular coffees and tell everybody upstairs the machines weren't working right. What the fuck—it's way too early in the day for this crap," I growl.

It's a guttural, subconscious flipping out, loud enough for those nearby in the line to stop their conversations and gape at us. The Woman With The Scarf's expression is aghast, now furious, brown eyes flashing with rage. I know she's about to erupt and yet I can't help thinking she looks pretty like that, teetering on the cusp of eruption.

"What did you just say to me?"

Her voice is soft yet unnerving, her gaze so intense I'm waiting for the lasers to shoot from her pupils and vaporize my head. I'd give my right pinkie to have her turn around and continue with her order.

"Look—"

"All I wanted"—her voice is slightly raspy now—"is to get the coffees on this list."

She taps the list in her hand repeatedly, poking a hole through it.

"Seven coffees. Seven. I appreciate the fact you need your caffeine fix, I know this line is awfully long, but it's not like I sat around upstairs trying to figure out, hmm, how can I make these coffees as ridiculously complex as possible? Hmm, let's see how I can aggravate every single person around me."

My ears are burning. Not metaphorically speaking; they're beet red and hot enough to fry an egg on.

"I don't even like coffee. It's vile stuff. Turns your teeth brown, you know. Changes your body chemistry and all that."

"It's not a big deal—"

"Shhh. Let me finish. So I wait in this line for twenty minutes, twenty valuable minutes wasted when I could be upstairs doing all sorts of empowering work. Photocopying and shredding and highlighting conjunctive clauses in thousand-page documents filled with small-type legal jargonese. And then when I'm sent down to complete a task worthy of the hundreds of hours spent cramming away to pass the bar, when all I want is for somebody to be nice to me because I'm having a really bad day"—here her voice trembles—"oh god, this has been such a horrific morning, all I get is attitude from everybody around me."

She turns back to the barista. "Can you please make the coffees on this list? I know it's not too hard; I'm sure you can figure them out. I'll be back in five minutes. I'm just heading outside for a quick nervous breakdown."

She nods once, sternly, like a soldier receiving orders, then walks briskly toward the exit, her neck scarf flapping behind her. The rest of the line watches her departure, then resumes their idle chitchat.

"You're such an asshole," the Defeated One says.

"Yeah," Clyde seconds.

The barista picks up the Woman With The Scarf's list and begins reciting the order. Everything is moving along as before.

"Gentlemen."

The Philandering Managing Director has snuck up behind us. Postal Boy gasps audibly. Jesus, he must have witnessed the whole thing.

"Whatever happened to her?"

He's not expecting anything in the way of an explanation. So he was distracted, didn't see how it all started. He gazes out the window trying to catch sight of her, grinning lecherously.

"Crazy broad, but she had a great set of—"

He catches himself and chuckles. The Philanderer reaches into a pocket and retrieves his wallet, handing Clyde a fiver.

"Order me a macchiato."

Then he's back to the sixty-year-old secretary, making her blush and giggle like a girl in junior high. Except her giggling gives off the impression her heart may soon stop abruptly, that she's going to keel over and collapse into the jars of biscotti.

"You've got to hand it to him," the Defeated One snorts. "He doesn't discriminate against any of them. An egalitarian man-whore. Probably sees her menopause as a hurdle to overcome."

"It's pretty anticlimactic," Clyde remarks. "We're expecting him to go apeshit and then that. 'Order me a macchiato.' All of Postal's freaking out for nothing."

The Defeated One shrugs, "The Bank works in mysterious ways."

We're up. Clyde orders a macchiato for the Philanderer and a Grande Americano for himself. The Defeated One and Postal Boy each get a Venti Bold. When it's my turn to order, I shake my head.

"Nothing."

The Defeated One grimaces at me. "Nothing? Why not? Don't tell me you're upset about that girl. She was just letting off some steam. Hates her job as much as you do."

"Don't be ridiculous," chimes in Clyde.

He's right; I am being ridiculous. Yet I can't quash this feeling of—I'm not even sure what it is exactly. Mortification, I guess.

"Stop being an ass. Here, drink this."

The Defeated One hands me a huge cup of coffee. I take a sip. There is a gospel choir breaking out in raucous hallelujahs somewhere. It's better than the Coke from last night, even. My discomfort over the Woman With The Scarf dissolves in this sudden jolt of caffeine.

So. Big deal.

♦

"Where were you? I came by your desk half an hour ago."

The Sycophant is seriously pissed. Somewhere within his tangled neurons lurks a memo to the Toad—our evil head of HR—waiting to be written, but frankly I don't really care. I'll care in five minutes, no question about that, but right now I'm floating on my caffeine high.

"We need sixty booklets of the investor presentation for the Brazilian mining deal. Color copies, bound. Get an assistant to help you."

He's referring to the Utterly Incompetent Assistant, a crotchety forty-something spinster who supports the M&A group. The Utterly Incompetent Assistant has a remarkably astute ability for screwing up the most perfunctory of tasks. Arranging a conference call, she'll send out the wrong area code. Photocopying documents, she'll print only one side of a double-sided document, but no matter, it will be for the wrong company anyway. The Utterly Incompetent Assistant should have been fired long ago, but incredibly, she's managed to survive the corporate reshufflings following the tech-bubble burst and post-9/11 financial armageddon. We're fairly certain she is sleeping with the Philandering Managing Director, which pretty much explains it.

Binding is a remote possibility. Under heavy supervision it might work out. Quite naturally, she's not at her desk. A quick perusal of the premises indicates the Philandering Managing Director is not in his office either, so there is a fairly good chance she'll be MIA for a while now.

Sixty booklets. Fifty pages each. It's not the end of the world. I give myself an hour and a half.

♦

Murphy's Law is in full effect at the Bank: When something can go wrong, it will *always* go wrong. A few general rules of thumb: If a printing job is required, then the printer will jam. Or be out of toner. Or stop functioning for no logical reason whatsoever. Binding machines and scanners and the Bloomberg terminals are just as temperamental.

As most of our senior managers veer toward procrastination bordering on lunacy, changing crucial numbers in a model five minutes before a pitch, it's not unusual to see Postal Boy careening at breakneck speed between the copy room and the boardroom, or the Star genuflecting before the massive color printer capable of performing a myriad of tasks, stapling and sorting and banding together with other highly functional color printers in a bid to take over the world.

Three hours later. The root of the delay: a missing toner. I spent an hour searching every cabinet in the copy room to no avail and half an hour ferreting out the Dirty Hippie Office Supply Manager, a lanky guy reeking of stale herbs, the only employee at the Bank permitted to wear tie-dye to work. Finally located him meditating on the Equity Capital Markets floor (always quiet this time of day), then spent another half hour rummaging through the same cabinets in the copy room, only to have the Dirty Hippie Office Supply Manager scratch his head, shrug, and promise he would put in an order by the end of the week. A few minutes I can't account for; possibly I fell asleep standing up by the binding machines. Snapped out of my reverie when Clyde dropped by, hunting down a pad of Post-it Notes, and followed him back to the M&A department, where the Utterly Incompetent Assistant was at her desk. Asked if she knew where the toners were kept and stood there like a buffoon waiting for her to finish gossiping on the phone, probably to a widespread network of Utterly Incompetent Assistants gossiping into their respective phones throughout the downtown core, before she located the elusive toner beside the Flavia packets of phosphorescent green tea. Very hygienic. Heh, nobody drinks the vile stuff, anyway. The Utterly Incompetent Assistant waddled off, clucking her tongue, as if I were an absolute moron for not having checked there before.

"What is this?" The Sycophant scowls, flipping through one of the booklets.

"Investor presentation for the Brazilian mining deal. Sixty color copies, as you requested."

"The Brazilian mining deal? No, that's been put off for another week now. Did I say the Brazilian mining deal before?"

"Yes."

He gives me that feral stare, those beady little eyes squinting once, twice.

"Are you certain? I'm confident that I asked you to print out the telecom presentation."

I'm not backing down.

"No. The mining deal. I'm, uh, certain of it."

I'd like my voice to come across as condescending and impertinent, but it doesn't; in truth, it's quaking under my own fear of confrontation.

"Well, either way, we're going to require sixty bound copies of the telecom investor presentation. Color. Put them on my desk before you leave tonight."

♦

Later that afternoon, I'm summoned to the Philandering Managing Director's office. He has his shoes off, feet on the desk, and he is stretching out one of those Koosh balls. The office is a complete pigsty: stacks of paper strewn everywhere, a pizza box from lunch on the floor, a beat-up *GQ* magazine propped underneath his phone. This is the sort of mess you'd expect from a theoretical physicist's office; it's kind of ridiculous coming from the Philanderer. For one, we're not even sure if he's literate. At meetings he'll flip through a pitch book and provide commentary on the color selections, the alignment of graphs and tables, as if formatting alone is of crucial significance. He is of the school of thought that the actual analysis doesn't matter one bit; it's all in the presentation.

"So Clyde, how are you enjoying your first week on the job?"

I've given up trying to convince the Philanderer that, no, I'm not Clyde, and secondly, that I've already been here two months. Apparently Postal Boy also goes by Clyde. A trio of Clydes. Not that it matters. The Philanderer doesn't really see us as separate entities to begin with; we're only this amorphous blob that manages to spit out whatever crazy analyses are required by the inner workings of the Bank.

"It's interesting."

"Good, good. It's a rewarding industry once you've found your bearings. Is this what you've always wanted to do?"

What a question. Would he really believe it if I quipped back, Yes, well, golly, I've always felt destined for this kind of existence, you know, lots of tedious work combined with intense sleep deprivation.

"Yeah, uh, banking has always interested me."

"Good, good."

A bout of silence as the Philanderer struggles to recollect why he called me into his office in the first place.

"The trucking deal. You know the one?"

Trucking deal. Trucking deal. Hmmm. The deal that kept me here all night? The deal that has required the model from hell?

"Yeah, I think so."

"Good, good. Anyway, we need to adjust the comps."

"Ah, what sort of adjustment were you thinking?"

"Hmmm . . ."

He's lost his train of thought. He whips the Koosh ball against the wall in frustration. Then his mouth twitches, and a dim light flickers on somewhere inside that head of his.

"We're going to require some European transportation conglomerates, get the Client thinking about consolidating some of the trucking industry in France and Germany."

This has to be the Philanderer's own idea. Who else would propose selling an international expansion to a client who has never ventured outside North America? A cowboy from Texas who sees Europe as a wasteland of clogged toilets, funny accents, and people wolfing down frogs?

"How many additional companies did you have in mind?"

"Let's say twenty. Yeah, twenty's a nice, solid number."

Thirty minutes a comp. No, it's European accounting, all the line items scrambled. Make that forty-five minutes. Damn Europe and its need to always be different; they deserve an ass-whipping for this.

"What is the timing?"

The Philanderer strokes his chin.

"I'd like to see something by tomorrow morning."

Combined with the Sycophant's binding mishap, it will be impossible to get everything done without pulling another all-nighter. I physically cannot do it. There is only one weapon remaining in the arsenal, a final bastion of hope—

The Push Back.

"I still need to put through some major changes to the model. Would it be all right if I had the comps done by early afternoon at the latest?"

The Philanderer removes his feet from the desk. The smile replaced by a haughty sneer. It's all over: He's recognized the Push Back.

"You'll have them on my desk by no later than eight tomorrow morning. And include the backup."

The Philander studies my face, perhaps for the first time realizing that, no, I'm not Clyde.

Fuck. I think I preferred the anonymity.

Two

Oh god, I've really got to pee. Pee real bad. Client has his eyes half closed; he's not even paying attention. We're holed up in a boardroom to run through the investor presentation for a Brazilian gold-mine merger. They begin presenting to the Street tomorrow and head off in a private jet for Boston and San Francisco next week. The Sycophant is scribbling furiously on a legal pad to my left. He is also surreptitiously glancing over to ensure I'm jotting down an identical set of notes.

Across from him is the Ice Queen, another vice president, a blond beauty just shy of six feet and sleek like a panther. She wears a beige sweater that is perfectly hugging her breasts, and there's a moist sheen to her lips from a touch of gloss, but despite this she's an absolute bitch. Beside her is the Prodigal Son, her Aryan male equivalent and the other analyst staffed on this deal. You know how difficult it is for one guy to comment on how another guy is good-looking. It's breaking an implicit rule of manliness, a sin against the testes. Suffice it to say it's the first thing that would pop into anybody's head when they saw him: Man, that's a good-looking guy.

To make matters worse, he is the son of a VIP at the Bank. I can't remember his dad's exact position in the hierarchy. Not that it matters; I'll never cross paths with him, anyway. No question the Prodigal Father has some immaculate office on the top floor, rare orchids from Thailand that get changed weekly, a private bathroom with gilded cherubs spewing water out of the taps.

The Prodigal Son flashes me a dazzling smile, his teeth so white they're almost blue, before sliding his pitch book across the table toward the Sycophant. The Sycophant picks it up and frowns, handing it over to me. On page 15 there is a subtotal circled, a column that doesn't add up properly. I feel a sense of dread until I realize this is one of the slides the Prodigal Son put together. I throw him my most menacing glare, but he counters with an indifferent shrug. Pinning the blame on me, the bastard. Fortunately, page 15 comes and goes without the Client detecting the error.

A sharp pang from my bladder—how much longer is this going to last? It's been thirty minutes already; probably another hour at least. I can't hold out that long. No fucking way. Damn the Defeated One for pressuring me into a Starbucks run right before a meeting with the Client.

The marvelous Client is a tall man in a suit so shabby it could have been stitched together in five minutes by a sweatshop laborer. Not at all what you'd expect from a guy who stands to pocket a cool sixty million bucks from the merger. The Client is slumped in his seat, head tilted back; any second now he is going to start snoring. It's actually pretty ridiculous. I mean, sure, all of this stuff is boring as hell, but that's sixty million bucks we're talking about. That's like six hundred years of being me, sitting here in this infernal boardroom with a bladder the size of a turnip and a Venti Bold banging on the exit channel.

"The Cu grade in the open-pit extension of the Alarmi main duct is very promising, and a concentration of 0.6 should yield our forecasts of 15,000 tonnes of Au byproduct before the end of the year . . ."

Boring Engineering Guy, the head of the Client's operations team, has been inundating us with industry jargon for the last fifteen minutes. It's perfectly clear his technical diatribe is meant only for other Boring Engineering Guys, none of whom will be attending any of the investor presentations, and thus his feasibility report will get axed before it has seen the light of day. Nonetheless, he keeps rattling on without anybody stopping him. I'm not sure of the reason. Perhaps it's for his ego preservation—let the Boring Engineering Guy bumble on about concentrates and smeltering because this is what he dreams about at night, and cutting him off would be like kicking a sad mongrel puppy.

Because of my perpetually weak bladder, disasters avoided by hurling myself into foliage or finding that stray bottle in the nick of time, I've learned a trick or two that act as a momentary salve in such dire situations. Right now I'm at the oh-god-I'm-really-not-going-to-make-it stage, timed about a half hour before the holy-fuck-it's-really-going-to-come-out-any-second-now, which usually gives me fifteen minutes until the real goods, the final outburst. It's too late for the most basic of maneuvers: thighs pressed together like a little girl; trying not to think about it (like that ever works unless you're a well-trained Zen master); crossing one leg so hard over the other you might as well be giving yourself a vasectomy.

Time for the Erecto-block. The Erecto-block is a relatively simple strategy that involves staring at the Ice Queen's beige sweater, pretending she's not such a total bitch and that she wants nothing more than to lunge over the boardroom table and tear my pants off, until I've blocked up my urethra. Shameful, yes, but you better believe it works.

Sort of. The Erecto-block is all about maintenance. When the Ice Queen crosses her arms and blocks my view, when my gaze travels up to her scowling face, the fantasy is gone and I come this close to losing it. Then the Client has directed a question at her and she's forced to flip through the pitch book frantically, providing an unobstructed view of the beige sweater—the Erecto-block back in full force.

And just as suddenly, the Erecto-block fades, a two-second leap from proud and throbbing to limp and pathetic. It's not just my nether regions that are sensitive to this subtle change. The Ice Queen wrinkles her nose, and the Sycophant sports this deer-in-headlights expression. It feels like somebody has cranked up the air-conditioning full blast. No, it's not so artificial; let's try this metaphor again: It's as if a cold wind has picked up off desolate mountain peaks, a remote place charred and lifeless and housing the odd peasant chipping at the frozen topsoil for a potato the size of a kidney bean, blowing over all manner of carnage before arriving, filled with this knowledge of the evil of man, into this tiny space, our investor presentation dry run, Boardroom 121.

The door creaks open, the hinges rattling from this terrible gust, and in walks the Coldest Fish In The Pond. We didn't come up with the nickname; none of us would have dared. The origins can be traced to a far-removed reporter from the *Wall Street Journal,* the paper's annual "Who's Who" of the banking world.

How does one provide an adequate description of this financial deity capable of invoking the heebie-jeebies in the bravest among us? All right, facts first. He's the head of the Bank. No, not just the head—he *is* the Bank. Founded it before he was thirty, a young Machiavelli who was the rising star in a hedge fund boutique before stealing the majority of their clients and opening up his own shop. Physically he is not so intimidating—on the short side, maybe five foot six or seven, and deeply tanned from a week vacationing in Palm Beach. He still runs marathons, even though he's pushing sixty, and has the type of sturdiness that gives the impression that if there was suddenly a nuclear fallout or a terrorist disaster, the only things left standing would be cockroaches and the Fish.

He settles into a chair at the head of the table and surveys the room, eyes masking the billions of computations per second shooting through his prodigious gray matter. The Sycophant whimpers softly, no doubt oscillating between the urge to flee and an instinctive desire to grovel by the Fish's Gucci loafers. When the Fish nods once in the direction of the Ice Queen, she visibly trembles and leaps from her seat to ferret around in the cabinets for a chilled bottle of Perrier water. Even the Client, on a level playing field, immensely powerful in his own right, chuckles nervously when the Fish precisely positions his black attaché case on the table. Only the Prodigal Son remains unfazed by his presence, stifling a yawn as he flips through a pitch book.

The Boring Engineering Guy, who hasn't completed his feasibility analysis, clearly doesn't know what to do. He is standing at the front of the room looking like he's about to crap his pants.

"Sit down," the Coldest Fish In The Pond demands.

The Boring Engineering Guy shuffles back to his seat with immense relief. The Fish opens the attaché case, removes a pad of legal paper and a gold fountain pen, and arranges them carefully beside the bottle of Perrier.

"Now," the Fish directs at the Client, "we are going to do this properly. In the next sixty minutes you will convince me why this deal is a suitable mandate for the Bank. By the end of your presentation, if I think it smells funny, then I will advise you to peddle your wares somewhere else."

It's the sort of command that is unheard of in this industry. Banking is all about sycophancy in some form or another (though rarely resembling the absolute epitome of this, the Sycophant himself), business won through courtside basketball tickets, Smith & Wollensky's bloody porterhouses, and bottles of Moët bubbling among the eastern European strippers. If everything goes off without a hitch, the Bank will pocket a twelve-million-dollar advisory fee on this single deal. The Client has every right, financially speaking, to be outraged. To go berserk. To demand we suck his toes, shine his shoes, and pelt him with truffles simultaneously.

Nonetheless, he spreads his hands on the table and stares guiltily at his well-manicured nails, nodding in humble agreement. The power of the Coldest Fish In The Pond is staggering.

"Well . . . um . . . let's begin," the Client says, shuffling his papers.

Then he is rehashing the same boring speech that started this meeting forty-five minutes ago. With the Erecto-block gone, forever flaccid with the added tension of the Fish's presence, I've officially entered the holy-fuck-it's-really-going-to-come-out-any-second-now stage. Fifteen minutes left in the gas tank. It's inevitable at this point, etched in stone, a predetermined event marked on the golden threads of those hoary Fates. Before, there was a remote possibility I'd muster up the courage to slink out of the room before disaster struck. Now, with the Fish writing meticulously on his legal pad, it's impossible to make my escape without crossing his field of vision.

My BlackBerry. A potential salvation.

From: Me@theBank.com

To: TheDefeatedOne@theBank.com

You have to help me, man. Sitting in Boardroom 121 with the Fish and Client et al. and am this close to pissing myself. 100% serious. Do NOT treat this as shit and giggles. Knock on the door and come up with an emergency.

Two minutes later, my BlackBerry vibrates.

From: TheDefeatedOne@theBank.com

To: Me@theBank.com

ha ha ha ha ha ha ha ha ha ha ha ha ha ha ha ha ha ha ha ha ha ha ha ha ha ha ha ha ha ha ha ha ha ha ha ha ha ha ha ha ha ha ha ha ha ha ha ha ha ha ha ha ha ha ha ha ha ha ha ha ha ha ha ha ha ha ha ha ha ha ha ha ha ha ha ha ha ha ha ha

ha—another one for added emphasis

ya big loser

Jackass.

From: Me@theBank.com

To: TheDefeatedOne@theBank.com

Half my bonus. Twenty sets of comps. Whatever it takes.

From: TheDefeatedOne@theBank.com

To: Me@theBank.com

What if your bonus really blows? There's a rumor going around that the Toad is considering cutting back on junior analysts' comp this year . . . FYI, even the Star is laughing his head off right now.

A minute later there is a cautious rapping at the door. Thank the lord. The Sycophant, who's closest, opens it a crack and pokes his head out. A muffled interchange and then the door creaks shut, the Sycophant returning to his seat, a stern glance in my direction before he's back to jotting down his notes.

Oh god.

Oh mother of god.

From: Me@theBank.com

To: TheDefeatedOne@theBank.com

What the hell just happened?

Any camaraderie I once shared with the Defeated One is terminated from this point on. The response comes a few seconds later:

From: TheDefeatedOne@theBank.com

To: Me@theBank.com

Told El Sycophant your grandma went into cardiac arrest this morning. Your family calling here like crazy requesting you get your ass down to the hospital pronto. Sycophant said, and I quote: If she's already dead, there's no reason why she can't wait.

It's like somebody's knocked the wind right out of me, and I'm not at all easily offended. Granted my grandma is not really dying on a hospital bed right now—she's probably slouched on her paisley couch fantasizing about Bob Barker, or drinking her daily gin & tonic under the mulberry tree in the yard—but just the notion that if, hypothetically, my grandma's heart had catapulted itself out of her chest cavity, if she really was on the verge of leaving this world and all she wanted was one final glimpse of her dearest grandson, for the Sycophant to deny her that basic human privilege . . .

From: Me@theBank.com

To: TheDefeatedOne@theBank.com

Evil little SOB. Thanks for the effort. It's going to happen any minute now; I'm well past the point of no return.

> You'll know when you hear the shattering of glass as I hurl myself through the window.

I experience a moment of serenity as I accept my fate: I'm really going to piss in my pants. The next few minutes will be turbulent, horrendous, but life will go on, nobody is going to die from this; at most, in fifty years it will be an amusing story whispered about at some wedding or reunion.

Fifteen seconds left. It can't just be the one Venti Bold doing such disproportionate damage. It feels like a couple gallons sloshing around in my bladder, the Venti Bond asexually reproducing, splitting off into millions of little cappuccinos and lattes, and now there's enough Starbucks flowing through my intestines to caffeinate the entire Bank.

Five seconds. One final clench before the bittersweet release.

An abrupt knocking. The Sycophant leaps up from his chair to let in Unadulterated Sex, the Fish's gorgeous assistant, who sashays over to her boss and whispers something in his ear. The Fish frowns and slips his notepad back into the attaché case.

"We're adjourning this meeting for five minutes," the Fish decrees.

Then he's out the door, Unadulterated Sex slinking after him with the half-finished bottle of Perrier. I channel all my energy into reversing the flow of urine through my body. A spot is forming on the crotch of my pants but it's not too large; I manage to hold out for a few seconds longer.

I dash out of Boardroom 121, ignoring the flinty glare of the Sycophant, a full-on sprint to the bathroom, and blessed be the lord, there is nobody at the urinals. Leaning forward and resting my palms flat against the wall, my entire body shuddering. The zipper miraculously doesn't get caught or else there could have been a premature disaster.

Exquisite release.

♦

Lunch with the Defeated One. We have a new policy of going outside for two, at most three, minutes, to enjoy the final dregs of late-summer weather before bringing the usual congealed teriyaki chicken up to our desks. Clyde and Postal Boy both have pitches this afternoon, so they're doing the requisite twelfth-hour scrambling around to put through the inevitable last-minute upheavals. A young couple clean and preppy enough to be in a Gap commercial, the annoying one where everybody's snapping their fingers, strolls by, grinning away like the Cheshire cat.

"It's fucking Tuesday." The Defeated One scowls in their direction.

He snaps open a Coke and gulps it down in six seconds flat, following it with a raucous burp.

"How many of those do you drink a day?"

"Five, six. Who are you, my goddamn dentist? Anyway, back to more important subjects. Tell me, what was the goddess wearing?"

The Defeated One, despite having a girlfriend of many eons, is unapologetically obsessed with Unadulterated Sex. Not that any red-blooded male could blame him. She's tall for a woman, five foot nine or so, with black hair and olive skin, even though she grew up in the cornfields of Kansas. Her body has a voluptuousness that's girlish and natural; there are definitely no silicon components. She's unattainable, of course (it's rumored she's engaged to the son of a Russian oil czar who is waiting around for his inheritance), but that's all part of the mystique. Nobody is entirely sure what she's doing at the Bank. You'd expect her to be jetting off to private islands, tanning topless on massive yachts raced by Speedo-clad European tycoons, not spending her days shuffling the Fish's Perrier bottles around.

"White sweater. Tight black skirt. Looked really expensive."

"Did her nipples show through?"

"Sorry, man, didn't have time to check. I was kind of distracted with the whole raging bladder thing. It was insane. I'm telling you, I was this close."

The Defeated One chuckles. "It would have been priceless. Pissing in front of the Fish."

"It would have been awful." I shudder. "And on top of that, there's the Prodigal Son trying to pin yet another of his errors on me. God almighty, I really hate that fucker."

"Yeah," the Defeated One says, crumpling up his can of Coke, "he did the same thing to Postal last week. Anyway, did you catch a glimpse of his new watch? Apparently it's a Patek Philippe. Swiss, of course, a present from Daddy Warbucks. That's a cool quarter million strapped right there on his wrist."

Another thing about the Defeated One: He's absolutely nuts about money. The guy probably gets off at night rubbing crisp bills against his genitalia.

"Jesus. That's like—"

"A Bentley Arnage T with a dozen high-class call girls and a magnum of Cristal thrown in for good measure. I've already done the math."

He checks his own watch, a Timex.

"Come on, let's go back up and eat. I don't know if I can take any more of this sunshine crushing my spirit."

We both take one last appreciative glance at the sky. It's achingly blue and crystal clear, perfect weather for wasting away an afternoon munching pretzels on a park bench somewhere. The Defeated One and I sigh simultaneously.

♦

Three o'clock I get a call from my college roommate. Mark is on a save-the-world career track, currently teaching some inner-city kids how to play hopscotch before he jaunts off to Bulgaria next week with the Peace Corps. Apparently a bunch of our mutual friends are meeting up for drinks later tonight to send him off. My initial reflex is to decline—it's a Tuesday night, for god's sake—but aside from a set of comps to scrub for the Sycophant, a few kinks to iron out in a leveraged buyout model, it could be a definite possibility. I tell Mark this.

"Yeah, I think I can manage it."

Mark sounds genuinely pleased. "You're never around anymore, man. I know everybody's going to be so excited to see you."

"Likewise. Anyway, what time were you thinking?"

"Ten or so, I guess."

"Cool. I should be finished up here by then."

"Great. Really looking forward to it."

♦

The next few hours pass with a heightened level of anxiety. Every time Outlook pops open with a new message, every time my phone rings, it's the potential for a Work Bomb capable of derailing my drinking plans. It would almost have been better for my psychological well-being to decline in the first place, saving myself the potential aggravation of having to cancel at the last minute.

Despite this paranoia, I'm excited at the prospect of meeting up with Mark and the rest of our crew. It's been far too long, at least a couple weeks now, since I've seen anybody outside the Bank, save for the homeless turning the sidewalks into their dormitories after midnight. By eight o'clock the Sycophant has already left to watch his son's soccer game, and the Philandering Managing Director is knocking back twenty-dollar cocktails in some overpriced Suits bar. As soon as I've fixed this LBO model—two hours I give it—I'm good to go.

♦

Nine o'clock I get another call from Mark.

"Just wanted to give you the heads-up that the Ex-Girlfriend is also going to be there."

"And she knows I'm coming as well?"

"Yeah, she knows, and she's cool with it. Actually, she told me she's kind of excited to see you."

Very interesting; I wonder what that means. Bullshit, I know exactly what that means. She misses me. It makes plausible sense because I miss her too.

"Oh, really."

"Yeah, I'm not shitting you. Are you seriously going to make it? Man, you've got to get out of that place."

"Tell me about it. Give me another hour to wrap things up and I'll be heading over."

♦

Nine forty-five and I'm packing up my stuff: arranging the papers on my desk into neat piles, sweeping any incriminating e-mail forwards into the recycling bin. The Defeated One returns from the washroom, sniffling. He sits down at his desk, legs spread wide, and mops the sweat from his forehead with a tissue.

"Das Wunderkind. Whatcha doin' at this ungodly hour?" he asks.

"Meeting up with some college friends. I don't have anything due tomorrow, and a buddy's heading off with the Peace Corps."

"So you're trying to tell me that you're takin' off at ten?"

I hate it when he pulls this self-righteous crap on me.

"Piss off. I haven't had a night to myself in the past month."

The Defeated One snorts. "Capacity."

I ignore him. All I have left is to e-mail the updated version of the LBO model to the Philanderer and I can jump in a cab—I'll make it to the bar in less than fifteen minutes—when there is a sudden *ping:* 1 New Message in Outlook.

It's so inevitable I can only laugh:

> From: TheSycophant@aol.com
>
> To: Me@theBank.com
>
> We're going to need some precedent transactions for U.S. beverage buyouts $50M-$300M. Need asap, first thing tomorrow morning.

Further down on the screen:

> From: TheSycophant@theBank.com
>
> To: TheProdigalSon@theBank.com
>
> Don't worry. I'll get somebody else on it. Have a good time.

At the beginning of the thread:

> From: TheProdigalSon@theBank.com
>
> To: TheSycophant@theBank.com
>
> A buddy of mine is off to Switzerland tomorrow and there's a massive party tonight. I'm not going to be able to get the comps done for the beverage deal. Can you get somebody else to finish them up?

"What the fuck—I'm going to kill that son of a bitch."

I slam my fist down hard on the desk, toppling over the computer speakers. I haven't been this angry in a very, very long time.

"Calm down, Mumbles," the Defeated One drawls.

I glower at him. I swear to god, if he starts with me now, I'm going to gouge out his eyeballs with a paper clip.

I dial Mark's cell phone. He picks up after three rings.

"You're not going to believe this," I start. "My boss— "

"Look, no need to make excuses. You're blowing us off tonight, right?"

I don't know what to say. I can't apologize; I've apologized so many times for this sort of thing that I no longer have any credibility.

"The Ex-Girlfriend is here already. She's not going to be too happy."

"Can I speak to her?"

Muffled sounds before Mark comes back on the phone. His tone is hushed.

"Look, she's pretty miffed. I think it's best if you just leave it for now. Are you sure there's no way you can make it down? Only for a beer?"

One beer. Fifteen minutes in a taxi both ways. Thirty minutes of drinking and chatting up the Ex. I could be done in an hour max.

God, who am I kidding? There's no such thing as one beer, and if the Ex wants to hook up later?

"I don't know. I have all these precedent transactions to finish up— "

"Don't worry about it. Anyway, I probably won't see you before I leave for Bulgaria, but be sure to stay in touch. You have my e-mail address?"

"Yeah."

I have a sense I'm dropping down one additional notch into this pit of despair.

"Hey, have a good time— "

Mark hangs up on me. Mark, even. I rest my head on the

desk and close my eyes. It's truly amazing; right when I thought I'd reached the nadir of this job, all of a sudden, there is this unprecedented low. A hand on my shoulder:

"There there, sweetcheeks."

I'm too upset to bother coming up with a retaliation. The Defeated One giggles erratically before heading to the washroom for another line.

Three

Many moons ago, before Christopher Latham Sholes invented the typewriter in Milwaukee, before gelatinous invertebrates slithered out of the oceans and evolved into prehistoric monkeys, the world was nothing more than a tiny speck. You could have carried it around in your pocket. Up a nostril. It was really that small. And when the world was no bigger than a fingernail, when it was nothing more than swirling hydrogen gases, there was no Bank. No time value of money. No bipedals buying and selling securities so they could cruise around in BMW 6 Series convertibles.

But I don't have to venture back to the beginning of time to make this point: It wasn't always like this.

♦

It's a Sunday afternoon and I'm surrounded by all of these aliens. They don't look like aliens, at least not the quintessential *X Files* variety, no pasty skeletons with bulbous sloping foreheads and hollow eye sockets, but they're aliens nonetheless. Here in this cookie-cutter suburban house, the aliens chatter aimlessly about needlepoint and seated lawnmowers, and about how the garbage should be taken out earlier in the week, on a Monday instead of a Tuesday.

One of the aliens, my aunt Penelope, whose fiftieth birthday is the cause of this extraterrestrial get-together, glides by in a yellow sundress and hands me a slice of chocolate cake. Picking at the colored sprinkles on the icing, I settle back in the fold-out chair and observe these life forms going about their day-to-day social norms: my uncle Bob stretched languorously on the couch like a giant cat; on the rug, a gaggle of vociferous cousins slamming down their Pokemon cards; my mom in the kitchen, chopping carrots for a salad; my dad smoking a cigar in the fenced-in yard beside dozens of identical fenced-in yards with Aunt Penelope's next-door neighbor, a husky man in galoshes. The aliens seem to go about their daily existence in this completely frivolous universe. No responsibilities, no deadlines, no ominous feeling that at any moment a cell phone could go off and next thing they know they're wasting the entire weekend putting together comps.

Aunt Penelope returns with two glasses of punch. She plops down beside me and tosses her head back, her long earrings tinkling like wind chimes.

"You look tired."

I've been keeping a tally; she is the eighth person who's told me some variant of this over the course of the afternoon. Even my gay uncle Tom, who usually comments on my developing physique while trying to grope a biceps, only shook his head sadly when we exchanged our hellos.

"I am tired," I mumble.

"What do you have to complain about? I tell you, it's not easy getting this old. Takes a hell of an effort."

She's been saying weird crap like this the entire afternoon, craving everybody's pity for living a relatively carefree five decades, marrying a quiet Deloitte & Touche accountant, and not having to work a day in her life—and now she's bored of it. The same house as everybody else, the same weeping willow in the yard, the same supersized groceries bought at Costco.

"How do you like the new job?"

"It's okay."

I have this policy: I try my best not to talk about work outside of work. It's really difficult to adhere to this. Because I have only this meager existence beyond the confines of the Bank, it's all too easy to derail any conversation I'm having, so I'm once again ranting about the latest outrageous request from the Sycophant, or how I constantly fantasize about shoving a pencil up a nostril and slamming my head down, killing myself the same way that Japanese student under the pressure of passing his entrance exams did once.

"How many hours are they making you work?"

"Ninety on average. Sometimes more."

Her head flies up, earrings jangling.

"Ninety a week? My gosh. Are you serious?"

I nod.

"That's downright obscene. Aren't there labor laws to prevent such a thing?"

I shrug. Aunt Penelope waves over Aunt Teresa and Uncle Tom.

"Can you believe it; they're making him work ninety hours a week! Isn't that crazy?"

Aunt Teresa and Uncle Tom bob their heads simultaneously.

"Crazy. Yes, definitely crazy."

It's not long before the entire roomful of aliens knows my work schedule. It's foreign to them, this ninety hours a week; it sets them debating whether such a thing is possible. Uncomfortable with the sympathetic stares thrown my way by every third cousin in the vicinity, I slip out to join my dad in the backyard. The fall air is crisp and refreshing, providing some relief from the smothering relatives inside.

"You look tired."

"Yeah," I mumble, "everybody else just told me the same thing."

"A bad week?"

"Each one worse than the last."

He puffs on his cigar thoughtfully.

"I hope you're not staying there because you feel obligated to stick it out."

"It's not that—"

"Because you know your mom and I would be proud of you regardless of your career choice. Hell, if you wanted to head off and play a flute in the woods, we'd still support that decision."

I know he means it. Even the flute thing. He's told me a million times he's having trouble figuring out why I'm doing this. The problem is, I'm not entirely sure why I'm doing this either. I'm pretty certain it's not the money, though the money is fantastic. Probably it's my fear of the abyss. You've ventured down this structured path since birth—grade school, then high school, then college, then recruiting—and you see the path's extension looming on the horizon: Work at the Bank for two or three years, take a break to get an MBA, return to climb your way up to the stratosphere of the industry, and retire by age forty-five with a home and a summer house and two Labrador retrievers. No matter that you're slowly being throttled by the invisible hand of crusty old Adam Smith. If I were to quit, to walk away from all this, it would be the equivalent of hurling myself into Nothingness. No stability, no steady flow of income, no guaranteed summer house, and no retrievers. A future plagued with way too much uncertainty.

I'm fully aware this is a pathetic standpoint. I've read *The Alchemist,* agree that humans can only hope to achieve inner peace by following their innate destinies. Still, I think my fear is valid enough. Think about it. Whose innate destiny is hanging on to the back of a truck and collecting other people's garbage? Scraping dead bodies from homicide scenes? *The Alchemist* maybe worked fine back in the agrarian days, when life wasn't so complex, when specialization of labor consisted of a decision between hunting wild boars or staying home and planting flax. But Ford and the Industrial Revolution changed all of that, bringing this whole notion of automation into corporate human behavior. Face it: *The Alchemist* just doesn't hold up in this modern age.

"I don't want you to waste any time. To spend even another year doing something that makes you so miserable."

Another puff. My dad is reaching the age when both of his parents died of cancer: my grandma with a tumor in her head, my grandfather with polyps all over his colon. It's making him acutely sensitive to the transience of things.

"Yeah, I know. It's like, standing here with you, I have this intuitive sense of what's good for me. But then the week starts, and I'm swamped with all this work, and suddenly my thinking is boxed in by their system. The Bank is like this evil vortex, sucking you in until you're one of them."

The tinkle of earrings. Aunt Penelope pokes her head out the screen door.

"Dinner's ready. It's all laid out buffet-style, so go right in and help yourselves."

While I'm scooping mushy carrots onto my plate, Uncle Tom creeps up from behind and pinches my left buttock.

"So, ninety hours a week, huh?"

I preemptively swat his hand away, avoiding another pinch.

"Yup."

"They must be paying you the big bucks?"

"Sixty base."

"That's it?"

"We get a bonus at the end of the year. Supposed to be another fifty or so."

"So you're, what, twenty-three and already pulling in over a hundred grand a year?"

Uncle Tom is really excited by this happy synaptic connection he's made. He's repeating to anyone who'll listen:

"Get this. He's twenty-three and making a hundred grand. He should be paying down our mortgages, right?"

Within seconds, the entire roomful of aliens knows my salary. It sets them buzzing like mosquitoes, the number rising up in disbelieving chirps. The rest of dinner is spent trying to persuade my preadolescent cousins not to pursue investment banking despite how many Pokemon cards they'll be able to afford.

As I'm forcing down the last piece of leathery brisket, Aunt Penelope, who's standing in the middle of the room, suddenly breaks out in uncontrollable sobbing:

"I can't believe I'm fifty and my life is like this. And the worst thing about it is everything's stuck. You can't change any of it."

It's pretty weighty stuff. Completely inappropriate, but weighty nonetheless. Nobody knows exactly how to react, so they do the awkward thing and gape at her in stunned silence until she's led upstairs by her embarrassed husband.

My mom giggles nervously. "That's our cue to leave."

On the way to the car, my dad betrays all the advice he spoon-fed me earlier, proving he too has succumbed to the alien mind-set:

"I just wanted to let you know that your mom and I, we're very proud of you. Pulling yourself up by your bootstraps, being entirely self-sufficient and all. This working hard now will only make you a stronger person later on. Trust me; stick it out for two more years and the world is going to be your oyster."

♦

The problem with my dad's logic is this: It's not going to be just the two years. We all start out kidding ourselves this way, swearing on our lives, on all good things in this world, that after twenty-four months we're going to step into that elevator and never go back. Never. Instead, we'll graduate from B-school and find a regular "industry" job with a decent enough salary, settling into upper-middle-class comfort: home by six, a hearty dinner of meatloaf and yams, coaching Little League or soccer practice on the weekend.

At least that's the theory. In actuality, demonstrated time and time again, the industry is not letting go; it nips at your neck like a pitbull on amphetamines. After suffering through the hellish experience of being the lowest of the low—those two or three years spent mastering the bricks and mortar of the trade—you're suddenly viewed by the industry as a precious commodity.

So this is how it works. By the time you're nearing the end of your second year in the banking world, your compensation has been juiced up to one hundred and forty thousand all-in. Analogously, you're also getting accustomed to the mind-numbing tedium of your position. You can crunch comps in your sleep, tame the two-hundred-sheet Excel behemoths, whip out perfectly formatted PowerPoint pie charts like nobody's business. Whether you like it or not, you're turning into the Star.

And let's not ignore the psychological aspect to it, the advent of Stockholm syndrome. The term originates from a bunch of Swedish hostages locked up in a bank vault for six days sometime in the seventies. The hostages gradually grew sympathetic toward their captors, resisted rescue attempts, and later refused to testify at the trial. The psychologists had a field day with this one. The prevailing theory is this: The human psyche is weak. In situations of duress, when we're surrounded by other humans who wield this awesome power over our ephemeral fates, we grow dependent on them. Dependency leads to affection; affection to love.

So in short, I love the Sycophant. Well, not yet, but I will.

♦

I'm all packed up after a long day and ready to crash at one-thirty—nothing too terrible, I'll still manage six hours of sleep—when the Defeated One returns from the washroom, sniffling. This time it's pretty bad, probably the worst I've ever seen him. A rivulet of guck trickles out one nostril. There's something about toiling away for sixteen hours straight that invokes a brutal honesty:

"You're a fucking mess," I say, shaking my head.

I brace myself for his retaliation. Though the Defeated One loves dishing it out, he's not so good at taking it. Instead, he sits down and belches out a wretched sob.

"It hurts."

He clutches at his chest in demonstration of this. It's actually kind of eerie; I've never seen the Defeated One genuinely upset before. Sure, he grumbles incessantly about his life, concocting never-ending plans to shove his head in an oven or impale himself on the modern art sculpture an achievable leap from our window. Still, there has always been a levity behind it, the overriding bullshit factor.

"What's going on?" I ask.

"I was up on the trading floor," he whimpers, "hunting down a can of Coke. Then I pass by this boardroom window and—"

Another wretched sob: "Oh god!"

"What?"

He's boring a pencil into his wrist now. A grunt later and he's managed to draw blood.

"Aren't you worried about lead poisoning?"

"If I should be so lucky. Besides, it's not lead, it's graphite."

"What about graphite poisoning?"

He rolls his eyes before another round of whimpering:

"Man, I'm telling you . . . it was *horrible.* The most horrible thing I have ever witnessed."

Even the Star's curiosity is piqued; he swivels around to listen.

"So what's going on?" I ask again.

"You're not gonna believe it—"

"Come on. Just tell us, already."

"All right."

The Defeated One takes a deep breath before moaning, "Unadulterated Sex. The Prodigal Son."

He rocks back and forth in the swivel chair, making a creaking noise. It takes only a few seconds for the neural connection, for pangs of jealousy to shoot through my abdomen. The Star, god bless him, seeks further clarifications.

"What do you mean? What were they doing up there?"

The Defeated One makes that creaking noise again. The Star ponders this for a moment, chewing on the eraser end of a pencil, before his eureka flash:

"Ohhhhhhhh."

He's got it now.

♦

"Do you have time to stay down for lunch?"

It's the end of the week, and half the senior guys in M&A, including the Sycophant, are tied up at a pitch for the next few hours.

"Always a risky proposition," the Defeated One says, scratching his chin, "but today's your lucky day, Mumbles. Let's go round up Clyde and Postal."

Clyde is a pushover. Postal Boy is putting up his usual resistance:

"The Ice Queen needs research reports pulled on every mining company in the Western hemisphere with a market cap greater than five hundred million. Half a day's work, and she wants it all done by the time she's finished her tuna wrap. I really can't."

The Defeated One puts up his hands in mock resignation. "Fine, fine. Sorry we bothered you in the first place."

Postal Boy's left eye twitches in relief as he swivels back around to his monitor. Clyde and I are walking out of the room when the Defeated One takes a running leap and lands a kick squarely to the back of Postal Boy's chair. Postal Boy lunges forward and collides with the edge of the desk, his glasses hurtling halfway across the room.

"Christ," he whimpers, getting to his feet.

The Defeated One is panting from the exertion. "Come on, Postal. You know that shit isn't going to work around these parts. Stop your whining and let's go grab some lunch."

Five minutes later there's the familiar electronic chime as we cross the threshold into Han's Blue Diamond Chinese Gourmet. There's no line, of course, because nobody in their right mind would subject themselves to this garbage: bins of glistening beef and broccoli, Kung Pao chicken and slithery noodles, our reflections all but visible in the sheen of the MSG coating. The pièce de resistance at Han's is Lunch Special No. 3 for $3.95. The General Tso chicken. Clumps of batter in an impossibly tangy red sauce enhancing the inner succulence of dubious chicken bits. Unbelievably tasty going in but leaving you an absolute wreck for the rest of the afternoon: fiery hiccups, your heart encased in an outer layer of gristle, the thick red sauce pumping lethargically through your veins.

The cardinal rule of eating at Han's Blue Diamond Chinese

Gourmet: You must order the Lunch Special No. 3, and extra sauce is mandatory. As the pockmarked teenager behind the counter ladles the General Tso onto a mound of rice, I shake my head.

"I swear to God, if I ever meet a girl who can finish an entire portion of this, I'll propose to her on the spot."

We settle into one of the cracked leather booths. Han's doesn't offer much in the way of atmosphere—oil stains on the linoleum floor, crumpled Fanta cans tossed in a corner, Postal Boy's elbow flying dangerously close to my jaw—but it's a tremendous indulgence, this shoveling in General Tso without a monitor blinking nearby and the Utterly Incompetent Assistant bitching about the smell if she's not out in the parking garage screwing around with the Philandering Managing Director.

Between mouthfuls of Lunch Special No. 3, the Defeated One imparts his boardroom discovery to Clyde and Postal Boy.

"We've got to get him fired. It's as simple as that."

"It's not that bad," Clyde says, then takes a swig of his Dr Pepper.

The Defeated One glares at him. "Not that bad? Not that bad? He gets to sleep around with Unadulterated Sex, violating a basic doctrine of human decency, and we're supposed to step back and take it? No fucking way. I mean, something's gotta be done."

"So what's the plan?" I mumble.

"Not too sure, gentlemen. I haven't come up with anything just yet. But we'll keep it in the back of our heads, figure something out eventually."

Postal Boy rubs at his eye. "I don't want any part of this. He hasn't done anything to me."

The Defeated One sneers in disgust. "He hasn't done anything to you? Give me a break. Who do you think has to clean up his comps while he's off screwing your mother?"

I shake my head. "Hey. Inappropriate."

"Fine, fine," the Defeated One mutters dejectedly. "But you guys are in, right?" Before Postal Boy can protest, he adds, "This is not a debatable issue."

He puts out his hand. Clyde puts his hand on top. Then my hand. Finally, with a sigh of resignation, Postal Boy joins our pile of hands. God, I feel like I'm in an episode of *Ghostbusters* here.

"Good," the Defeated One says, nodding. "We have until Christmas to accomplish the deed."

We've returned to wolfing down our General Tso, when we hear a familiar voice from the front of the restaurant:

"Lunch Special Number Three, please."

We all turn to gape at the Woman With The Scarf standing before the cashier.

"No way." Clyde squints in disbelief. "Isn't that the crazy chick from Starbucks?"

The pockmarked teenager behind the counter grins. "You special customer. You get extra meat."

He ladles a second spoonful of General Tso onto the rice. The Woman With The Scarf carries the heaping plate to a booth closer to the front of the restaurant.

"Fifty bucks she doesn't eat more than a third of her lunch," the Defeated One wagers.

None of us will take him up on it.

"Cheap bastards," he mutters.

We continue eating without bothering to put up a facade of idle chitchat. All eyes are glued on the Woman With The Scarf, who is angled in such a way that she can barely see us. Even the kid behind the counter is watching her with keen interest. She eats slowly and meticulously, pulling apart the lumps of General Tso with her chopsticks before placing the tiniest morsels between her lips. Her delicacy is incongruous in a place like Han's;

here you're meant to swallow first, chew later. After fifteen minutes at this pace, she's made a modest dent in her double portion of meat.

"I have to get back," Postal Boy says, beginning to panic. "The Ice Queen is going to have my head on a platter."

The Defeated One waves him off. "Look, she's showing no signs of fading."

At the twenty-minute mark, she's halfway there.

The Defeated One whistles. "Jesus, she's gone through a whole portion of Lunch Special Number Three, a *whole* frickin' portion, and not only is she not projectile-vomiting all over the walls but, look at that, she keeps on ticking. Gentlemen, we may be this close to witnessing a miraculous feat of human perseverance."

The Woman With The Scarf has devoured two-thirds of the plate, when there's a sudden grimace, a hand rushing to her mouth.

"Oh no!" The Defeated One giggles excitedly. "Thar she blows!"

The kid behind the counter is looking nervous, his hand already straying toward the handle of a mop.

And there it is: a hiccup. Perhaps a muffled burp. Either way, once it's expelled from her system, she's back to pulling apart the last few nuggets of General Tso.

The Defeated One shakes his head. "My god, she's on the homestretch now."

A few minutes later and the Woman With The Scarf has somehow managed the impossible. Plowing through a double portion is a feat worthy of spontaneous applause as raucous as Irish rugby hooligans', a thunderous standing ovation from every passerby on the street. The pockmarked teenager leaves the mop by the wall and slumps against the counter in relieved disbelief.

The Defeated One pushes me out of the booth.

"It's your turn to shine, big boy."

"What the hell are you talking about?"

The Defeated One turns to Clyde and Postal Boy.

"Didn't our young colleague just promise he'd propose to any fine lady who could eat her way through a portion of General Tso?"

Turning back to me, he adds, "That was double meat, Mumbles. No way you're pussying out on this one."

The Woman With The Scarf is dabbing at her lips with a napkin and doesn't notice my approach until I'm already standing over her booth. She eyes me quizzically.

"Yes?"

"I, um, I mean . . ."

The mumbling is out in full force now. I smile sheepishly. She's not smiling back. I hear the Defeated One snickering somewhere in the background.

"I'm not sure if you would remember me. A couple weeks ago, at Starbucks. You were in front of me in the line. I kind of, um, lost my cool."

She remains as impassive as a gargoyle.

"Anyway, I wanted to apologize. If you remember it, that is. I mean, it was just, uh, I was having this really terrible day. Didn't sleep well the night before. Didn't sleep at all, actually. And yeah, you were having a horrible day as well. I mean, I'm really not an asshole, at least not most of the time, it's just that I hate my job—"

"You can stop now."

"Oh."

"You're rambling."

"Yeah."

Then she makes this strange laugh. More of a grunt, really.

Leaning back in the booth, tucking a strand of hair behind an ear, she sighs.

"I wasn't always like this, you know," she says.

She's looking not at me but straight ahead at a small black-and-white television playing an episode of *The Dukes of Hazzard.* Or maybe it's the dusty bottles of chili sauce lining the wall.

"I used to like rambling. I mean guys who rambled. Whatever. Awkwardness as a sign of sensitivity."

I expect there to be more to this tangent, but that's it; the conversation has reached a standstill. After an uncomfortable silence, I think to say, "That was pretty impressive just now."

"What?"

"Getting through the double portion of General Tso. We"—I shrug back at the trio of yokels raising their glasses of water to us—"didn't think you'd be able to manage it."

She smiles. It's a feeble smile, no warmth behind it.

"Look, I know you meant well coming over here and apologizing—" She laughs nervously, wiping a spot of sauce from her chin. "I have no idea how I was going to finish that sentence. I guess what I'm trying to say is, well, I'm just really, really tired. And I don't know what you want from me, whether you're just being friendly or you're expecting something else—"

"Just being friendly." I nod profusely. "Hey, don't worry about it."

I look over at the Defeated One; he gestures to indicate they're ready to leave.

"Anyway, I'm really sorry for the whole Starbucks debacle. Well, it was nice running into you again."

I've already turned around, heading back to our booth, when she calls out.

"Wait a minute."

She rummages around in her handbag and comes up with a business card. She leans out of the booth and hands it to me.

"If ever our hectic schedules allow for it, we could go for coffee or something. At least I'll be assured you're not going to go apeshit on me in the line."

♦

Despite the Defeated One's jeering on the walk back to the office and Clyde's attempts to snatch the card from my pocket, I'm left with a testosterone-fueled halo of triumph. The three of them, they're mere boys building tree forts in the backyard. I, on the other hand, I'm your genuine, swaggering, chest-thumping alpha male. That is, until I return to my desk and find a Post-it Note stuck to my chair:

12:45 now. Checked with the Utterly Incompetent Assistant and she doesn't have a clue where you are. This is not good at all. Come see me as soon as you get in.

The Sycophant's note is from right before we left; the pitch must have ended early. Looking at the clock on my phone, I've been MIA for over an hour and a half.

Two words: Instant Emasculation.

Four

It takes two weeks for the Defeated One to hatch our plan against the Prodigal Son, and it's Lulu Heifenschliefen who catalyzes the process.

Excluding our Gang of Four, Frau Heifenschliefen is the only Bank employee I genuinely like. Lulu hails from across the Atlantic—Poland, the Netherlands, I forget which—and she's built like an ostrich: a long neck leading up to a blond, unruly mane; a small, puckered face with the exception of a prominent beak nose; a squat torso perched on two spindly legs. You know Lulu is coming down the corridor because her peculiar laugh, a shrill chortle capped off with a sneeze, always precedes her. And when she arrives, ruddy-cheeked and wearing her polka dots, a plastic flower struggling in the crow's nest of her hair, you're filled with an overwhelming sense of *goodness*. Freshly baked chocolate chip cookies and sun-kissed meadows and all that.

It's brought on by Lulu's naïveté, I think. While the Philandering Managing Director's getting tied up and spanked on the weekend and the Sycophant is pressing his face up against the TV to decipher grainy porn on the pay-per-view channels, you know Lulu Heifenschliefen's out and about on her brand-new shiny red bike, ringing her bell, her colored streamers flying in the breeze, a basket of fresh turnips up front, all the while laughing and sneezing and transcending this city's notion that you have to be kinky and achingly sophisticated to have a good time.

Lulu is technically the Events Coordinator, meaning she's responsible for organizing all of the Bank's corporate functions and retreats. Nonetheless, because the Coldest Fish In The Pond is a notorious tightwad, rumored to periodically inspect expense reports for any lavish transgressions, her official duties are minimal at best. There is the annual holiday party, for one, and the analyst orientation during the summer.

"Hello, my piglets," she coos, slipping into our office.

She's flushed and excited and wearing woolen boots despite the fact it's not all that cold outside. Minus the eccentricity, she gives you the familiar feeling of being greeted by your favorite aunt. Even the Defeated One breaks into a giddy smile, a stretching of his cheek muscles that looks like it's hurting his face. Lulu settles into the spare chair and pats down the creases of her orange-and-maroon-striped taffeta skirt.

She motions to something on my desk.

"Be a good boy-chick and pass me a tissue."

I hand it to her reverently, and she accepts it with a batting of her fake eyelashes. She blows her nose twice, deposits the tissue in a fold of her skirt, and beams at us with a beatific smile, her pupils as shiny as flecks of ebony. We've all swiveled around to face her, the tired gentry of Lulu's court. She holds a hand to her chest, releases a single brittle cough, and scrunches up her puckered face.

"Ach, this change in seasons always affects me like this. I trust you have all been in fine health?"

"Yeah, things have been all right," the Defeated One says, nodding.

It's not a very convincing response, and Lulu frowns, a tsk-tsk clucked under her breath.

"They work you too hard in this little department. Too much work and not enough play, *nein?*"

We stare at her in brooding silence.

"*Nein?*"

"All right," the Defeated One concedes, hanging his head. "It's been pretty bad."

"My poor little piglets," Lulu sighs.

"And what about on your end? How has the Toad been?"

Lulu shrugs. "The Toad, he is still the same pipsqueak. He thinks because we work in the same department, he can get all hussy-fussy on me. But I tell you, kittens"—here she smacks her palms together—"Lulu is having none of it."

"What a jackass," the Defeated One snorts.

"Language," Lulu scolds.

The Toad is the Toad for a reason: small and cute in a platonic pudgy way but filled with sacs of lethal toxins that enter your bloodstream and leave you brain-dead five minutes later. No antidote, no best friend sucking out the poison and bragging about it afterward on a talk show.

Aside from his HR duties, the Toad is the analyst liaison with senior management. Nonetheless, the Toad *despises* us lowly peons. If the Toad had his way, he'd want the Bank run as a Viking slave ship. Tied to our computers, peeing into plastic pipes, with nutrients injected into our forearms three times a day. Multitasking janitors lashing us across the shoulders. The Toad would all the while promise us raises, an extra five bucks for our dinner allowance, spewing forth his endless rhetoric that we're the most valuable asset in the Bank's hierarchal pyramid.

"Anyway, what brings you around today?" I ask.

She winks at me before snorting into the tissue.

"What, am I to be denied the pleasure of coming by and gazing at three strapping young boy-chicks like yourselves? Doesn't an old bag deserve a little fun?"

"Can it, Lulu. You're what, forty-five? Definitely under fifty?"

"Ach, if you say so. Fifty-seven as of last week."

We go around and dispense our birthday wishes. As Lulu checks her purse for a cough drop, the Defeated One motions for me to close the door. After it's shut, the Defeated One draws his chair close beside Lulu, and the two of them start whispering conspiratorially. This is Lulu's unofficial duty at the Bank: professional gossipmonger. Because Lulu is so off-kilter, her eccentricity incongruous among the immaculate professionalism of Ivy League MBA grads, people have no idea how to react to her. During these heightened moments of confusion, while you're distracted perhaps by the clunky rhinestone pendant swinging across her ample bosom, she'll peer at you with glassy honest eyes, and very soon you're seeking comfort for the crappy bonus you just received, your suspicions the wife may have more than just a passing relationship with the landscaper, for how the assistant you were screwing around with earlier in the month gave you an itchy present down below.

Yet it's a known fact: While all of the Bank's dirty little secrets have at some point filtered through Lulu Heifenschliefen's eardrums, she knows to propagate them with utmost discretion. All the heavy stuff, anything with the potential to wreak havoc if left to fester out in the open, is locked up in some secure chamber of her cerebellum. Everything else, though, the frivolous triviality with loads of entertainment mileage, is fair game.

"The Sycophant, it is just *sooo* terrible; the man wears tighty whities! Even in Europe the men would not dare it!" she whispers ecstatically, putting a hand to her mouth to stifle a fit of giggles.

Lulu knows all our nicknames, a meager trade-off for her wealth of knowledge. The Defeated One snickers.

"How'd you figure that one out?"

"Eyes, chickie," Lulu says as she shakes a bejeweled finger at him. "A crumpled-up pair sticking out of his gym bag."

"It's a darn good thing they weren't modeled for you directly. That would have been some scary shit."

Lulu Heifenschliefen snorts devilishly. She's definitely in her element. In a hushed tone, she continues:

"This is nothing compared to the Philandering Managing Director. That man is *veeery* naughty, yes, into far more filthy undergarments."

"Oh god, you've got to tell us!" giggles the Star.

"Patience, boy-chick." Lulu rubs her hands together in glee. "First I require a juicy morsel or two to widen my big fat mouth."

The three of us stare at each other and shrug. Then the Defeated One leans in close beside Lulu's ear. I can't really make out his whispering, but I think I hear it punctuated with the names of the Prodigal Son, then Unadulterated Sex.

"Are you sure that's such a good idea?" I interrupt.

The Defeated One scowls and waves it off. Lulu listens attentively, nodding her head slowly. When the Defeated One is finished, she purses her lips together and absentmindedly wipes at her forehead with the snot-soaked tissue. I hand her a fresh one.

"Thank you, piglet."

Exhaling sharply, she says, "That is really quite something. *Mein Gott,* I was not expecting that at all. She is engaged, wouldn't you believe it, to a Russian."

She furrows her forehead as if processing this new information carefully.

"But he is such a young boy. She must be off her rocker, right, piglets?"

She sighs in exasperation. The Defeated One winks at me, an unspoken understanding: Lulu also thinks their tryst is wrong. We have a third-party opinion to support our determination to get him fired.

"The Russian, he will be coming to the holiday party. This name you call her—what is it, Unadulted Sex?—yes, she said she will bring her fiancé. I am certain this is the case. Which reminds me—"

Lulu pulls a heap of waxy envelopes out of her purse and hands us each one. Palm trees sway on the cover of an invitation.

YOU AND A GUEST ARE CORDIALLY INVITED TO
THE BANK'S ANNUAL HOLIDAY PARTY.

SHERATON HOTEL, DECEMBER 14, 8:00 PM.
DRINKS AND HORS D'OEUVRES WILL BE SERVED.

PLEASE RSVP NO LATER THAN NOVEMBER 20.

THEME: LUAU!!!
DON'T FORGET YOUR FLORAL SHIRT OR HULA SKIRT!!!

"A Hawaiian theme? Lulu, how could you?" the Defeated One chides.

Lulu shrugs. "Don't give me that. It will be fun. Leis, coconuts, plastic palm trees. We'll be drowning in kitsch, piglets."

The Defeated One mentioned this party in passing. It's a pretty wild time, apparently: open bar, decent finger food, an opportunity to watch the Sycophant make an ass out of himself trying to get the steps down to the electric slide. As a party teeming with investment bankers has its natural limitations—the Toad acting as chaperone, analysts quivering in fear lest they drink too much and do something really stupid in front of their bosses—the Bank has typically been clever enough to invite its umbrella of other divisions: the cantankerous old drunks up on the bond trading floor; the Tech Support team always showing up either grossly underdressed or grossly overdressed; and, most fascinating of all, the back-office employees, those forgotten souls tucked away in the basement doing risk analysis and credit profiling and god knows what else. There is otherwise no recognition for these subterranean critters, no chance at glory, only this one annual party, a single foray into the Bank's public eye.

Needless to say, the pressure is too much for them. Dusting off their sixties chiffon prom dresses, donning their tweed suits, they venture forth into the limelight to provide hours of top-notch entertainment: being the first ones on the dance floor, inevitably drinking too much, vomiting all over the bathroom walls before one of them knocks over the punch bowl. A burst of greatness before slithering back to their dank and muted cubicles, forgotten for another 364 days.

"Back office got the invite, right?" the Defeated One asks, grinning.

Lulu titters behind her hand; even she appreciates the insinuation.

"Of course, boy-chick. It would not be a party without them."

"Are we doing one of those videos again?"

The Defeated One mentioned this as well. It's one of the Bank's long-standing traditions (meaning it was initiated two or three years back) that the analysts are supposed to get together and film a witty-yet-within-the-bounds-of-good-taste video to be screened at the party.

"Yes, I believe the Toad mentioned something about it this morning. As a senior analyst, boy-chick, I think you might be in charge."

"Jesus," the Defeated One groans, "like my job isn't difficult enough without having to force a chuckle from Stepford wives."

Lulu is no longer paying attention, struggling to shove the remainder of the envelopes back in her purse.

"It was lovely, my piglets," she says, bolting up from the chair, "but duty awaits."

She holds the edges of her skirt and does a little curtsy, then bounds across the room, still trying to stuff the envelopes back in her purse.

"Adieu, adieu."

Before she slips out the door, she adds, "Oh my, I nearly forgot. It's a G-string, by the way. Zebra print. I noticed it when the Philanderer bent down to pick up some papers."

After we're done shaking off that horrible mental image, I turn back to my monitor. It's been a few days since I ran into the Woman With The Scarf at Han's Blue Diamond Chinese Gourmet, and social etiquette dictates it is now permissible for me to send her an e-mail without coming across as too desperate:

> From: Me@theBank.com
>
> To: WomanWithTheScarf@GoodmanWeisenthal.com
>
> Hey—you gave me your card at Han's a couple days ago. Double portion day. Was wondering if you were up for coffee this afternoon. If not, another time.

A Shakespearean sonnet it's not, but you better believe it took twenty minutes to craft that e-mail. Her reply is immediate:

From: WomanWithTheScarf@GoodmanWeisenthal.com

To: Me@theBank.com

Oh yes, I could definitely use some caffeine right now.

Starbucks in fifteen?

I whip off an affirmative: Three o'clock it is.

I begin reviewing an annual report. When I look over my shoulder, the Defeated One is still facing away from his desk, scratching his chin with the nib of a pencil. Suddenly he smacks his knee and starts laughing hysterically.

"Gentlemen, I do believe I've got it!"

"Got what?"

"The plan, Mumbles, the plan!"

The Defeated One gets to his feet and starts pacing the room. He's babbling animatedly.

"We're going to capture it on tape. They've done it once, they'll do it again. We'll hide the camcorder in the boardroom or something. Come the holiday party, projecting it on the screen, the two of them rutting in front of each and every employee at the Bank, including her Russian fiancé"—the Defeated One pulls at the sides of his receding hairline in his excitement—"it's fucking brilliant!"

The Star and I stare at him stoically. The Defeated One grimaces.

"Huh? Don't you appreciate the genius behind it?"

"So, we're going to get this all on tape?" the Star offers meekly.

"Yes! Detectives do it all the time."

"And you're fully comfortable broadcasting this in front of everybody at the Bank? What about the fallout? How's the Prodigal Son not going to suspect it's us behind it? Have you even stopped for a second and thought about the consequences if anybody catches us?" I ask. "We'd be served our pink slips faster than—"

The Defeated One shakes his head sadly. "Mumbles, stop being such a pansy. We'll get some scapegoat to cover the rest of the editing and splice in the clip right before the party. Don't worry about the minutiae; we'll figure out the kinks in due time. So, you guys are in, right?"

The Star has already swiveled back to his monitor.

"Heh"—the Defeated One turns to me—"he wasn't meant to be a part of it anyway. Are you in?"

It's a feasible plan, I'll grant him that. There is ample room for potential fuckups, the punishment for failure being severe, but also a sliver of a chance we might be able to pull it off.

"Aaargh. You won't let up on this until I agree, will you?"

"Not likely."

Leaning back in the chair:

"Fine," I mumble, "I'm in."

"Great!" The Defeated One beams. "I'm going to run it by Clyde and Postal later this afternoon, see what they think about it."

I check the clock at the bottom of my monitor. Two minutes to three. I open a complicated-looking spreadsheet and strew some papers across my desk.

"All right, boy-chicks, I'll be back in fifteen minutes or so. If anybody asks, tell them I'm taking a dump."

"Where are you off to?" the Defeated One asks suspiciously.

"Coffee date with that girl from Han's."

"You're sneaking away for an afternoon fuck. Way to go, stud," the Defeated One snickers.

"Piss off."

I've just located my wallet hidden under a pitch book, when the phone rings; the Sycophant's extension shows on the caller ID. I consider not answering it—surely it can wait fifteen minutes—but for some stupid reason I do. The Sycophant is snappy and clearly frustrated, explaining how the Utterly Incompetent Assistant needs help with some filing and it has to be done within the hour. Resisting a primal urge to scream expletives into the receiver, I tell him I'll be right on it.

As I hang up, the Defeated One shakes his head in mock pity.

"The Sycophant cock-blocked your little coffee date, huh?"

"Jesus, I should have known better," I sigh, slumping back in the chair. "I mean, you'd think I'd be used to it by now, you really would. But fuck, it still stings every time. Does it ever get any better?"

The Defeated One flicks a rubber band at me. "Nope."

I pick the rubber band off the carpet and add it to the rubber-band ball I've been forming since I started here. So far it's no bigger than a golf ball, only a meager few dozen rubber bands, but I'm inspired by the mammoth aluminum-foil ball that used to roll into *Pee-wee's Playhouse* before the guy crushed our youthful naïveté by wanking in a movie theater.

I dash off an e-mail:

> From: Me@theBank.com
>
> To: WomanWithTheScarf@GoodmanWeisenthal.com
>
> My humble apologies. My VP is in a crunch and needs some immediate assistance. Impossible to get away right now. Hopefully you haven't gone down already. Anyway, would really like to reschedule—perhaps later in the week?

A couple minutes go by and I still haven't received a response.

Fucking hell.

♦

I don't understand it. I really don't. I'm kneeling beside the Utterly Incompetent Assistant, mountains of paper surrounding us, and I've just seen her slot a Prudential Securities report in the D folder. It's simple: Prudential, P. It's the umpteenth time she's messed up since we started, the first time I'm going to muster the resolve to say something about it.

"Why'd you just do that?"

She stops filing and stares vacantly at me.

"What?"

I'm trying my best not to come across as too antagonistic.

"That report was clearly for Prudential Securities. Right at the top of the first page. And yet you put it in the D folder."

Her expression is vapid.

She shrugs. "I made a mistake. I'm human."

She goes back into the D folder, removes the Prudential Securities report, and drops it in its rightful spot in the P folder. Less than five minutes later, I see her slotting an SBC Communications pitch in the Z folder. It's too much. I reach into the Z folder and slam the SBC pitch on the floor beside her.

"That's an S," I bark. "*S.*"

My attempt at authoritativeness comes out forced, a little too abrupt. Perhaps it's a deficiency in my character—I'm a notorious conflict avoider—though it could also be the inherent awkwardness of a twenty-three-year-old having to bitch out a woman who is already pushing her midforties.

The Utterly Incompetent Assistant glowers at me, putting her hands on her hips.

"What's your problem?"

I'm flabbergasted, truly.

"What's my problem? *My* problem? I'm asked to help out because you're too stu—"

I catch myself before I cross a line. Though it's an objective truth—the Utterly Incompetent Assistant is as dumb as a doorknob—my stating this explicitly would have severe repercussions. No doubt she'd send off a complaint to the sticklers at HR and then I'd be booted out, the Utterly Incompetent Assistant left to gloat over a file cabinet in complete disarray. Justice duly served.

"I just don't understand it, that's all. I mean, you *know* the SBC Communications pitch should be filed in the S folder. You have to know this. And yet you put it in the wrong folder."

I'm expecting some moral outrage, a defense mechanism kicking in, but instead she's back to that irritatingly vapid expression.

"What I don't understand is why you care so much."

I stare at her in stunned silence, but she ignores me, going back to her filing. I pick up another report and drop it in the correct folder, and yet I can't seem to brush off what she just said. I'm sure she didn't intend it to be profound, but it is somewhat, now that I'm thinking about it: Why do I care so much? What makes me different from this middle-aged woman who is perfectly content going about her daily business making all sorts of negligent errors, returning home to her cats and her *Reader's Digest* and a Lean Cuisine popped in the microwave? Why do I care so deeply about getting these reports and pitches into their correct folders, given that nobody's going to pat me on the back for the effort?

Two years: the average lifespan of an i-banking analyst. That's all it's going to be. Kneeling here beside the Utterly Incompetent Assistant, I make a commitment to myself: No matter what's thrown my way, whether it be a ludicrous salary increase, a promotion, or the promise of a brilliant letter of recommendation to the prestigious B-school of my choice, I'm going to walk out that door after twenty-four months, never to return.

For now, it's more of the same. I notice the Utterly Incompetent Assistant slotting a Coors Brewing Company report in the

K folder. At least she got it right phonetically. I don't bother reprimanding her; she's chosen her path, just as I've chosen mine. I reach in and correct her mistake, both of us silent until our task is done.

♦

The Defeated One is testing out the eyepiece of a digital camcorder.

"Lulu was right," he says, filming me walking across the room and sitting down at my desk. "The Toad came by while you and dimwit extraordinaire were filing away and put me on video crew. The quality on this is fantastic."

I open up Outlook.

> From: WomanWithTheScarf@GoodmanWeisenthal.com
>
> To: Me@theBank.com
>
> Didn't get your e-mail until too late. My sincere thanks for sending it out one minute before we were supposed to meet up. Waited at Starbucks for a good half hour before I realized you'd be a no-show. Maybe this coffee thing wasn't such a brilliant idea. Anyway, not the end of the world. Perhaps I'll run into you in the elevators.

There's nothing unexpected here: Of course she was going to get my e-mail too late; of course she was going to blow me off as a result. Perhaps I'm finally adopting the required mind-set for this job, though this isn't exactly the most comforting thought.

"I ran our plan by Postal and Clyde already. Clyde thinks it's a great idea, and Postal's being Postal, meaning he's a bit squeamish right off the bat. Nothing a few rounds of good ol' peer pressure won't fix. All right, so we're all in. Next step is being on the lookout for a filming opportunity."

"Cool," I mumble.

The Defeated One is unperturbed by my lack of enthusiasm.

"I can't believe how genius this is. We're going to pull this off, we really are, and it's going to be brilliant!"

"Yeah."

This time he senses my malaise.

"Dude, I wouldn't worry about that chick. Face it, if she's going to get all pissy about missing one coffee date, imagine how she's going to react when you fail to show up at her birthday party, or an anniversary, or something like that. An inevitability if you start dating."

"Yeah," I say, shrugging. "You're probably right."

"You've got to start doing some coke, man. Trust me; it makes this life a little more bearable."

I'm not anti–drug use by any means—to each his own—but I tend to like doing that stuff when I'm feeling good about things, not as an escape mechanism.

"No, thanks."

The Defeated One shrugs.

"Well, you know it's available. Just say when."

I've already swiveled back around to add footnotes to my pie charts.

Five

Filming begins earlier than expected. It's two in the morning, less than a week after Lulu's visit, and the Defeated One has gone to pick up some rancid coffee from the Most Depressing Donut Store in Downtown, the only place that's open at this ungodly hour. Run by a portly Vietnamese woman and reeking of stale cigarette smoke, the dimly lit hovel is a meeting ground for old men literally weeping into their cups of tepid coffee when they're not coughing up phlegm or gnawing away on chocolate-glazed crullers.

My phone rings. Before I've even put the receiver to my ear, I'm bombarded with urgent instructions from the Defeated One:

"Prodigal Son and Unadulterated Sex spotted heading into an elevator together. This could be our golden opportunity. Grab the camcorder and boot it to the boardroom off the Equity Capital Markets desk. Hopefully they'll be going to the same place as the last time. Hide the camcorder somewhere discreet and get the hell out of there."

I interrupt his barrage. “Hey, I didn’t agree to the actual filming.”

After a moment of silence the Defeated One snaps at me, “You said you were in on this. You damn well agreed to this plan. I’m telling you, this could be our last chance. Don’t fuck this up, Mumbles.”

I sigh audibly, but the Defeated One knows he’s got me.

“You have two minutes.”

Then he hangs up. It’s difficult to shrug off my two-in-the-morning lethargy as I grab the camcorder, then speed-walk down the corridor and climb the stairs two at a time. The boardroom off the Equity Capital Markets desk. There are two rooms, one straight ahead, the other a bit to the right. A fifty-fifty probability I’ll get the right one. I slip into the dark room to the right and close the door.

Where to conceal the camcorder in hopes of getting the money shot? Behind the potted fern in the corner? Above the projector-thingy that nobody knows how to use properly, not even the IT guys? I hear footsteps approaching and I have about six seconds, max. I switch on the camera and crudely position it on the cabinet facing the boardroom table, hurling myself into the closet just as the door squeaks open. I’m panting hard, adrenaline racing through my veins, with the exhilarating feeling that comes from being a sneaky shit-disturber. Crammed in between a tower of Coca-Cola cases and boxes full of Bank giveaways—umbrellas and fleeces and packets of mints with the Bank logo stamped on the tins, whatever the marketing team concocts to justify its existence—I hear the door shut behind them.

“Oh fuck, yeah.”

A deep male voice, then a forceful sucking sound.

The closet has louvered doors with slits down the front, allowing for moderate visibility if you press your face up close.

Peering through the cracks, I have a decent enough view of two shadowy figures moving around on the other side of the room.

"I want to look at you, babe."

The lights flare on. Apparently there is going to be very little foreplay involved: Unadulterated Sex is leaning back on the table, the Prodigal Son standing between her splayed legs. He hikes up her skirt and she groans, a rumbling emanating from deep within her chest.

Oh god.

Oh fucking god.

The envy rears up like a colossal wave and pierces the fuzzy bubble of my exhaustion. I mean, they don't even sound like real people anymore. It's an avant-garde cacophony of biting and moaning and animalistic grunting, the acoustics of cannibals tearing at the succulent flesh of unsuspecting pilgrims. I'm not going to open my eyes. I'm not going to subject myself to this. Think Zen thoughts: stalks of bamboo swaying in the breeze, delicate rice paper calligraphy, lotus petals fluttering across the surface of a pond filled with fat goldfish.

But suddenly my eyes fly open of their own accord, drinking in the full spectacle before them: the Prodigal Son standing at the edge of the boardroom table, his unbuttoned shirt revealing rippling abdominal muscles contrasting sharply with my own recently developed squishiness, thrusting into a glistening expanse of perfect humanity stretched languorously before him. My throat parches instantly, my breath coming out in wheezing gasps. And yes, I've got a throbbing hard-on. I hate myself for it.

It's just not right, that's all. You're struggling to hold on to a youthful idealism, an earnest belief that everybody exists on a fairly level playing field, that a woman like Unadulterated Sex is truly unattainable, that she lies in bed clutching a teddy bear and pining for some regular schmo who sat in front of her in remedial algebra, and then something like this happens and suddenly you've got cracks splintering all over your belief system.

"Your fiancé screws you this hard, huh? Takes you right on the boardroom table?" the Prodigal Son pants.

Unadulterated Sex is whimpering incoherently.

"That little Russian with his small little dick making you feel this good, huh?"

"Nooooo," she moans.

The Prodigal Son chuckles, wiping the sweat from his forehead.

"Yeah, that's right, babe. There just ain't no competition."

There's not much I can do but keep gawking at this spectacle. I'm waiting for an event that will precipitate my catharsis: the Prodigal Son getting off too soon, Unadulterated Sex suddenly shameful of her infidelity and kicking him off her. I'd even take something slapstick, like the Prodigal Son banging his head on the videoconferencing control panel, or Unadulterated Sex accidentally rolling off the table. Anything to disrupt the unconscionable pleasure they seem to be deriving from each other.

"Oh yeah, this feels awesome."

The Prodigal Son leaps onto the table, repositioning Unadulterated Sex so her upper body is now dangling off the edge. It's a beautiful position from my vantage point, her breasts hanging there in plain view, until I realize her head is a mere ten inches away from the camcorder. She opens her eyes and there is no way she's going to miss it.

Oh shit.

Unadulterated Sex rasps, "I'm getting close."

The Prodigal Son is silent, focusing all his energy on bringing her over the edge. Literally. Half her body now dangles acrobatically off the table, her head no more than six inches away from the camcorder. My god, she could just reach out and touch it.

Their breathing becomes more erratic now, like an asthmatics,' and I can't say I'm entirely immune to their imminent climax. Beneath this web of rational thought—my genuine fear of getting caught, the suffocating envy, the bitter loss of my naive worldview—is the undeniable physical aspect of a steel girder in my pants. I know they're teetering on the verge of orgasm when they've entered the realm of monosyllabic communication:

"Ohhh."

"Yeah."

"Christ."

"Fuck!"

"Ahhhh!!!"

"Yeahh!!!"

"Ahhhhhhhhhhhhhhhhhh!!!!"

"Fuuuuuccccccckkkkkkkk!!!"

"Ahhh."

"Ohhh."

"Yeah."

"Uhmmm."

"Ahhh."

"Christ."

It's a painfully erotic sixty seconds, and thank god when it's finally over. Unadulterated Sex remains lying half off the table, eyes closed, until the Prodigal Son yanks her up into a sitting position. I'm too emotionally numb to appreciate the end of her close call with the camcorder. As with their lack of foreplay, there's not much in the way of postcoital activity: They slide off the table and dress in silence; a minute or two later and they're out the door. Brute animalistic rutting, that's all it was. Goddamn lucky bastard. After cleaning myself up with a Bank-monogrammed fleece, I grab the camcorder and scurry back downstairs.

The Defeated One quickly shuts the door behind me, snatching the camcorder out of my hands and trying to watch the replay in the eyepiece. He's already assembled Clyde and Postal Boy, who are both more giddy than I've ever seen them. Clyde cuffs me on the shoulder.

"Great job, man."

Postal Boy's left eye is twitching like crazy, but he's grinning away like a kid who's just found his older brother's porn stash.

"Yeah, way to go, buddy."

I can't really deal with them right now, but I manage a weak nod. The Defeated One looks up from trying to get the camcorder to work, and, perhaps noticing the gravity of my expression, says, "Holy shit. You witnessed the whole thing."

"I couldn't get out in time," I say, then shrug sheepishly.

"*Sheeeet.* It's painful, I know. I'm really sorry, Mumbles."

"Whatever."

"Anyway, a small sacrifice made for the betterment of your corporate existence. And ours."

The Defeated One figures out the replay. There is a stretch of uncomfortable silence before the Defeated One puts down the camcorder, grimacing.

"Fuck, it's horrible. I mean, it's perfect, you got them both right on camera, Unadulterated Sex is, like, right up there in your face, but still it's just awful, you know?"

I shrug again. The Defeated One eyes me sternly before extending his hand. It's a stiff shake:

"You've done well for your country tonight, comrade."

♦

There's a palpable feeling of victory over the next few days. The Defeated One is in particularly high spirits: whistling in the bathroom, chuckling over the latest economic indicators in the *Wall Street Journal,* even going so far as treating me to a cappuccino one morning, which is saying a lot, because he's a cheap bastard.

We might have to rename him the Eternal Optimist, though it doesn't quite have the same ring to it.

There have been more of those Starbucks excursions as well, as many as twice a day now. Mostly it's to discuss progress on our little film project, or, rather, the weirdness of the Star editing it for us. A real mind-fuck, I assure you. While we were sitting around discussing the editing job one morning, realizing none of us knew our ass from our elbow when it came to digital software, the Star made the unfortunate mistake of mentioning an undergraduate film class he'd taken for half a semester. Needless to say, after the Defeated One threatened to tamper with the Star's meticulous library of Visual Basic macros if he refused to help out, he finally caved on the condition we'd never disclose his involvement. A pinkie swear later and he was in.

♦

I enter the office a week later to find the Defeated One and Postal Boy huddled before the Star's computer.

"Quick"—the Defeated One waves over his shoulder—"close the door and get over here."

On the monitor, a miniature Prodigal Son is biting the neck of a miniature Unadulterated Sex. They're positioned a little off-center, but the clarity is good enough for them to be easily recognizable. A seventies porno beat wafts softly from the speakers. Then the screen shifts to a close-up of the penetration. The Defeated One throws his hand before his eyes and turns away.

"Jesus, easy on the hard-core."

The Star swivels around in his chair, as skittish as a Japanese schoolgirl in a Tarantino movie.

"It's a new function on these digital camcorders. You can zoom in anywhere on the image and it doesn't really affect the pixel quality. Awesome, huh? Look at that penetration . . . woof!"

The Star rubs his hands together in glee. Even Postal Boy throws me a stern glance. It's like we've created a monster: one part gadgetry geekiness, two parts sexual frustration.

The action shifts so Unadulterated Sex is now lying half off the table, her face filling the entire screen. It's the close call with the camcorder witnessed from this strange new vantage point. Her features are contorted into a look of lust, yes, no denying that, but—dare I say it?—an element of vulnerability as well. Maybe there was a brief moment when she was remembering her Russian fiancé, how he sits in his armchair beside the mother-of-pearl lamp and augustly turns the pages of a Dostoyevsky novel. Perhaps only then does she appreciate the meaninglessness of their sex, a purely physical rutting devoid of any emotion. Maybe I'm just plain fooling myself and what I interpret as vulnerability is really Unadulterated Sex wallowing in enormously gratifying pleasure. Either way, I've found my catharsis. I put my hands on the Star's shoulders.

"That, comrade, is a job well done."

The Star giggles and takes a bow in his seat.

"Hey, where's Clyde?" I ask.

Postal Boy shrugs. "Not sure. He didn't come in this morning. Maybe a sick day?"

Sick days at the Bank are only slightly more acceptable than vacation days, meaning they should be taken with the utmost discretion: a ruptured appendix is fine, a strange tumor growing out the side of your neck, fine, but flu symptoms or a nasty hangover are out. And if you think this job is bad enough, try doing comps after a night of gratuitous tequila shots to send a colleague off to B-school, then puking in a mailbox before passing out fully clothed on your grimy kitchenette floor. Done that once; it's not an experience I'm hoping to repeat.

"Starbucks time," the Defeated One declares, turning away from the monitor.

"You up for coffee?" I ask the Star.

He blinks at me in disbelief and gratitude. That's right, I forgot—we excluded him from our Starbucks runs long ago, considering most of our coffee-break banter revolves around how much he pisses us off.

"I, um, I'm trying to cut back on my caffeine intake, but I *really* appreciate the offer."

"How 'bout a muffin or something?"

"I ate breakfast already. But thanks."

"Cool."

We head downstairs. While waiting in the line, I happen to glance back in the direction of the lobby and glimpse the flash of a white scarf.

Fate, I'm telling you.

"Hold on a minute, guys."

She's nearing the elevators, and I make a wild dash for it. I reach her just as the doors slide open, my breath coming out in great wheezing gasps. Underexercised investment bankers and spontaneous sprinting: not the cleverest of combinations. I place my hand on her shoulder, spinning her around.

Shit. It's a fifty-year-old crone with the nose of a hawk. At least I got the scarf down pat.

"Sorry," I mumble, "thought you were somebody else."

She eyes me suspiciously, fingering the end of her scarf until the elevator doors glide shut in front of her.

♦

Clyde isn't in the next day either. Or the day after that. It's the third day when, walking in with my morning coffee, I notice the Defeated One engrossed in the newspaper. Nothing strange about that; he always checks his stock quotes for at least a solid half hour each morning before he actually gets down to doing any real work.

"Hey," he calls over, "check this out."

He hands me a page of the newspaper.

"Huh?" I ask. "What's so interesting about Norwegian scientists growing tumors in laboratory mice?"

"No, jackass," he says, grabbing the paper out of my hands, "look here."

He's pointing to a small article in the bottom right-hand corner:

LOCAL CONSTRUCTION MAGNATE KILLED IN PLANE CRASH NEAR AIRPORT

Oct. 23—Charles P. Bakerfield, CEO of Bakerfield Construction Inc., was killed Monday afternoon in a plane crash five miles north of the airport. The National Transportation Safety Board confirmed that the tail number on the plane was registered with Bakerfield Construction. The plane was reported lost at 4:33 p.m. Around this time, local residents near the crash site—

"Holy shit. Isn't Clyde's last name Bakerfield?"

"I think so. Didn't he say his dad was in construction?"

"Yeah, he is."

I slump back in my chair.

"Christ, this is terrible."

We sit in stunned silence. A plane crash is the type of tragedy that is so sudden and random that you can only shake your head and wonder at the fragility of existence—you're planning away, meticulously diversifying your portfolio, your liquid cash funneled into an ING Direct 2.5% savings account, and then *poof:* a cloud of smoke and you're gone.

"Do you think we should try and get a hold of him?" I ask.

The Defeated One scratches his chin.

"I don't know, really. Maybe he wants to lay low for a while, not have to deal with anybody from work."

"What about a card?"

The Defeated One snorts. "All right, why don't you just run down to Hallmark and grab the 'Happy Fiery Plane Crash' one. Make sure you get the cartoon fireball on the front; I hear it's pretty darn cute."

"Piss off. You know what I mean. A quick note, keeping it simple."

He nods. "Okay. That could work. You want to take the reins and write it up?"

"Sure."

The Defeated One shakes his head and takes a deep breath.

"That's rough."

"I know."

He rocks back and forth in his chair.

"It's like, you've got all these things you still want to do, fucking and drinking and buying a house and a nice car—"

My phone rings; it's the Sycophant's extension. He's the last person in the world I want to speak to right now.

"Hold that thought for a second."

The Sycophant is his usual snippy self, so I doubt he's heard the news about Clyde's dad. Scratch that; I wouldn't put it past him to have learned about the crash and shrugged it off a moment later, his eyes narrowing into slits—*at least it wasn't me, ha!*—before turning back to fidgeting with his BlackBerry.

"I'm going to need your immediate assistance with some archiving over the next few hours. It has to be done by early afternoon."

"What do you mean, archiving?"

"A few old files and boxes. You'll rearrange everything and take it down to the archiving department somewhere in the basement. Ask one of the assistants for the exact details."

This has bitch work screaming all over it. There's something about Clyde's dad, this sudden sensitivity toward my own mortality, that has me quipping back.

"Isn't that why we have assistants— "

"Excuse me? Is this going to be a problem?"

"I'm only saying— "

"Because if it's going to be a problem, then *we're* going to have a problem on our hands. Maybe we should sit down with HR this afternoon and discuss it with them."

"No. If you need help, then of course— "

"Good. Come by in five minutes."

He hangs up on me.

I lean back in the chair, rubbing at my eyelids.

"I'm going to kill him, I really am. One day we'll be standing at the top of a cliff and he's going to squint at me the wrong way. Fuck, he's never going to know what hit him."

"It could be worse," the Defeated One reasons. "You could be charred up beside the fuselage of a plane right now."

"Aaargh. Tell me about it. But then the Sycophant comes along and makes you want to rip the skin off your frickin' face. I swear to god, I understand why people go crazy here."

"Don't stress about it."

After a minute or two of procrastination spent checking my Hotmail account (no messages), I stand up.

"All right, off to the latest degrading task he has lined up for me."

I knock on the Sycophant's door. When it opens, a pile of paper scatters across the floor. Not that it matters, as the office is a complete disarray of manila folders and pitch books. The Sycophant has put no effort into keeping things orderly; he must have just shaken out his filing cabinets and let everything settle into a big messy heap. This is going to take most of the day, and I have loads of other work due for tomorrow.

"Do you think I could ask one of the assistants to help— "

"They're all busy finalizing client invoices this week," he says, squinting at me. "This is a job you should be able to manage by yourself. Are you certain we don't need to have a talk with HR?"

I can't even look at him. I'm scared I'll do something really crazy, like strangle him with his necktie or give him a roundhouse kick to the buttocks, sending him flying over this mess of papers.

"No. That's fine."

♦

I devote six hours exclusively to the archiving until I have everything organized into twenty boxes. Six hours shot to hell when I could have been sourcing the data for the LBO model the Philanderer expects by the end of the week, or scrubbing the next run-through of a telecom pitch due first thing tomorrow morning. Fuck, it's going to be another really late night. At least the Sycophant is out of the office in a meeting for the afternoon; otherwise I would have been down on my haunches, wading through this sea of paper as he squinted at me from behind the desk. A tad humiliating to say the least.

Now I have to trudge down to the archives with these boxes, which, according to the Dirty Hippie Office Supply Manager, involves taking the elevator to the lobby and walking across to the stairwell, down three flights of stairs, and along a narrow corridor. Of course, as the boxes are crammed full of papers that will never again see the light of day, each one is back-breakingly heavy. I ask the Utterly Incompetent Assistant if there is a mail cart around somewhere, but she snaps her gum, throws me that vapid expression, and goes back to the Minesweeper on her monitor.

Invoices, my ass.

Fine, I can manage this. I stack two of the boxes and lean down to pick them up. I hear a disconcerting popping sound from the general region of my spine. Alrighty, then; I'm not going to manage this. I lift one of the boxes and head toward the elevator.

I'm fairly sweaty by this point: two huge pit stains sloping down my white shirt, my pants soaked through along the waistline. I drag the box into the elevator and push "Lobby." A karate chop just as the doors are closing, and they open once again to reveal the Prodigal Son.

Fan-fucking-tastic.

We begin our descent and the Prodigal Son snickers.

"Getting pretty soaked there, huh?"

I do this mock-sigh thing that sounds really put on.

"The Sycophant has me boxing up every paper he's ever read and schlepping it to the archives down in the basement."

The Prodigal Son chuckles hoarsely and crosses his arms, stretching the shirt's fabric with the girth of his biceps.

"Yeah, he's quite the little fucker."

Uh-uh; I refuse to get into this with him. To vent successfully, to feel fully satisfied via your venting, there has to be a shared sense of mutual subjugation. And in truth, I wouldn't put it past him to repeat everything I said straight to the source.

We descend the remaining floors in an awkward silence (awkward for me, at least; I'm sure the Prodigal Son isn't attuned to it), and when the doors glide open, we part ways by exchanging stiff half-nods. I'm so distracted watching him exit through the revolving doors, no doubt for an afternoon tryst with an ex-cheerleader now hawking overpriced body gels in a nearby department store, that I manage to barrel into somebody, my view mostly obstructed by the box I'm lugging. A female voice cries out. Dropping the box, I hurry over to a hunched-over form.

"Ow! My ankle!"

Of course. The forces of the universe wouldn't have it any other way.

The Woman With The Scarf.

"Jesus, I'm so sorry."

She looks up and rolls her eyes.

"You again. God, it's like we're in this crappy Sandra Bullock romantic comedy over here."

I help her up. As she's smoothing out her dress, she admits, "It wasn't your fault. These stupid heels— "

"I'm really sorry. I should have been paying more attention."

"Relax," she says, waving it off. "It's not a big deal."

Giving me the up and down, she scoffs, "What's with all the sweat? You've been working out with your shirt on?"

I'm abruptly brought back to my pit stains. I pray I'm wearing enough deodorant.

"My evil VP has me bringing these boxes down to our archives in the basement. Not the most pleasant of tasks, I assure you."

"Don't you have assistants or mail clerks to help out?"

"Exactly what I said, but this VP's had a major stick shoved up his rectum as of late. Wife left him for the cable guy, we think."

"Never the best of domestic situations. But then again, he probably deserved it, right?"

"Oh yeah."

We chuckle quietly.

"Look, I'm really sorry about before, standing you up like that."

"Hey, it happens. Don't stress about it."

I smile sheepishly. She stifles a yawn. She seems just as exhausted as I am.

"Well, I should let you get back to your archiving. I've got some hefty photocopying awaiting me upstairs, but I think your grunt work has mine beat."

I glance back at the box, half concealed behind a potted floral arrangement.

"How about getting some coffee? I mean, we're already down here; it would only be a couple more minutes."

She mulls it over.

"Yeah, a jolt of caffeine would be great."

As we stand in the back of the line, an interminable length to the baristas, I'm beginning to regret my initiative. We're smiling at each other, and I know she's waiting for me to dazzle her with witty banter, but my brain keeps latching onto work-related trivialities, and who in their right mind wants to hear about the copy speeds of our color printers? Maybe it works on the type of girls the Star picks up.

"I'm sorry," I mumble, "it's just that I, uh, I don't know—"

"Tell me about your work."

"But it's boring."

"Work is supposed to be boring. Anyway, it has to be better than watching you struggle to impress me or whatever."

She smiles encouragingly.

"All right. Well, today for instance, I'm supposed to be bringing these boxes down—"

Getting started on the injustices of the Bank is like breaking the urinary seal when you're completely sloshed, and my self-consciousness dissipates under a torrent of relieved babble. I bitch about the Sycophant, and then she regales me with tales of her own boss, a Maggie Thatcheresque ballbuster.

"She sounds like an absolute tyrant."

"Wouldn't you believe it. We call her the PMS Express."

"So you guys do the nickname thing too."

"But of course," she says, winking demurely. "Doesn't everybody?"

We pick up our coffees from the Asian barista with the Coke-bottle glasses. The cappuccino foam is dense and perfect. Fortunately there is an empty table discreetly tucked away in the corner. We sit down and she takes a sip, smiling blissfully.

"Oh lord, I really needed this. I didn't get to bed until two last night."

"Why? Did you go out or something?"

"On a weeknight?" she snorts. "Please, I haven't been able to pull that off since college. Nah, I just couldn't sleep for some reason. There were a few episodes of *The Joy of Painting* on television, though, so my insomnia wasn't a complete bust."

"Bob Ross! That guy's a genius."

"Yeah," she says, grinning.

" 'Every tree needs a friend' and all that."

"He's dead, you know."

"No shit."

"I'm totally serious. Died of lymphoma a couple years ago."

"Oh. That's too bad, I guess."

We stir our coffees in silence. Then I think to ask the dumbest question ever.

"So, you must have hated me that first time we met up here, huh?"

She sips the cappuccino, getting some froth on her upper lip.

"Hmmm. Hate is such a strong emotion. I definitely thought you were a jackass, though."

"Fair enough."

She chews on the end of a stir stick.

"Though sort of cute, mind you."

"Sort of?"

"Definitely easy on the eyes. Nice ears. Anyway, I had to have thought you were *sort of* cute; it's not like I hand out my card to just any guy who approaches me at Han's."

Nice ears; all right, I can deal with that.

By the time our coffee cups are empty, I'm trying to figure out how to end this appropriately. Would it be acceptable to just lean over and kiss her, a quick peck on the cheek? I settle on moving my hand slowly across the table, a tentative path until it gingerly brushes up against her fingers. She looks down at my skittering hand curiously. I blush, quickly drawing it away.

"You're thinking way too hard about this," she says, laughing.

She reaches across and wiggles her fingers against mine, sighing breathlessly. I chuckle despite my embarrassment. Getting up from the table, she says, "A pity we have to go back to work after this. I could definitely use a nap right now. Much obliged for the coffee, kind sir. I'll have to return the favor."

"So, we can do this again?"

She smirks. "What, some good ol'-fashioned finger stroking?"

"I was thinking more along the lines of another coffee."

Tightening the scarf around her neck, she nods briskly.

"Yes, I do believe it could be arranged."

♦

On Monday morning I pass Clyde in the corridor.

"Hey, man," he asks casually, "how was the weekend?"

"Not too shabby. Worked the entire Saturday but had a couple hours off on the Sunday. Managed to get some laundry done."

It's such a nonchalant exchange, Clyde so his usual self, that it's not until after I've arrived at my desk and hung my coat on the hook that I realize the weirdness of it and address the Defeated One.

"Hey, Clyde's back already."

He looks up from his stock quotes.

"No shit, Sherlock."

I'm flabbergasted. "But I mean, I just saw him in the corridor. And it's as if nothing ever happened. Everything exactly the same as before."

The Defeated One shrugs. "We all deal with things differently."

I shake my head at him and say, "But his dad died just a few days ago. Wouldn't that fuck you up for at least a couple weeks?"

"You're not a psychologist, Mumbles. I'd leave it if I were you."

I chew on the eraser end of a pencil, contemplating the strangeness of it. Is this the Bank's influence, a malevolent vortex sapping Clyde of his regular emotions, preventing us all from behaving like rational human beings?

"It's just so messed up."

"Leave it."

"Fine."

♦

Clyde comes by an hour later.

"Anybody game for Starbucks?"

The Defeated One doesn't look up from flipping through a tower of pitch books, ensuring all the pages are in the correct order.

"Sorry, man, have two pitches due this afternoon. Would love a double macchiato, though, if you're taking orders."

"Sure thing, boss. And yourself?"

A part of me wants to decline, unnerved by this discomfortingly numb Clyde, but then I also want to get to the bottom of his stoicism.

"Yeah, I'll join you. Where's Postal?"

"Bogged down in the copy room. Investor presentation going out in the next half hour."

I grab my wallet and we head to the elevators. Clyde's whistling something or other, more Spice Girls, I think. I know I should probably heed the Defeated One's advice and mind my own business, but I really can't help myself; it just seems too unnatural not to say something:

"I, um, I mean, if you ever want to talk about it— "

Clyde stops whistling and peers at me intently. The blood rushes up to my ears.

"I mean, we read in the paper— "

A momentary breather as we step into the elevator. When we begin our descent, Clyde is still peering at me funny, the tension crackling like if you scuttled across the carpet and shoved your finger in an electrical outlet.

"What did you read in the paper?"

Okay. This is getting bizarre.

"The plane crash— "

Clyde crosses the small elevator space and gets right up in my face. He doesn't look like Clyde anymore; his mouth is clamped in an inverted U, and he narrows his eyes menacingly.

"Haven't you figured it out, Mumbles? I really don't want to get into this right now. The Bank is horrible enough without having to drag your personal issues into it as well."

I nod apprehensively.

"No more talk of this around the office," Clyde warns.

Just in time, the elevator comes to a smooth halt. Clyde winks at me as he props the doors open.

"After you."

Six

November ephemerally passes into December: The barely legal *Pattaya Fun-Fun Girls* calendar mail-ordered from Thailand by the Defeated One, hidden away in an upper filing cabinet, turns a page. There's only the most delicate rustling of cotton-candy-pink panties and almond-shaped eyes, a *shhhh-shhhh* whisper, drowned out by the clatter of thirty fingers racing across ergonomic keyboards.

Outside, there are tremendous happenings. The sky beyond the window is getting dark earlier. As with every change in season, the city belches out a new wave of human eccentricity: a man who's lived at the top of a tree for twenty-odd years; another who's been hoarding an exotic menagerie—a pair of leopards, a boa constrictor, several fluorescent amphibians smuggled in from Brazil—in a dilapidated low-income housing project; a blind woman demonstrating her artistic talents on public-access television.

Locally, the hot-dog vendor on the street corner north of Han's Blue Diamond Chinese Gourmet has begun hawking his roasted chestnuts. Nearby, the homeless lady who inhabits the bus shelter with her shopping bags full of her worldly possessions, the only person I routinely see on my walk to the subway in the wee hours of the morning, suddenly disappears without a trace. Though I hope for the best, a migration to the sunny beaches of Florida, perhaps, I can't rid myself of a horrible conviction that she's wasting away from some Dickensian disease in a dark alley somewhere, consumption or the bubonic plague gnawing at her brittle bones.

Venturing outward now, beyond the city walls, beyond the strip malls of suburbia, beyond the sprawl of suburbia's suburbia, skimming across an ocean toward the other side of the world, we watch as a country is invaded. Then there is a second invasion purely through happenstance. Weapons of mass destruction are found, then lost, then found and lost all over again. More personally, my cousin Ruth in Prague gives birth to twins, and this makes me do a double take because she's only, what, seventeen months older than me?

Inside the Bank, time is far more unassuming. Flakes of skin fall away from our microscopically crumbling bodies. They collect in little piles in the cracks of our desks and behind messy stacks of annual reports and pitch books—wherever the cleaning lady with the golden caps on her teeth neglects her early-morning wipe. Market prices on Bloomberg take a slight beating and then healthily veer back up again. The knob connecting the swivel to the base of my chair loosens, so now there is a creaking noise when I lean all the way back. We close one deal that makes a client a millionaire, another deal that makes another client a billionaire. In our neck of the woods, the Philandering Managing Director starts screwing around with a new assistant. My ball of rubber bands grows to the size of a puny organic tomato.

Despite this stagnation, I haven't for a moment lost sight of the end goal: eighteen months, seventeen days, four hours, and sixteen minutes remaining until the expiration of my contract. And when the clock winds down, when it's finally time for that faux-bittersweet farewell e-mail—*good-bye all, it's been such a blast!*—I'm going to race through the streets, knocking on random doors, bellowing at the top of my lungs: I'm alive! I was dead, but now I'm alive! And people will emerge onto their fire escapes, blocking the glare of the sun from their eyes, wondering what the heck is causing all that racket, and then they'll see me barreling along, really gunning it, and they'll smile wistfully, because they'll understand what it's all about.

♦

A shorter countdown is kicked into gear whenever my eyes stray toward the palm trees tacked beside my telephone list: Only a week remains until the Bank's annual holiday party.

"Hey," I ask the Defeated One, leaning back in my chair, "are you bringing your girlfriend to this holiday party?"

The Defeated One swivels around to face me.

"Of course. It's mandatory stuff. You don't think the senior guys aren't itching to judge you by your date so that they can form all sorts of conclusions about your management potential based on what she looks like?"

"You make it sound so appealing."

"It's the truth," he says. "My girlfriend absolutely despises these Bank events. But there's pretty decent alcohol at least, none of that bottom-shelf crap."

I shift around in the IKEA swivel chair, and it makes its horrible groaning sounds, its fragile Scandinavian being shuddering under the weight of my Krispy Kreme–enhanced buttocks. Note to self: Remind the Dirty Hippie Office Supply Manager to reenter the cycle of rebirth and order me a new chair.

"You'd think they'd cut us some slack. It's not like we have all this time to go out, meet a great girl, and cultivate a meaningful enough relationship that she's willing to tolerate the Philanderer trying to sniff out her panties."

The Defeated One holds up his hands. "Hey, I didn't write the rule book of this industry. What about the chiquita you've been going on all those Starbucks runs with? The one who always has that fuck-with-me-and-you-die scarf tied around her neck?"

An interesting proposal, not that I hadn't considered it already.

"I don't know. I'm thinking it might be a bit too early to subject her to our guys. And lay off the scarf. I kind of like it."

"Of course you'd like the scarf, you submissive little bitch."

"Piss off."

"Which reminds me. Hey, Starsy— "

The Star swivels around on command.

"Yup?"

"How's our video project coming along?"

The Star opens a drawer and pulls out a CD case. Tossing it to the Defeated One, he says, "Finished as of last night."

The Defeated One wiggles his fingers together.

"Excccellent."

"Check out the last thirty seconds. Wait until you see the detail on the penetration . . ."

"Uh-uh-uh," the Defeated One says, raising his hand. "We will have none of that, please."

The Star hangs his head sadly and swivels back around. The Defeated One kisses the CD, reaches up to his bookshelf, and hides it between the pages of an *Introduction to Option Pricing* textbook.

♦

"So, any chance you'd be interested in coming to this party?"

The Woman With The Scarf sips her cappuccino thoughtfully.

"Hmmm. I'll be perfectly honest: I don't really want to go. I mean, I'm kind of curious to get some visuals to back up these crazy stories you've been telling me, but on the other hand, it might be a bit much at this stage in our relationship. What's it been, only a few coffee dates now?"

"Yeah, I figured you'd say that. Thought I'd give it a shot, though."

"Look, if you really want me to— "

"Hey, don't worry about it. Not a big deal."

A blur of Armani in my peripheral vision: Five Managing Directors from the Bank's telecommunications group stride into Starbucks. My instinctive behavior is to reposition my chair so I'm facing the window. The Woman With The Scarf eyes me curiously.

"What's going on?"

"Nothing," I mumble.

Fortunately the line isn't too long. The Managing Directors get their coffees and exit without noticing me scrunched up by the window. She must have followed my line of sight.

"You're nervous about being spotted by your colleagues, aren't you?"

I don't answer.

"That's what it is, isn't it?"

When I don't answer again, she smacks me on the shoulder. "It's official. You are the biggest dork *ever!*"

I hang my head. "I'm sorry."

"Anyway, you're *my* dork," she says, grinning. "So, are we still on for dinner this Friday?"

"Fingers crossed."

"You better not cancel at the last minute again."

We were supposed to see a movie last weekend, our very first non-Starbucksian date. The plans got nixed when my BlackBerry vibrated ten minutes before showtime. Damage control was moderately successful—lunch at Han's Blue Diamond Chinese Gourmet on the Monday—but I think she's still a little miffed about it.

"Work has been slow lately. Maybe a five percent probability something might pop up toward the end of the week, but that's it, honest to god."

She sticks her finger in her coffee cup, licking off the last of the foam.

"Okay. But do try to make it."

"I will, I promise."

♦

After I return to my desk, it's back to the task at hand: Who am I going to bring to this party? I ponder it for a few minutes, puzzling over my mental list of acquaintances and third cousins, but now it seems like every female I've ever known has faded into the woodwork, all through my own doing: e-mails or calls I never returned, parties or dinners cancelled at the last minute. Just as I'm about to resign myself to stagdom, Outlook pings: 1 New Message. An e-vite to Steph's twenty-fifth birthday at some bar I've never heard of in the Village.

Steph.

Steph.

Who the hell is Steph?

It takes a moment of intense concentration to place her: Steph from a Suits bar at the end of the summer where I was out one evening with the rest of the analysts from the Bank. What was the occasion? Ah yes, sending the summer students back into the wild. It was your classic Bank social outing: a swarm of Brooks Brothers–clad nerdlings drinking overpriced bottles of Amstel Light and fidgeting nervously with their BlackBerrys. Interspersed, a bunch of heavily madeup high schoolers getting off on the fact they're intimidating the hell out of guys at least seven years their senior. And then there was Steph, half Chinese and half German, dancing on the bar in a slinky miniskirt. Reaching down, grabbing a hold of my Ferragamo tie, the one with the penguins, pulling me toward her, and slurring in my ear: *I just looove bankers. Especially bankers with busssby eyebrows.* One thing leading to another, scribbling down our e-mail addresses on a shredded napkin, the sort of exchange you never expect to lead to anything much. And now this.

My mind racing: Could it work? Would I want it to work? Before I start doubting myself, I whip off an e-mail letting Steph know I'll try to show up at her party (on a Wednesday night—not likely), and also drop a casual reference to the holiday party, wondering if she'd be interested in joining me for a drink or two. The Defeated One flicks a rubber band at me from across the room.

"All right, man, let's grab Postal and Clyde. Coffee time and then you boys are going to help me pick out a present for the old lady. Big b-day this evening. I need to find something special, as she's been kind of pissy lately."

I pick up the rubber band and add it to my rubber-band ball.

"Why?"

The Defeated One shrugs. "Heh, the usual gross negligence."

Postal Boy is the only one at his desk. He doesn't look up from plugging away at his spreadsheet. Postal Boy has been getting his lashings extra severely as of late, single-handedly shouldering the brunt of two projects that both exploded over the last couple of weeks. I'm fairly certain he hasn't slept a wink in the last thirty-six hours, slaving away until seven in the morning, going home to shower and change into a fresh shirt, and being back in the office by eight. It's the type of schedule that's crushed many a lesser mortal. While Postal Boy definitely looks the part of the living dead—rings around his eyes, his skin turning a peculiar shade of ashen gray—the fact that he's still functioning is testament to an exceptional perseverance.

"Postal," the Defeated One barks at him, "time to get you some juice. Starbucks convoy is leaving in ten seconds."

Postal Boy doesn't even turn around, waving us off.

"C-a-a-n-n'-t r-i-g-g-h-t n-o-w-w"—he's barely capable of stringing syllables together by this point—"m-u-s-s-t f-i-i-n-i-i-s-h c-o-o-o-m-p-s."

The Defeated One is already gearing up for a flying kick to the back of Postal Boy's chair. Just as he's about to launch off, I step forward and block his path, and the Defeated One stumbles backward from the fruitless exertion. I shake my head and push him out the door. Postal Boy keeps typing away, oblivious to his near-brush with the edge of the desk.

As we're walking toward the elevator, I chastise him. "Christ, that would have been so goddamn inappropriate. Postal's on the verge of losing it and you're going to fuck with him now. Don't you ever know when to stop?"

The Defeated One sneers at this. "Since when did you develop scruples, Mumbles? And no, I don't support any of us descending into lunacy because of this job."

He pushes the elevator button.

"Look, you've lost the game unless you can always keep a level head and remember: Nobody's going to die from this"—the Defeated One pauses to enunciate each syllable—"*No-bo-dy's go-ing to die.* Think about it. We're not emergency-room surgeons, just glorified paper pushers. And so, no, I will not pander to Postal turning into a basket case whenever the Philanderer snaps his sticky fingers."

Getting into the elevator, I'm unconvinced.

"Easier said than done. You *know* how difficult it is to finesse the Push Back. And let's not forget who he shares his office space with. The glorious Prodigal Son, who's out all day porking high school cheerleaders and playing squash with the board of directors. Oh yeah, and then there's Clyde."

The Defeated One blinks rapidly when I mention the name.

"What do you mean by that?"

It's weird; I'm suddenly conscious of the fact that over the last month, the Defeated One and I have never spoken about this explicitly.

"You know what I'm talking about. Disappearing for hours at a stretch during the middle of the workday. Surfing for porn while the Utterly Incompetent Assistant lurks right outside the door."

The Defeated One shrugs. "He's always done that."

I eye him sternly.

"Tell me you haven't picked up on it getting worse ever since his dad died. I mean, how normal was that? Plane crashing and a week later he's back in the office, la-da-da-da-da-da, look at me, I'm completely unaffected."

We grab our coffee and walk through the lobby toward the gift shop.

"It's the Bank," reasons the Defeated One. "You can't show any signs of weakness. What do you expect from him, to go seek counseling from the Sycophant?"

He flips through his money clip.

"Crap; all I have is a twenty. Can you spot me anything?"

I only have two cents in my pocket, the change from our coffees.

"Sorry."

As the Defeated One haggles with the cashier over a bottle of perfume, I continue:

"I confronted him in the elevator the day he came back, you know. Tried to do the Good Samaritan thing and let him know I'd be there to listen if he ever wanted to talk about it. And then he practically ripped my head off."

He's barely paying attention.

"That's what you get for being the Boy Scout."

The cashier won't budge on the perfume, so the Defeated One settles on a box of Ferrero Rochers and a stuffed Teddy Bear with an American flag printed on its belly.

"She's going to kill me," he mutters. "If this doesn't have Duty Free afterthought written all over it, then I'll be damned."

As the cashier hands the Defeated One his change, I turn to exit the gift shop and spot a familiar flash of red hair.

"Speak of the devil."

The Defeated One shoves the change in his pocket and joins me in observing Clyde strolling briskly out through the revolving doors.

He shrugs. "So? He's probably taking a smoke break."

"Clyde doesn't smoke. Cigarettes, that is."

"Give him the benefit of the doubt."

I'm already walking toward the exit.

"Let's see where Clyde runs off to during the day, why don't we?"

We push through the revolving doors. The cold air pierces the thin cotton of our shirts, our suit jackets left upstairs so as not to arouse suspicion while we sneak off on our coffee breaks. We've exited into the courtyard at the rear of the building, which is packed during the summer with assistants chowing down on their tuna wraps and fruit cups but a deserted wasteland come the end of autumn. A herd of modern-art cow sculptures droop their forlorn bronze heads over the empty flower beds.

Across the courtyard, beside a pillar, Clyde is shooting the shit with a bike messenger.

"Look at that," the Defeated One says, slapping me on the back. "Clyde is *sooo* busted. Sneaking off and fraternizing with the *help*, huh? The Toad would be absolutely livid."

He's already turned toward the revolving doors. I wave him back.

"Give it another minute or two. There's something peculiar about this."

We're standing in plain view; Clyde and the bike messenger could easily catch us spying on them.

"Let's make this a little less obvious," the Defeated One snorts.

We hide behind one of the pillars. After another minute, the bike messenger reaches into a pocket hidden somewhere within his sleek spandex tights and pulls out a plastic bag and hands it to Clyde. In turn, Clyde passes him a couple bills. Then a shaking of hands, the transaction completed, and the bike messenger strolls off with a lopsided gait.

"Bull's-eye!" I exclaim.

The Defeated One is unimpressed.

"What's wrong with you, man? Look at us hiding away behind this pillar. Are we playing narc now? So Clyde does drugs; we knew that already. And so do I, and so do you, and so does everybody at the Bank. Take that back; probably not the Star. Anyway, what's the big deal?"

It's a valid point, but I'm not willing to brush it off so easily.

"The big deal is that there's a fine line in this industry, a tacit understanding of what's considered inappropriate. Like, for example, you know when it's okay to sneak off to the bathroom and do your vices, but you also know when you've got to buckle down and crank out some comps. We live and die by the line. And though I like Clyde, I really do, and I understand why you're being so protective of him, he's crossing that line every single day now. I mean, look at him"—Clyde is brazenly rolling a joint, only partially concealed by one of the bronze cows—"and it's not even lunch yet, for Christ's sake."

When the final licks are in place, Clyde deposits the joint in a pocket and saunters away in the opposite direction of our office tower.

"You think he's heading off to grab a burrito? Because I'm getting hungry myself," I say.

The Defeated One scowls.

"I'm sorry." I step out from behind the pillar. "It's not like I'm getting off on this. It's just that I'm worried about him, and I think you are too. And if all this bullshit doesn't stop, then, well, I'm concerned that everything's going to come crashing down on Clyde's head. The senior guys must have already noticed it."

"Don't overestimate their interest in us. As long as the work gets done . . ."

Even he doesn't seem too convinced by this.

"Let's go back inside," the Defeated One murmurs.

♦

I sip my bourbon & ginger, a little umbrella nestled between the blocks of ice, and observe Steph circulating through the crowd of black that mingles around the plastic palm trees lining the Imperial Ballroom of the Sheraton Hotel. From the waist up she's dressed fairly conservatively in a Maoist shirt, a severe high-collared satin affair with an ornate golden dragon circling around the back. Below the waist, though, she's definitely no love child of the Cultural Revolution in a skirt with two dangerous slits in the sides, almost up to her panties, along with saucy black stilettos.

"Where the hell did you find her?" Postal Boy gapes in amazement.

"End of the summer. That night we took the summer kids out before their release into freedom."

"Yeah, she's pretty smoking," Clyde acknowledges. "Not at all what I expected from you. And look at her network; just wait until she gets slipped your promotion."

"That's not all she's gonna get slipped," the Defeated One cackles, taking a swig of his beer.

I gulp down my drink.

"Hey, at least I brought somebody to this," I mumble.

The Defeated One shrugs. "I can't help it if the old lady came down with a last-minute case of strep."

We're all in awe of Steph's magnificent cocktail party prowess. She is truly a mistress of the schmooze, able to flit effortlessly from one group to the next and blabber away on a diverse range of topics: firewall protocols and sleek new motherboard designs with the zealous IT guys; the latest income-trust taxation laws with august senior bankers; the smoothest brand of peach schnapps with the elderly lushes from up on the bond trading floor; manufacturing growth indicators with the economic strategists; even where to buy durable yarn at rock-bottom prices with the taffeta-draped back-office dowagers. Steph has mastered the wisdom behind the schmooze, namely that it's not all that important to actually know what the hell you're talking about. As long as you nod enthusiastically and lubricate the small talk with a couple words interjected here or there, you'll survive the requisite five minutes until you're off to the next circle.

Of course, it's the application of this wisdom that's the tricky bit. I tried my utmost to keep up with her, towing by Steph's side for the first half hour of the evening, but my enthusiastic nodding was more of a jerky twitch, and any attempt to add to the conversation only led to a pervasive awkwardness for all parties involved. Eventually worn out from cramping Steph's style, I slinked back to the safe haven of our Gang of Four stationed at a comfortable reach from the bar.

Steph has a competitor in the schmoozing department: the Prodigal Son. I'm trying my best to ignore him, but he's impossible to miss, hovering above everybody else in the room and making the otherwise sullen wives titter shamelessly as they try to accidentally brush up against his bulky musculature. It doesn't help that his date is a willowy blond goddess in a strapless silver dress.

Then again, who cares? This social incompetence thing is not the biggest deal in the world. And it doesn't hurt that I'm already beginning to feel a wee bit sloshed. We've been at this party for less than an hour, just two drinks deconstructing my system, but the bartender has been mixing them up pretty stiff this evening. Perhaps it's the desperation in our eyes as we order another that has this bald guy in the black vest and John Lennon glasses intuiting our need for instant liquid courage before any attempt to venture more than an arm's length from his mahogany countertop. And Lulu Heifenschliefen's brilliance in scheduling this for six o'clock isn't helping anything much; an open bar is stocked with an AA group's wet dream—Grey Goose and Cuervo, a slew of Merlots and Cabernet Sauvignons—before anybody has had an opportunity to grab a bite since lunch. A handful of elegant hors d'oeuvres float by on silver trays, but they're flimsy nothings (slivers of exotic vegetables, spoonfuls of ahi tuna tartar, tiny mushroom spring rolls no bigger than a baby's pinkie), incapable of soaking up the torrents of booze flowing about this room.

The Star passes by with what has to be his female counterpart, a freckled woman with barrettes in her hair and argyle stockings.

"Were you able to splice everything in okay?" he asks nervously.

The Defeated One gives him a thumbs-up.

"Yup. Your brilliant handiwork is soon to have an audience."

The Star scuffs his foot.

"Are you sure you want to go through with this? I mean, if anybody finds out, we can get in a lot of— "

"Starsy," the Defeated One says as he swigs his beer, "don't worry your little head about it. Just try and have a good time tonight."

As if on cue, a flurry of pastel-colored taffeta and earth-toned tweed whizzes past, this J. Crew montage now distinguishing itself as a dozen or so members of the back-office tribe, rushing the dance floor to boogie down to the opening strains of the Macarena. It's evident that they're already this side of rip-roaring drunk. One guy has the classic telltale tie wrapped around his head, and another has stripped down to an "I ♥ Cancun" T-shirt and Bermuda shorts.

Apparently the back-office groove is a series of rapid convulsing movements somewhat resembling a choreographed fit of epilepsy. Their leader, a determined heavy-set woman with a hula skirt bulging around her girth, is trying to demonstrate the correct hand movements. Just when it seems like her troops have gotten the hang of it, the man in the Bermuda shorts lurches forward and retches into one of the plastic palm trees. As the rest of the dancers scurry to his aid, scandalized reactions break around the room: very senior management furrow their brows in displeasure; less senior management try their hardest not to spew up their drinks; the Stepford wives either sneer vapidly or giggle vapidly, depending on their spousal connection. The Defeated One clutches at his abdomen, tears welling in the corners of his eyes.

"Score one for the good guys! And so early in the game too."

He's regained his composure by the time we hear a familiar shrill chortle capped off with a sneeze: Lulu Heifenschliefen glides by, clutching a cosmopolitan. She's encased in a ruffled yellow dress, a hodgepodge of loopy ribbons and multicolored polka dots, and hair that is gelled down heavily to her scalp. The flattened look is a bit strange on her; it accentuates the smallness of her head relative to the rest of her body.

"Good evening, boy-chicks," she cries upon noticing us, whipping leis around our necks. Fanning her heaving, pasty bosom, she says, "*Mein Gott,* aren't you all looking hubba-hubba tonight."

Postal Boy, his cheeks flushed from too much alcohol, over-extends himself by feigning a Southern twang: "You're lookin' real perty there yourself, Lulu. Like the new 'do."

Lulu giggles and sneezes, patting at the sides of her head. She brings an empty martini glass to the bar and almost immediately has another. A trick of perception, maybe; I could have sworn the first one was almost full when she arrived just moments ago.

"So," the Defeated One asks, "did you catch the premier back-office blow-out of the evening? Hopefully the first of many."

Lulu smiles impishly, batting her fake eyelashes.

"But indeed. That was Alfred Mulligans, senior risk analyst supporting the bond desk. Thirteen years at the Bank, wouldn't you believe it? Alfie's a sturdy goat; I wouldn't worry too much about him."

Clapping her hands and turning to me, she coos with excitement. "But piglet, you must tell me all about your better half. She's the geisha in the naughty dress, yes?"

"Christ, Lulu."

"What?" She fingers the lei around her neck. "Everybody this side of Honolulu's already gotten a good peeking at her panties."

We all turn to watch Steph working the other side of the room. As if she has a sixth sense for when she's the topic of conversation, Steph eases away from her current circle and points her stilettos toward us. Upon arriving at our cluster, she does an annoying half-curtsy thing and throws an arm around my waist. She's clearly a bit sloshed as well.

"Why did you just desschert me like that?"

An attempted guilt trip doesn't work too well when you giggle hysterically at the end of it.

"I'm schorry," she apologizes.

"I guess you just seemed like you were having a great time, and I didn't want to get in your way or anything—"

"Don't be succch a silly gooshe! You sshouldn't have left me to meet all those big, powerful, successchful"—each adjective is uttered in a breathless exhalation—"men all by mysschelf. And most of them said they didn't even know you when I mentioned I was your date." Steph hiccups.

I chuckle wearily. It's evident from her half smile that she thinks she's helping me, furthering my career by hobnobbing with these gasbags. No doubt they're encouraging such a mentality by flattering her to no end, dropping not-so-subtle innuendos when the wives are turned the other way. I'm drunk and disproportionately irritated for some reason, and there is a sadistic side to me that wants to throw Steph off her game, to see how she'd handle a curveball.

"Yeah, well, maybe I don't want to meet any of those big, powerful, successful"—I adopt the same whimsical breathlessness as her initial delivery—"fuckers to begin with. Maybe I think they're all a bunch of arrogant pricks."

Steph blanches at this. Hands on her hips, her slurring now upping itself to a full-fledged whine, she replies, "How can you say ssshomething like that if you've never even met them?"

I shrug nonchalantly. "Just call it a hunch."

An awkward silence follows until Lulu intervenes, grabbing hold of Steph's hand.

"Come, kitten, it's time for another drink."

"Be easy on her," I say. "She looks like she's already well on her way."

Steph sticks out her tongue as Lulu drags her off to the bar. After they're gone, the Defeated One pats me on the back.

"Way to pounce on your date, Mumbles, for having the balls to chat up a few of these people."

"Shouldn't have left the leash at home," Clyde snickers.

Yeah, I'm a big jackass. Scratch that; a fairly drunk jackass.

"Steph's a big girl," I mumble.

Indeed, she's already staked herself beside the bar, cosmopolitan in hand, and is entranced by Lulu folding a napkin into an origami ship. I'm distracted by Lulu pressuring the bartender to wear the ship as a hat, when the Defeated One exalts giddily, "Holy crap, that's him!"

I follow his gaze to some palm trees clustered in the corner of the ballroom. Huddled between the plastic trunks, radiant in a flowing red dress, is Unadulterated Sex.

"God," I rasp, my breath getting lodged in my throat.

Clyde whistles. "Hot damn."

The Defeated One is temporarily lost in a similar daze before he shakes his head vigorously, wiping the drool from his chin.

"No, no. Ignore the dress. Beside her, gentlemen, is the fabled Russian fiancé."

Dazzled by the blinding perfection of Unadulterated Sex, we find it difficult to shift our attention to the tall, tanned man in the well-tailored suit by her side. He's sporting one of those old-school mustaches with the waxed tips, the facial hair you'd expect from Colonel Mustard, but otherwise his physical presence is nothing so extraordinary.

The Defeated One checks the time on his BlackBerry.

"All right, have to stay focused. Only fifteen minutes until showtime. I'm going to check with that kid"—he motions to an analyst setting up the projector—"and make sure everything is working on the technical front. Postal, you go schmooze Unadulterated Sex and the Russian fiancé. Don't let them leave the room until the video is finished."

Postal Boy gapes at him in disbelief.

"You expect me to just go up and make an introduction? I'm just a little turd to her probably."

The Defeated One shakes his head and rests his hands on Postal Boy's shoulders.

"Postal, it's time for you to become a man. Search deep inside yourself and make it happen."

Postal Boy peers at him slack-jawed.

"Huh?"

"Just go." The Defeated One pushes Postal Boy in their direction.

"What about us?" Clyde asks.

The Defeated One ponders this for a moment.

"You guys just stay put for now and deal with any fuckups as they come our way. Cool?"

"Fine," I mumble.

After he sets off to check on the projector, it's just me and Clyde. Partners in crime. Best of chums.

Talk about awkward.

Fortunately it's not too long before a goose bump–inducing voice wafts over the microphone. The Coldest Fish In The Pond is standing at the front of the room.

"I'd like to thank you all for joining us tonight . . ."

I order another bourbon & ginger and tune out for the next few minutes, snapping from my reverie when the lights begin to dim.

"And now," the Coldest Fish In The Pond states gruffly, "as per the Bank's annual tradition, the analysts have prepared a video for our viewing pleasure."

The Coldest Fish In The Pond steps away from the microphone to a smattering of applause. A hush floods the room, and all eyes turn to the screen at the front.

The video is actually quite accomplished, believe it or not. The theme is "Bank: After Dark," a tongue-in-cheek showcase of the stupid shit we supposedly get up to after the senior guys call it a night: pushing each other around in the mail cart, chugging beers in the boardroom, tinkering with the height adjustments of the Fish's swivel chair. Halfway through, the frame cuts to a close-up of Clyde smoking a joint on the Equity Capital Markets floor. It's the real goods; plumes of smoke escape from his nostrils. It elicits the loudest applause from the clip so far, even raucous hollering from the IT guys, and I glance over to spot Clyde taking a bow.

From across the room, the Defeated One flashes me the peace sign. I point to my wrist and he holds up three fingers. Three minutes. Oh god. Despite having reached full-blown inebriation, I'm getting really nervous about this, my stomach doing these strange rolling movements. Not far from the Defeated One, Unadulterated Sex leans against the wall, laughing along with the rest of the crowd. A little ways off, the Prodigal Son is feeding a California roll to his blond date, that marvelous creature clutching at his waist and opening her mouth like a baby pigeon.

Too late now. What's done is done.

The picture on the screen jumps, a flash of white, and there it is: my very own camera work in all its big-screen brazen glory. It sobers me up instantly. The shot depicts Unadulterated Sex's bare midsection writhing on the table, nothing overtly pornographic yet. Then the camera trails up her tanned abdomen, those perfect breasts swinging from side to side. An eerie silence settles over the crowd.

This doesn't last long; a moment later and there is a loud crunching sound from the direction of the projector. A flash of sparks, the projector fizzling out of control, and the screen at front goes blank. The analyst who's on technical duty scurries over in a panic.

Suddenly another crashing sound: Across the room, the Defeated One has dropped his drink. He's still staring straight ahead, entirely oblivious to the vodka dripping down his pant leg. Like a team of NASCAR pit mechanics, a fleet of waiters swoops down on the scene, armed with their brooms and dusters.

Then somebody starts clapping, and then another, and very soon the whole room has erupted in unabashed applause. It takes a minute to register what just happened: the Bank's minions thought the brief porn clip was a farce, just another vignette of the original "Bank: After Dark" video. And there weren't any faces displayed just yet, so the porn clip could have been sourced from anywhere.

The lights come back on and the Coldest Fish In The Pond stands flintily before the microphone.

"Thank you, analysts," the Fish deadpans, "for that interesting film. No long-winded speeches from me; my wife promised she'd kill me if I even attempted it"—there's polite chuckling here and there—"so I'll end this by advising you all to eat, drink, be merry. To the analysts scattered around the room, this might be your last social outing for a very long time"—more polite chuckling—"so make the most of it. From all of us at the Bank, happy holidays."

More applause. The Defeated One walks briskly from one corner of the room, Postal Boy from the other. When the four of us are assembled by the bar, we stand there staring at one another, none of us knowing exactly what to say.

Finally the Defeated One croaks, "Fuck."

He's on the verge of tears, his lips trembling and eyes blinking rapidly.

"A blown fuse?" Postal Boy shrugs meekly.

I shake my head. "God only knows."

I hear a fit of giggling directly behind me. It's a very drunk Steph, propped up by Lulu's shoulder.

"Heellloo gentleschmen," she says and hiccups.

"Lulu," I scold, "she's wasted. Why didn't you stop her before she got to this?"

"What?" Lulu shrugs. "I was drinking two cosmos for her every one. It's not my fault these American kittens can't stomach their alcohol."

I sigh, turning to the rest of the Gang of Four.

"All right, I think I better take her home. We'll talk about *it* tomorrow."

They nod solemnly. I reach out to take Steph's hand, but she recoils at my touch.

"Nooooooo!"

"What?" I hiss.

"We're going to the afffshterr-party."

"What after-party?"

"Hiiish afffshhterr-party."

She points out into the crowd. I follow her dangling finger to a man in a black suit surrounded by an entourage of women. He's facing away, but I recognize him immediately: the Philanderer.

"Oh no," I say, reaching for her hand again, "you don't want to go to *that* after-party. Trust me."

Steph scrunches up her face.

"Butt I wantt tooo gooo!!!"

As I'm about to reach for her again, Lulu pulls me aside.

"I'll take care of her, boy-chick. We'll drink some water, have a little munch, and then in a taxi she goes. I'll make sure she gets home all right."

I'm truly grateful.

"Lulu, thanks for doing this. Are you sure it's not going to be—"

"Shhh," she intones gravely. "You don't think your Lulu will get fired if she allows some chick-a-dee to get vomity at one of her parties?"

She reaches into her bosom and hands me a sweaty taxi voucher.

"Sweet dreams, boy-chick."

Outside, it's cold and drizzling. The bellman informs me there is a short delay for taxis and directs me to a bench where I can wait. It's only after I've sat down, careful to avoid a cigarette butt, that I become aware of a woman at the other end of the bench. Most of her face is draped in shadow, but I recognize the blond hair and the sleek black dress—the Ice Queen.

Goddammit. I was really hoping for a smooth exit.

I needn't have worried. When she glances at me sideways, I realize she's so blitzed she's hardly aware of my presence. The drizzle turns into a heavier downpour and I pull my suit jacket over my head. As I stare out into the darkness, listening to the soothing drone of water smashing against pavement, my thoughts turn to the Woman With The Scarf. I wonder what she's doing right now, whether she is still at work, highlighting away under the jaundiced overhead lighting. Or curled up in a plush armchair at home, thinking about me, perhaps, as she rests her head contentedly against the armrest. Maybe I should drop by unexpectedly with some hot chocolate. Nah, it's getting late; she might have fallen asleep already.

I've forgotten about the Ice Queen until there is a retching sound to my left. Turning my head, I see she's puked all down the front of her dress. She's not done quite yet, apparently, as another jet of liquid shoots out of her mouth.

She glances in my direction, her eyelids droopy. Wiping at her mouth, in her cold monotone, she says, "God, I just hate when that happens."

Seven

I stand at the foot of my enemy's gate. It's a nice gate, I'll admit: wrought iron, ivy crawling up the trellis work. Across the well-manicured lawn, down a cobbled path, sits a red-brick two-story dwelling, the architecture simple and sturdy without coming across as too ostentatious. Not exactly what I expected from the Sycophant's residence, truly. I had imagined something more along the lines of a solitary turret rising up from the scorched earth of a gnarled hill, gaunt dogs yapping miserably and licking at the open sores on their legs, perpetual storm clouds hovering overhead.

This sojourn is the latest demeaning request from El Sycophant, an hour-long ride through suburbia to hand-deliver his son's passport to the incommunicado wife because they're about to head off to Barbados in a few hours. I tell the company driver to wait for me, and I unlatch the gate, walk down the path, and ring the doorbell. I hear the sound of slippers shuffling, and then the door opens a crack, the chain still in place, and the inner sanctum of the house releases a faint whiff of potpourri. So the Sycophant is apparently a fan of lavender. Or was. A blond head is barely visible.

"Yes?"

"I, um, I work with your husband. He's asked me to deliver your son's passport . . ."

The sound of the chain being removed.

"Oh, yes." The woman swings open the door. "He called me about it this morning. Please come in."

It's astounding, really: The Sycophant's wife is actually not that bad-looking. At least, much better than any of the preconceived notions we'd formulated back at the office, which pretty much amounted to the Sycophant with longer hair and a touch of eyeliner. The Defeated One is going to be devastated by this news. As I stand beside the shoe rack, my nasal passages struggling to adjust to the stench of her citrusy perfume, I'm taking in the early-eighties bulbous blond hair, the toothy grin, and the gawky lankiness in limb that suggests she must have gone through a fairly awkward puberty. Despite overdoing it on the perfume, the Sycophant's wife seems to radiate good health, her skin slightly tanned as if in cheerful defiance of the onset of winter, and there is a prominent muscle running down her forearm that hints she either plays a lot of tennis or sweeps the house obsessively.

"I, um, I've got the passport right here."

I fumble around in my jacket pocket and hand it to her. She looks it over with complete disinterest before depositing it beside a vase of lilies on a side table.

"Can I offer you something to drink?"

"I have a driver waiting outside. It'd probably be best if I get going . . ."

"Please," she says, shuffling off in her slippers, motioning for me to follow her down the hall. "I've just brewed some fresh iced tea."

I make myself comfortable on the sofa in the living room while she slips into the kitchen. Though I'm itching to explore the lion's den, to snoop around the closets for rotting corpses or studded leather ensembles, it's impossible to deny that the room has a soothing pleasantness to it. Long, airy drapes, a gleaming hardwood floor, a ceramic urn of dried roses beside a canvas print of a famous impressionist painting.

On the mantel straight ahead rests a smattering of framed pictures: the Sycophant dressed in ski gear at the top of a chairlift, the Sycophant smugly holding up a large trout, the Sycophant and his family grinning away in a Jacuzzi. Either his wife hasn't finished her housekeeping yet or there's still a chance at salvaging the relationship. I'm feeling dirty looking at these pictures, a shameful voyeur. I'm reminded of the time I ran into Mr. Gilbert, my third-grade teacher, at the Baskin-Robbins with my mother one summer. He was with his two kids, and it was a real creepy experience. I mean, I didn't want to know that Mr. Gilbert's favorite flavor of ice cream was mint chocolate chip, or that he wore shiny basketball shorts, or that he was one of those paternal figures who had no qualms calling his son Squirt. I wanted him banished immediately to the classroom, with its popcorn strings and paper chains dangling from the walls and cubbyholes with our name tags above them, to have no other facets of personality beyond being my third-grade teacher. It's the same way with the Sycophant, I guess.

His wife emerges from the kitchen with a tray laden with two glasses of iced tea and a plate of chocolate chip cookies. After positioning the tray carefully on the table, she joins me on the couch. Not all the way at the other end but with only a finger's length separating us. As we drink our iced tea, the house is as silent as a mausoleum, the stillness only disturbed by the occasional clinking of ice cubes in our glasses or the crunching sound from trying to gnaw at an overbaked cookie.

Fortunately she takes the initiative.

"They're not very good, are they? My son likes them rock hard for some crazy reason. I prefer them chewy myself."

I grin, trying to mask my discomfort. "No, they're fine. A nice texture, good ratio of chocolate chips to batter . . ."

She laughs off my attempt at being polite. Settling back into the cushions, invoking an image of a svelte jungle cat, she asks, "So, do you enjoy working at the Bank?"

I give my typical prefabricated response: "Yeah, it's all right."

"And you like working with my husband?"

What a question. Another of my prefabricated responses:

"Yeah, he's a decent guy."

She's unconvinced, rolling her eyes.

"He's an absolute shit. Really insecure. I can just imagine his behavior at the office, groveling to the senior guys while giving you young bucks a load of crap."

Bucks. Weird choice of noun. I shrug and pick up my glass. She reaches over and pats my thigh.

"I understand. You're just being a good boy. Trying to protect yourself."

More uncomfortable grinning from my end. The problem is this: A minute or two passes and she still hasn't removed her hand from my pant leg. It rests perfectly content on my thigh, even being so bold as to make a suggestive circular motion.

"I, um . . ."

While I've never technically been propositioned by an older woman before, I've watched *The Graduate* a few times and have a vague notion of how this seduction is supposed to transpire. Inviting me in for a glass of iced tea, a hand on my thigh, rolling around in the upstairs bedroom, sending framed pictures of the Sycophant crashing to the floor. Yet despite Anne Bancroft's fueling the odd masturbatory session, I can't seem to shake off who this woman is: bearer of the womb that incubated the Sycophant's progeny, she who has witnessed him in all his bare-ass naked grotesqueness and lived to tell the tale.

She winks at me coyly and suddenly the reality of the situation—*the Sycophant's wife has her hand on my inner thigh!*—smashes into me like a kamikaze pilot's final *sayonara.* Holy fucking crap. The Sycophant's wife is unfazed by my tension. She scoots over, nonchalant, as if seducing the young'uns is a part of her daily routine, until our legs are squeezed firmly together. She's wearing a sheer blouse and I'm certain I can decipher the outline of a nipple—*the teat that has nourished the Sycophant's children!*—and even the surrounding areola, this hyperreality really kicking in.

All right; I'm putting a stop to this.

Just as I'm about to push up off the couch, the hand on my thigh continues its upward trek, venturing boldly to my crotch and probing at my trousers. I'm not fully erect—I'm way too nervous to achieve that level of turgidity—but the hand seems content probing at my squishiness.

"I love your ears," the Sycophant's wife purrs from close by. "Do you mind if I touch them?"

Before I give my consent, she reaches over and starts stroking an earlobe.

"Oohhh," she moans, "the skin is just so supple."

With one of her hands fingering my earlobe and the other on the verge of a handjob, I'm definitely approaching the point of no return. Do I really want this? Rationally, no. Too many complications for a quick roll in the hay. And then there's the Woman With The Scarf to think about.

"The driver. He's still waiting outside . . ."

"Fuck your driver," she moans, licking the side of my neck.

Enough with the rationality. It's been way too long since anything more serious than those tentative kisses at Starbucks. And when it boils down to it, I'm getting mad bragging rights for this.

She gasps as my tongue pushes between her teeth, invading her tonsils. My hands are all over the place: tearing at the buttons on her blouse, fumbling with the clasp of her bra, squeezing a breast, trying to worm their way inside the waistband of her slacks.

"My god," she chuckles throatily, "you're so positively . . . *virile*. I forgot about the pleasures of youth."

All I can manage is a pretty inane "Yeah, baby."

She slides down the couch, pulling me on top of her. Grinding into her pelvis, I'm overwhelmed by my insatiable horniness. I have to slow down or I'm going to get off too soon.

My fingers reach their final destination and she's squirming underneath me like a fish fresh out of water. Gone is the awkwardness that she's the Sycophant's wife, gone the awkwardness that she's at least twenty years older than me. All this awkwardness dissipates under a primal lust, an impending orgasm. I dry-hump her ferociously into the couch, rubbing my hardness against her stomach.

We're really getting into it when there is a knocking at the door followed by a little boy's voice:

"Mommy, Janice dropped me off early."

She stiffens beneath me, then tries to hurl me off her—except for the fact that my hand, entangled in her panties, won't come loose from her slacks, and her bucking below me isn't making this any easier.

"Oh fuck," she hisses, fumbling to reclasp her bra.

"I'm sorry. It's my fingers, they're stuck—"

"Just get them fucking out!"

We're interrupted by the appearance of a short blond boy with egghead glasses.

"Mommy, what are you doing?"

With a burst of panicked strength, she yanks my hand out of her crotch, sending the top button of her slacks flying. She leaps off the couch and smooths down her hair.

"We were just wrestling, honey."

"*Wrestling?*"

The boy peers at my open fly with obvious disdain.

"Who's *he?*"

The Sycophant's wife is superbly collected, as if she's had a lot of experience with these close calls.

"He's one of Daddy's business colleagues."

The boy doesn't look too convinced.

"He's got stick-out ears," he says, scowling. "Much dopier than Daddy's. Where is Daddy, anyways?"

The Sycophant's wife strokes the top of his head.

"Daddy's very, very busy with work right now. We'll only be gone for two weeks and then you'll see Daddy again."

The boy stares at me with the youthful manifestation of sheer hatred before bounding up the staircase. The Sycophant's wife puts a hand to her forehead and stares wistfully at the ceiling. Then she walks me out with minimal eye contact, neither of us saying a word.

♦

Back at the office, the Star's monitor displays a little girl jumping up and down on a trampoline. The Defeated One is hovering over it.

"What the hell is this?"

"My sister's birthday party. My folks wanted it on film, and the camcorder was just lying around, and, uh, the clip had already been transferred to the CD . . ."

"Fuuuuck," the Defeated One moans.

"I thought we didn't need it anymore," the Star whimpers.

The Defeated One puts his head in his arms.

Hanging up my coat, I ask, "What about the file on the CD?"

"All gone." The Star puffs out his bottom lip. "Somehow the projector corrupted the data when it crashed. I tried everything, but it's no longer extractable."

I shrug. "We can always try filming them again?"

The Defeated One looks up woefully.

"I'm not even sure if they're sleeping together anymore."

The Star guiltily hands the CD case back to the Defeated One, who tosses it on his desk. We observe a moment of silence to mourn the plan's failure before I suggest a Starbucks run to lift our spirits. The Defeated One and I head down the hall to round up the rest of the troops. As per usual, Postal Boy is the only one around. He's rooting through Clyde's desk, frantically opening and shutting drawers.

"Postal, what are you doing?" the Defeated One asks.

Postal Boy ignores us, removing piles of paper and dumping them on the floor.

"What the hell is going on?" the Defeated One asks again, raising his voice.

When Postal Boy reaches into the back of Clyde's filing cabinet and tosses a tattered *Swank* magazine across the room, the Defeated One grabs hold of one of the swivel chairs and pushes it in Postal Boy's direction. It nudges into the back of his legs, causing him to stumble forward and bash his knee against the edge of the desk. Postal Boy emits a strangled, unnatural "Aaarrggghhhhhhh."

He whips around to glare at us, his shoulders hunched forward and fists clenched in the stance of an avenging zombie in a B-grade horror flick. In a voice I've never heard before, one shaking with rage, he says, "Do you know what I'm doing?"

The Defeated One throws me a bewildered glance as Postal Boy lumbers toward us.

"Going through Clyde's desk?" I offer.

Postal Boy shakes his head and sneers, "I'm trying to find a pile of research reports on alternative-energy firms. You know why I'm looking for these reports?"

His left eye is twitching so rapidly that *fluttering* is a more apt description.

The Defeated One mouths at me, "This is it. The moment we've all been waiting for."

Postal Boy continues:

"I'm looking for these reports, mind you, because I just got called into the Philanderer's office. Seems like Clyde has been doing some shoddy work of late and they're getting nervous he's going to screw this one up. So, with infinite wisdom, they decided to pass this project along to yours truly. Four sets of comps to be completed by Thursday morning. This on top of the one-hundred-and-twenty-hour weeks I'm pulling on these other projects."

Then Postal Boy really loses it, grabbing a stapler and hurling it against the opposite wall. It strikes a cabinet beside the Prodigal Son's monitor and erupts in a gale of shiny silver crescents. The Defeated One glances at me and makes the hand movements of an explosion.

Postal Boy leans against the edge of the desk, panting hard, looking forlornly at the staples on the floor. Then he gets down on his knees and crawls under the desk, curling into a fetal position beside the buzzing computer and power cords.

"I just can't take it anymore," he whimpers.

My immediate instinct is to quickly shut the door. Pragmatism, I guess. My second instinct is to stand there wringing my fingers, not knowing how I'm supposed to react to the long-awaited event of Postal Boy finally going mental. With a gentleness that surprises me, the Defeated One steps over and leans down beside the desk.

"Come out of there, buddy."

After some reluctance, Postal Boy slowly gets to his feet, dusting off his pant legs. Though he isn't tearing up, the desolation etched on his face is heart-wrenching in its own right. The three of us sit in the empty swivel chairs in the room.

"I'm sorry," Postal Boy croaks, "I'm not sure what just happened."

"Hey," the Defeated One assures him, "we all lose it every now and again. Consider it part of a banker's rite of passage."

Postal Boy manages a weak smile.

"I'm just so fucking exhausted."

"I know."

"And I've got to clean up those staples."

"Yeah, you do."

Postal Boy runs his hands through his hair, further disheveling the crow's nest.

"I don't know how I'm going to handle it. It's like . . . I can't physically meet all these deadlines. The comps for the Philanderer, the LBO model for the telecom group, this alternative-energy crap. It's not humanly possible— "

"Relax," the Defeated One urges, repeating his mantra, "you have to remember: Nobody's going to die from this."

Postal Boy slumps further in the chair.

"I think I'm going to speak to the Toad this afternoon," he says. "Tell him that it's getting to be too much. It's hard enough picking up the slack for the Prodigal Son, but now Clyde as well— "

"You are not going to sit down with the Toad." The Defeated One rises from his chair. "You choose to confide in him and what's going to happen? The Prodigal Son remains, because he has his head firmly lodged up the Fish's anal cavity, and Clyde will get the boot. Where does that leave you? Right back where you started, shouldering the work of three analysts, albeit with no sympathy from the rest of the junior employees because you're about to be known around these parts as the whistle-blower. The guy who is not to be trusted. And don't forget the Toad really hates a whiner, interprets sniveling as a sign of weakness. A couple thousand bucks docked from your bonus for all your troubles."

Postal Boy remains quiet, considering this angle. Putting his head in his arms, he acknowledges, "You're right, but it can't go on like this. The Prodigal Son is a write-off, but Clyde . . ."

"Let's leave Clyde out of this for now," says the Defeated One.

I snap, "No, let's bring Clyde into this. We've had this talk already; enough with the denial. We've been patient, we've given him his space, but forget it, man. Clyde is now at the point where he's a liability on the rest of us. Look at Postal; he hasn't slept in the last week. There's frickin' mildew growing out the side of his head."

"That's just fluff from my tie."

"Whatever. Maybe it *is* a good idea to bring it up with the Toad. At the very least, it'll give Clyde a kick in the pants."

The Defeated One slams his hand on the desk.

"NO!"

The veins in his neck bulge out prominently. This only makes me equally pissed, and I shout at him.

"Why the hell are you so loyal to him, anyway? Why are you so perfectly content letting him get away with this bullshit?"

The Defeated One scowls. "It's like this, jackass. We slave away at the Bank, these missiles of excrement hailing down on us from all of the senior guys, and there's not a single moment of reprieve: no time for our families, our friends, not even five fucking minutes when we get home to satisfy that basic human craving for sex. And so, let me ask you this: What do we have left if we turn on one another? I'll tell you—*zip*. Nada."

He takes a deep breath, turning to Postal Boy.

"Look, I'm not trying to be Clyde's protector, and I'm not going to force you to stay away from the Toad. If you really feel the need to lie down on his couch and unburden your woes, then I won't stop you. But think about what's helping us survive here—not the Toad, not the Sycophant. It's the ability to rely on one another."

"Kumbaya, my lord," I hum, but I stop when the Defeated One throws me a menacing glare.

"I don't know . . ." Postal Boy sighs.

The Defeated One sits back down.

"Postal, I'm just not willing to give up on Clyde after only a few weeks. Granted he's not dealing with his father's death in a perfectly natural way, but I'm telling you, that sort of shit has to mess with your head."

Again I find myself getting snippy.

"That's all fine and dandy, enlightened one, but you're not working one-hundred-and-twenty-hour weeks cleaning up after his mess."

I expect a moral outburst, but instead the Defeated One leans back, scratching his forehead.

"Okay, how about this? I'll handle the LBO model for the telecom group, and Mumbles"—he nods in my direction—"will take care of the alternative-energy comps. That should ease some of the burden for now."

"Gee, thanks for volunteering my services," I mutter. "Like I'm not busy enough with everything else I have on my plate."

The Defeated One ignores me, swiveling around to ferret through the Prodigal Son's desk for a piece of gum. Anyway, it's not like he really needs to say anything; one glance at Postal Boy, his left eye twitching in a display of infinite gratitude, is enough to confirm that, ah, fuck it, I guess I'm stuck with those comps.

♦

There is only one method for staying moderately healthy in investment banking. Because your daily exercise routine consists of nothing more rigorous than walking back and forth between your desk and the copy room and flexing your wrist muscles using the binding machine, you have to make do by improving your diet: copious amounts of iodine-enriched seaweed and lumps of raw fish full of protein and low in fat.

Nonetheless, it's an acquired taste. The Sushi Progression works like this:

- *Veggie Rolls.* Your first brave foray into this alien cuisine. Speckling your shirt with soy sauce because of those damn chopsticks and realizing the weird pink flakes aren't just for decoration, you struggle to keep down the cucumber and avocado while the more advanced sushi eaters effortlessly drop nasty blobs of raw fish down their gullets.
- *Fake Crab Rolls.* Fake, you surmise, as in processed out of a taro potato? Those crafty Japanese; you wouldn't put it past them. It's not until after you've wolfed down a six-pack of California rolls, ready to swagger up and down the joint with your chest puffed out like a peacock, that somebody at the next table wonders how they're able to make other types of fish taste so convincingly like crabmeat. Right at this very moment is the crucial hurdle of the entire progression: You either make a beeline for the restroom and eject such foulness in a torrent of doubly reconstituted pseudo-crabmeat or you shred the list of things you're willing to swallow and boldly venture forward in an unblinking free fall . . .

- *Rolls with Tiny Shreds of Fish Inside.* You've overcome the non-crab crabmeat and you're going to give this your best shot. Maybe your second-best shot: tiny pieces of fish rendered completely tasteless by clumps of rice, soy sauce, those weird pink flakes you're beginning to like, and dollops of wasabi.
- *Rolls with Big Chunks of Fish Inside.* Hey, this raw fish thing isn't too bad.
- *Nigiri—Strips of Fish on Rice.* Really, this raw fish thing isn't too bad.

Finally, after you're officially addicted to the $7.99 lunch specials (including miso soup and salad):

- *Sashimi—Strips of Fish Without the Rice.* Screw the carbohydrates, Aki, my man, and pelt me with more raw tuna.

♦

We're both at the nigiri level, the Woman With The Scarf and I, awakened to our burgeoning craving for raw aquatic matter but not yet ready to forgo the rice altogether. It is essential for two people to be at a similar point in the Sushi Progression to truly enjoy their meal together; otherwise there's always going to be one enthusiastic person with lips smacking—oh, man, you've really gotta try this!—while the other sits back and makes glum faces.

The Woman With The Scarf delicately swallows a piece of unagi. She closes her eyes and sighs.

"My god, this is so delicious."

Of course she's going to love the barbecued eel. According to Aki, the one-eyed sushi chef slicing and dicing behind the bar, the secret ingredient is maple syrup.

Preparing a second piece with a shard of ginger and a fleck of wasabi, she says, "So, tell me again why you're a banker. You don't exactly fit the mold."

"And what, pray tell, is the mold?"

"Now you've put me on the spot," she says, smirking. "I don't know: brash, arrogant, myopically materialistic—"

"Myopically materialistic?" I cock an eyebrow.

She waves a chopstick at me threateningly.

"Buzz off, mister. Let me get back to reducing your creed to a cardboard stereotype. Let's see . . . Armani-wearing, Mercedes-driving, *Wall Street Journal*–skimming, summerhouse-tripping, sushi-eating . . ."

"What are we doing right now?"

She shrugs. "Hey, lawyers are just bankers without the bulging wallets. At least the junior ones."

I reach for a squishy mound of fatty tuna.

"I guess I could make something up, try to pretend I find something noble in it, greasing the wheels of capitalism to crush the corruption behind communism or whatever, but the truth is, it's just a lack of integrity."

The Woman With The Scarf smiles.

"But it's true, right?" I continue. "I mean, you're finishing up your undergrad in econ or poli sci or the mating habits of Eskimos, and everybody is competing for the same top-tier jobs, consulting and banking, and though you might have a disconcerting inkling that perhaps you're meant to draw comic books or round up elephants in Tanzania, still, you kind of just shrug it off and get swept up in this need to succeed according to other people's expectations. I'm sure this is all really obvious."

"Yeah." The Woman With The Scarf nods. "But it's nice you can admit to it. You're not in denial or anything. Though I don't think people studying the mating habits of Eskimos are going to be seriously pursuing investment banking careers anytime soon."

"Probably not," I agree, grinning. "Anyway, I can't see myself doing this forever. Only two years at most. What about you—I mean, why are you a lawyer? It doesn't exactly seem like you're too happy with your profession either."

The Woman With The Scarf laughs.

"Touché. Well," she says, taking a sip of her Asahi Super Dry, "I can't say I'm coming from the exact same place as you. I really do like the law; I think there's something respectable in its practice. I honestly believe it's the legal system that sets us apart from other animals, this ability to govern our societies. But somewhere along I guess I was lured away by the prestige and money as well. Look at me . . . I'm a tax lawyer. I can't exactly argue I'm forging a more noble society while sitting behind a desk assisting corporations exploit tax loopholes, can I?"

"I'm sure you do the best you can."

"Yeah, here's to ambiguous accounting scandals."

We clink our glasses and settle into a really comfortable silence. It's weird to have reached this stage so early in our relationship; normally it takes a few solid months before I stop feeling the need to say stupid things in order to fill the awkward gaps in a conversation. When the check comes, I whip out my credit card. The Woman With The Scarf puts up a fuss, but I put up a greater fuss. It helps matters that I'm not really forking for this anyway, expensing dinner for myself and the Prodigal Son (who's never around, hence the default when we go over our allotted allowances).

We grab our coats and exit into the first snowfall of the season. Flurries of white whirl gracefully through the sky and land on our noses and fingertips. We walk a couple more blocks, tentatively holding hands, then holding hands more naturally, before she turns to me.

"This is going to sound very brash, and I don't normally do this, especially after I've only known someone for a short while . . . all right, enough with the justifications. I'd really like it if you came back to my place. You know, for some hot chocolate and stuff."

"Now?" I gulp.

Those alternative-energy comps I'm supposed to put together for Postal Boy are due first thing tomorrow morning and I haven't even started them yet.

She nods. "Yeah, now. Right at this very second."

She grabs onto my loosened tie, narrows her eyes, and yanks my head toward her. We've kissed before at Starbucks, a quick peck or two before heading to the elevators, but this is something else, taking things up to the next level. I reach out and touch the dangling ends of her neck scarf. She slaps my hands away.

"Don't touch the scarf."

"All right . . ."

"I'm just messing with you," she snickers.

Then she pulls me toward her again. We go at it for a couple more minutes, the snow falling on our heads, passersby without their winter hats scowling or smiling depending on whether they're lonely or not.

"That was great," she beams.

"Yeah."

She's shivering, hugging herself and looking insanely beautiful.

"So, you're up for that hot chocolate?"

"I, um—"

And in the duration of a stammer, the mood comes crashing down on our heads, the romance replaced by a jarring unease.

"You don't have to."

"No, I, uh—"

She's already turning away.

"It's not that big a deal."

I walk in stride beside her.

"I'm not letting this turn into a cliché situation. You walking away before I can speak my piece. I promise, there is nothing I want more in this world right now than to have a hot chocolate with you. 'Hot chocolate' as a euphemism for—"

She eyes me sternly.

"Okay, just double-checking. But look, I also promised this colleague of mine who's in a tight crunch that I'd help him out tonight. If it was my own work, to hell with it. But I don't know—"

"It's fine. I sort of understand."

She definitely doesn't understand.

"It's not like—"

But she's already strolling off, waving her fingers without looking back. I stand there peering after her, snow settling on my ears, until she's turned the corner.

Eight

Bonus time is rapidly approaching and the Toad looks like an absolute wreck: sagging bags under his eyes, a gallon of coffee in hand, tie askew, and suit jacket covered in wrinkles. It's all part of the Toad's underlying strategy, the Defeated One's explained to me: Exude an aura of extreme haggardness to suggest he's sticking around the office till the wee hours of the morning (try till 6:30, which is at most half an hour later than the rest of senior management), painstakingly determining whether Postal Boy really deserves that extra five hundred dollars or not, all designed to detract from the painfully obvious reality that he's really just useless overhead. Seriously, even the janitors are more value-added scrubbing the piss from our urinals.

This is not to say that coming up with junior employee bonuses isn't an incredibly important task. Because the economy is plodding along nicely right now, with everybody shrugging off the sluggishness of the post-9/11 bear market and embracing a return to obscenely lucrative profits, attrition rates are shooting through the roof. A fundamental truth: There isn't a modicum of loyalty in this industry. I once mentioned to the Philandering Managing Director in passing that I really felt the Bank was becoming my home—god knows what I was thinking; probably sucking up early in the game when I didn't know any better—and he unabashedly laughed in my face. Come Thursday, as we're shepherded into the Toad's office to receive our manila envelopes, we will all be weighing our options carefully, a toss-up between following one or another of several stepping-stones on a banker's generic quest to undermine income equality and crush the rest of the financial world: defection to another Bank with higher pay; a perhaps risky move to a hedge fund started up by an older brother; or, if you're especially lucky, if you have great contacts and know how to work them, the holy grail of the trade, the shuddering multiple orgasm for every B-school graduate, Private Equity. Sell side. The ability to triple your salary and cruise around in a private jet while the clients come begging you for money, not the other way around. Thus, it's all up to the Toad to prevent a mass exodus of liberated analysts.

Nonetheless, despite acting like Atlas with the weight of the world on his shoulders, it's not like he's in this alone. Every bank on the Street has its own Toad equivalent responsible for determining junior employee bonuses, a squat doppelgänger sighing and grumbling and despising the little piss-ant analysts who are all too eager to defect should anybody wave an extra thousand bucks in front of their noses. Over the next few days, this consortium of Toads will sneak into their respective offices and covertly call each other. After some collusion and coercion and crumbling under peer pressure, they'll arrive at an allowable spectrum for junior bonuses that is compressed into a narrower band. It's then up to each individual Toad to determine where they want to hit.

According to the Defeated One, our Bank aims for low to middle of the road.

"You'll walk away feeling cheated, a bit nauseated in the pit of your stomach, but not bad enough that you'll sprint toward the nearest exit. It would almost be better if you really got screwed over; then you'd be forced to come up with a feasible escape plan."

I've been trying to finagle him into tightening up my forecasted range. Right now it's fairly open-ended. I've decided upon an absolute minimum of $20,000 for six months of work—anything below that would be unacceptable, though I still haven't worked out the consequences of this—and an optimistic peak of $32,500. Including my base salary of $60,000, this amounts to an annualized all-in of $100,000 to $125,000. It's tempting to think this isn't too shabby for a twenty-three-year-old fresh out of an undergraduate degree. Yet, as the Toad hands you that envelope, all the crap you've put up with over the last few months is focalized on the sparse piece of paper folded neatly inside: weekend after weekend shot to hell; all non-Bank relationships deteriorating into oblivion; slaving away with flu symptoms at three in the morning; acting as designated whipping boy for cretins like the Sycophant.

"Why won't you tell me?"

"I can't," he says, leaning back in the chair. "It's against company policy. The Toad would have my head."

"Give me a break."

"What's your best estimate?"

"Twenty as the minimum—"

He snorts.

"As the minimum? What, you think a couple months as an analyst is worth—what's that over the year?—a hundred grand?"

"Piss off."

The Defeated One revels in these sadistic mind games. As I'm about to swivel back to my spreadsheet, he asks, "And what's your upper bounds?"

I'm reluctant to tell him.

"Give it up, Mumbles."

"Thirty-five. No, thirty."

He guffaws, slapping his knee.

"Thirty-five? Over a hundred and twenty for the year? You've got to be kidding me. What the hell do you think we're doing here, neurosurgery?"

He looks around the room.

"Because I ain't seein' no deconstructed brains around these parts, are you?"

"I hate you."

"Awww, Mumbles has his feelings hurt."

"I'm not kidding. I'm beginning to seriously hate you."

The Defeated One shrugs before swiveling back around.

♦

Two thousand and forty minutes until the day of reckoning . . .

I'm trying for the hundredth time to make sense of our ultra-sophisticated fax machine, a Hewlett-Packard capable of collating and stapling but never seeming to manage what it's technically supposed to do, in this case, transmit a client invoice halfway across the world. Invoicing is typically an assistant's job, but the senior guys no longer entrust the Utterly Incompetent Assistant with the task after she neglected to bill the federal tax on a million-dollar fee. A mistake costing the Bank a hundred grand, more than double her annual salary, and yet she's still sitting at her desk, a box of Krispy Kreme doughnuts poking out her top drawer. It's truly amazing what sleeping with the Philanderer will get you.

As the fax machine spits out my page yet again, I can't help but wonder if she knows how to work this contraption. It's a bit of a stretch, but the Defeated One has already gone to grab lunch, and the Client was expecting this five minutes ago. I brush aside my humility and interrupt the Utterly Incompetent Assistant licking the icing sugar off her fingers.

"Could you help me fax this?"

She rolls her eyes and snatches the page out of my hand. Sauntering over to the fax machine, she pushes a few buttons, her fingers a blur, and the device hums to life. Of course she'd be able to get it right, if only to exude this irritating smugness. As the page is fed through, she shakes her head slowly, eyeing me up and down like I'm a complete invalid.

"Thanks," I mumble.

"Whatever," she grunts.

♦

One thousand five hundred and thirteen minutes . . .

From: Me@theBank.com

To: WomanWithTheScarf@GoodmanWeisenthal.com

Apologies again for the conclusion of our evening a few nights ago. I always seem to be apologizing for things, don't I? Guess that's the eternal curse of the investment banker. Anyway, I saved my co-worker's ass; now that the Good Samaritan bit is out of the way, I was wondering if you had time for coffee this afternoon? Let me know.

Two hours later and there is still no response.

♦

One thousand three hundred and ninety-three minutes . . .

The Sycophant bursts into our office, one notch down from full-fledged nuclear meltdown.

"What the hell is going on? Where are those comps, already?"

He's stumped me for a moment. Which comps?

Then I realize he's referring to the comps he dropped on my plate less than fifteen minutes ago. Give me a break; even three Stars laboring away concurrently couldn't have pulled it off in less than an hour. I struggle to keep my voice level.

"I'm going to need a bit more time."

He's been unreasonably demanding like this the entire week, more so than his usual repugnant self. It's because of bonuses, the Defeated One's hypothesized; the Sycophant hopes a few days of acting all bossy will compensate for being a spineless creep the rest of the time, his sudden authoritativeness earning him that ever-elusive promotion. Sure enough, I spy the Philandering Managing Director schmoozing the Utterly Incompetent Assistant just beyond the door frame, well within earshot.

The Sycophant leans over my shoulder and peers at the monitor. He's picking at his teeth with the end of a paper clip.

"That TEV/EBITDA ratio is blatantly incorrect."

I haven't even calculated a TEV/EBITDA ratio yet.

"And why didn't you include Dodge Phelps in your list of North American producers?"

I'm this close to pushing off the edge of my desk and propelling my chair backward, and then, when the Sycophant is knocked down, quickly wheeling back and forth over his head, reducing it to pulp. I can't imagine it being all that difficult. Easier than a watermelon, I'll bet.

"Fix this up and have it to me in fifteen minutes."

He tosses the paper clip toothpick to the carpet and storms out of the room. No pulp, then. Heh, I'll have to content myself with the knowledge I nearly screwed his wife.

♦

Three hundred and ninety minutes . . .

I'm guzzling down caffeine with Postal Boy and Clyde at two-thirty in the morning. The Defeated One copped out early in the hopes of smoothing things over after a nasty scrap with the girlfriend.

"So, we're going to tell one another our bonuses, right?"

Clyde cocks his head back and lets loose a resounding belch. Wiping at his mouth, he says, "Yeah, I don't mind."

I raise my can of Coke to him. Clyde's behavior has drastically improved lately: showing up to work at a reasonably punctual hour, not smoking up on the job, and keeping his disappearances to a minimum. I'm almost positive the Defeated One chatted with him after Postal Boy's breakdown, though nothing has been mentioned explicitly. Postal Boy, as per usual, is the voice of dissent:

"I don't know, guys. I don't think I'm comfortable with this."

"What's the problem?" I ask.

Postal Boy removes his glasses and blows on the lenses.

"What if you guys get more than me? Then I'm left feeling like crap. Maybe it's better if we just keep it to ourselves— "

"But knowledge is power," Clyde interjects. "Postal, wouldn't you want to know if you got royally screwed over? Sure you'd feel terrible if the Toad gave you the short end of the stick, but is that worse than not knowing the injustice of one of us potentially getting a fatter check than you?"

"I guess you're right," Postal Boy sighs.

"So, you're in?"

"Yeah," Postal Boy agrees.

♦

And finally, the day of reckoning is upon us . . .

> From: TheToad@theBank.com
>
> To: Analysts; Associates
>
> After an excellent recovery over the last few months, I'm pleased to announce we will be distributing year-end bonuses and reviews throughout the day. Please see the attached schedule.

I'm allotted an afternoon appointment at 3:30. The Defeated One is scheduled in at an earlier 12:45. He rubs his hands together gleefully.

"So, are you excited, Mumbles?"

"Yeah, ecstatic," I deadpan.

I'm actually shitting my pants, in all honesty. I know it's kind of unfounded, but what if the Sycophant gave me a really horrible review? Despite busting my ass over the last several months, jumping through all sorts of demeaning hoops, I wouldn't put it past him.

"Don't get too excited by the Toadian language," the Defeated One instructs. "We had an 'excellent recovery' last year as well, and bonuses were still flat."

"Great," I grumble.

"Awww," he says, pouting. "You're worried you won't be getting that big fat bonus check for thirty-five grand."

"Leave me alone."

"Mumbles, you know I'm just fucking with you."

Then he starts giggling hysterically, unable to restrain himself:

"But thirty-five thousand! My god, what tailpipe are you sniffing?"

♦

Eons have passed by the time the Defeated One is getting ready for his appointment. Despite all the big talk, he's looking nervous as he takes a deep breath and strides out of our office like the royals being prodded along to the guillotines.

Fifteen minutes later and he's slumped in his chair with the manila envelope on his lap. He looks downcast at the envelope before hurling it against the window.

"Goddamn."

"That bad, huh?"

He shakes his head and points to his stomach.

"Gets you right here, didn't I tell ya?"

On that ominous note, by the time the clock flickers to 3:25, my nervousness has manifested itself as a physical nausea. I arrive at the Toad's office just as an Asian associate rushes out. She'd make a brilliant poker player; there is nothing in her expression that betrays whether she's pleased or devastated by the manila envelope she clutches in her hand.

The Toad sits regally behind the desk, his posture painfully erect in an attempt to boost his five foot two inches above the stack of envelopes piled neatly before him. A shaft of sunlight breaks from the murky clouds beyond the window and illuminates the glistening expanse of his receding hairline.

"Please sit down."

He's clearly eating up this full day of intense power-tripping egomania. There is one envelope separated from the rest of the pile; I imagine that's mine.

The Toad presses his hands together and clears his throat. He has this peculiar habit of spreading his arms real wide when he speaks, like he's maximizing his surface area for optimal windpipe clearage before he finally utters a peep. After such a physical production, you're expecting a supernatural baritone, Barry Manilow reverberating out of his tiny frame. Instead, it's choirboy falsetto, a squeeze toy held down too long. He could use a misshapen beret with a feather in it. Silken tights. All hail the great orator, Sir Venomous Toad.

He rambles on about how the year started off in the dumps but ended respectably, how I should be very proud of my contribution to the Bank's performance, how senior management doesn't take for granted the immense importance of us flea-ridden monkeys humping the base of the totem pole. At the end of this two-faced monologue, the moment of truth has finally arrived. He hands me the manila envelope. The first page is my review scorecard, mostly a bunch of 3's and 4's. Not great, but not as terrible as it could have been.

On the next page, halfway down, there is the number:

$22,000.

It's not my minimum, I grant you that, but it's definitely not something I'm going to cream my pants over. Before I've looked up, the Toad is narrowing his eyes; he's perceived all of this in a flash. A stern shaking of hands and then I'm dismissed with a nod of his gleaming head, off to commiserate with the Defeated One.

♦

"So, we're going to pull them out one by one and write the numbers on a piece of paper, right? Nobody will know for sure exactly who got what."

I shake the hat with the three strips of paper, each containing our scribbled bonus amount. Clyde rolls his eyes.

"Like this isn't going to be painfully obvious."

The Prodigal Son saunters in right as I'm about to unfold the first strip. He collapses in his chair, arms behind his head.

"Hey, boys."

"You're here late." Postal Boy's monotone wavers with contempt.

It's only 5:30, a ballsy comment coming from him.

"Yeah, tell me about it, dude. Just forgot my wallet. Headin' home in fifteen minutes."

He scratches his belly and yawns.

"Anyway, what's in the hat?"

"We're comparing bonuses," Clyde answers matter-of-factly.

"Cool." The Prodigal Son stifles another yawn. "Hold up a minute."

He writes something on a piece of paper and folds it. Tossing it in the hat, he puts on his jacket and swaggers out of the office.

"Fucker," Postal Boy mouths after him.

"Back to business."

I shake the hat again. After unfolding the four pieces of paper, I write the numbers in a column:

$22,000
$27,000
$22,000
$22,000

"There it is, gentlemen."

"Congratulations, Postal." Clyde slaps him on the back.

Postal Boy doesn't even flinch at the smack. He's gone white as a sheet, literally, all the blood draining from his cheeks. He peers at me quizzically, his left eye twitching in disbelief.

"Did you get more . . . ? "

I look over at Clyde. He shrugs.

It dawns on all three of us simultaneously.

"Fucking hell," Clyde roars.

♦

From: Me@theBank.com

To: WomanWithTheScarf@GoodmanWeisenthal.com

So we just received our bonuses. I'm still trying to work out whether it's adequate comp for being a slave to the Bank; figure probably not. Nonetheless, it's a decent enough excuse to celebrate. Any chance you'd be up for grabbing another dinner sometime? Come on, write back.

♦

My original idea was to celebrate my bonus with a low-key affair, wings and beer and a few rounds of Texas Hold'em with a few friends who had miraculously survived my extreme negligence. However, Lulu popped by all flustered this afternoon and sabotaged my happy plan, weaseling us into attending the WETI Society Annual Winter Gala this evening. It happens all the time: The Bank purchases a table at one of these hoity-toity charity events, and if it's for a boring cause, meaning it doesn't involve hobnobbing with the industry's finest, then the Bank fills the thousand-dollars-a-plate chairs with sullen analysts.

"What does it stand for again?" Postal Boy swigs from his personal-size bottle of Moët. "Women for the Ethical Treatment of . . ."

"Iguanas," the Defeated One slurs.

"Inuits," Clyde chimes in.

I down my champagne irritably. Aside from the frustration of not having heard back from the Woman With The Scarf over the past few days, this gala reeks of pretension: elegant women scuttling around, blowing air kisses at one another; the fun-size bottles of Moët; the pecan-encrusted catfish and garlic broccolini that tastes no better than rubber chicken and overcooked spinach.

A woman in a brown dress resembling the pecan-encrusted catfish taps the microphone at the front of the ballroom, then immediately breaks into a militant tirade.

"We must stand by the men in our lives who feel the insecurity of satisfying us, who roam through this world limp and vulnerable— "

"My god." The Defeated One grimaces. "Women for the Ethical Treatment of *Impotence?*"

"Relax." Clyde passes him another bottle of Moët. "It'll make for a great story one day."

The Defeated One turns to an analyst on his left, a guy who eerily resembles Postal Boy. I wonder if they've always looked similar or if it's the Bank's evil doing, converging their physical identities like those Borgs on *Star Trek*.

"So brotha, what trouble are you getting up to with your bonus?"

The guy doesn't even hesitate and says, "I'm investing it."

"All of it?"

"Yup."

"But, dude," the Defeated One reasons, "if you don't treat yourself to anything, if you just save it all, then it's almost as if it never happened."

The guy frowns. "Look, I'm really trying to pay attention to this, all right?"

It's hard to believe, truly, and I'm reminded of why I rarely make any social effort outside of our Gang of Four. The catfish lady's voice rises over the microphone:

"And now I'd like to introduce the venerable Mr. J. P. Reynolds from Sotheby's, who will commence the auction of more than twenty lots of stunning American Indian art and textiles. A gentle reminder: Ten percent of all proceeds will be graciously donated to fund programs coordinated by the WETI Society."

The catfish woman exits the stage to vigorous applause. An elderly man in a tuxedo takes her place before the microphone.

"Thank you, Evelyn. Please note the bid cards arranged on each table . . ."

It's not long before the auction is in full swing. It's actually somewhat exciting, believe it or not. Our participation is restricted to voyeurism, as the auction is anything but child's play: The first item, a Tsimshian mask, sells to a flamboyant man in a mustard-yellow blazer for eighty thousand dollars. The room claps enthusiastically as the man pumps his fist victoriously.

"The cheese has slipped off their crackers," the Defeated One says, shaking his head. "Frothing at the mouth over a faded strip of cotton."

He's referring to an authentic Navajo woven shawl, bid up to sixty thousand dollars before it's finally won by a beautiful woman who doesn't look all that much older than us. She shrieks in excitement and hugs an equally breathtaking socialite beside her.

One of the final lots is a painting only slightly larger than a postcard of two Indians paddling across a lake. As soon as it's brought onstage, a murmur starts up in the room. The Defeated One and I exchange a glance and shrug; neither of us can figure out what gives. Perhaps it's the final work of a European master who grew bored of painting cherubic ladies sprawled under apple trees and decided to immortalize the brown-skinned natives frolicking around the forest, earning him an arrow through his gut for not minding his own business.

The bid starts at eighty thousand dollars.

"Ninety thousand?"

The man in the mustard-yellow blazer shoots up his bid card.

"Ninety-five thousand?"

By the time I've polished off my fun-sized Moët and beckoned the waiter over for another, four socialites in ruthless competition have bid the paddling Indians up to one hundred and forty-five thousand.

"One hundred and fifty?"

From a landing directly above us comes a brash "Hell, yeah!"

All eyes in the room glance upward. That voice—

"One hundred and sixty?"

The man in the mustard-yellow blazer grits his teeth and holds up his bid card.

"One hundred and eighty?"

Again from above our heads:

"You betcha!"

The murmuring reaches a feverish pitch. My gaze flits to the Defeated One, then to Postal Boy. The three of us bolt from the table simultaneously, rushing out so we can have a better view of the landing. Visual confirmation: Clyde is slouched over the railing, twiddling the bid card between his fingers.

"Holy shit," the Defeated One curses.

As we race toward the stairs, the man in the mustard-yellow blazer, clearly frustrated, reluctantly holds up his bid card. The crowd is eating this up; there's a smattering of applause even before the auction is over. We're halfway up the staircase when Clyde has spotted us.

"Hey, guys," he says thickly, obviously drunk off his ass.

"Going once," the auctioneer intones gravely.

"Clyde, don't be a fucking moron," the Defeated One bellows.

"Going twice."

Clyde grins goofily, waving us over with the bid card.

"Check this out. I'm gonna get me something for my wall."

The crowd gasps in disbelief.

"Two hundred thousand?"

The man in the mustard-yellow blazer shakes his head and sits back down. The room breaks into thunderous applause. The gavel strikes down just as Clyde unloads his catfish all over the plush carpet.

"Sold, to the man on the landing for two hundred thousand dollars."

♦

The next day it's damage control at Han's Blue Diamond Chinese Gourmet. We're in no particular rush, as the Bank has settled into an eerie calm following the distribution of bonuses.

"What do you mean, you didn't inherit all that much?" the Defeated One implores him.

Clyde gingerly caresses his temple.

"Stop screaming, dude. My head is totally pounding."

"Screw your fucking hangover," the Defeated One growls. "What happened to your dad's money?"

"I don't know," Clyde says, wincing. "He gave most of it away to the ethnic Albanian refugees, I think. Wanted me to pull myself up by my bootstraps."

I pick at my General Tso, but I'm not all that hungry. The whole situation is ridiculously absurd—you kind of want to laugh about it, but at the same time, it's gravely serious. My god. On the hook for two hundred thousand dollars.

Clyde puts his head on the table.

"Jeez, what am I going to do?"

The Defeated One doesn't look all too pleased.

"How much did he leave you?"

"A hundred grand."

"And what about extending your personal line of credit?"

"Checked this morning. The Bank is only willing to lend me thirty."

The Defeated One furrows his brow in consternation.

"So you're in the hole for seventy."

Clyde closes his eyes and begins to whimper.

"Shut up," the Defeated One barks.

Clyde stops whimpering.

"All right. You've got fifteen after tax from your bonus. Fifty-five left. This is how it's going to work. I'm willing to lend you twenty-five thousand; you pay me back when you sell the painting, or fork it out of your next bonus, whichever comes first. That leaves a gap of thirty."

He turns to Postal Boy and me. Postal Boy's mouth gapes open and shut, but I know he's not going to say anything. That leaves me to take the reins.

"No."

The Defeated One balks at this.

"What do you mean, no?"

"Simple. I'm not lending Clyde the money."

"Why not?"

Clyde still has his head down on the table; it wouldn't surprise me if he's fallen asleep. I slip out of the booth and motion for the Defeated One and Postal Boy to follow me to the front of the restaurant.

"I don't trust him. At the rate he's going, what if he gets fired? If he doesn't get his next bonus, then we're seriously fucked."

"Haven't you noticed him getting better?"

So, the jackass did talk to Clyde without mentioning it to us.

"I don't know about this," I say, crossing my arms.

"What about you, Postal?" the Defeated One asks.

Postal Boy shrugs. The Defeated One turns back to me.

"It's all about faith, man. You *know* Clyde's back on track.

Look me straight in the eye and refuse to acknowledge it. He'll pay you back in a year, tops."

I have a really bad feeling about this.

"Come on, Mumbles."

The Defeated One glares at me with determined conviction. Before I can stop myself, I crumble under the pressure.

"All right. Fine."

The Defeated One takes one look at Postal Boy, and without even waiting for his response, says, "Good. You boys have made me proud today."

Nine

I formulated my list of New Year's resolutions during a hazy reunion of sorts in Montreal, the city of shameless debauchery. After three days of getting plastered with Francophone schoolgirls and licking champagne off a stripper's taut belly and chugging down way too much Fin du Monde lager, I was eventually rewarded for my efforts with a puddle of regurgitated *steak et frites* spread across the hotel lobby. Good times, I tell you.

The list of resolutions is as follows:

1. *Restrict coffee intake to four cups per day, two in the morning and two in the evening. An emergency cup is appropriate when the shit really hits the fan.*
2. *Learn how to use that stupid fax machine.*
3. *At least once a week, make that extra effort to contact a regular human being existing somewhere beyond the confines of the Bank. This includes: mother, father, brother, friend, remote acquaintance. This does not in-*

clude: pizza delivery guy, taxi driver, the Korean dude who always squirts way too much mayonnaise when preparing our Subway sandwiches.

4. *Speaking of Subway, no more of those ridiculously addictive M&M's cookies.*

And finally:

5. *Be positive. Enough with this self-pity bullshit. Only seventeen more months and you're out of here. Seventeen months; it's really nothing to get that worked up about. A phase in your life that is relatively inconsequential in the grand scheme of things. Bottom line: Don't become as bitter as the Defeated One.*

♦

It all begins on my first day back. Hanging up my coat, my forehead pounding from my self-imposed dearth of caffeine, I do my best at bidding the Defeated One and the Star a chipper good morning. It comes out sounding forced; normally we've never bothered with any exchange of pleasantries. The Defeated One swivels around on instinct.

"What's up with you, Mumbles?"

My first test of commitment: the inevitable confrontation with this beacon of negativity. I stretch my face in what should come across as a beaming, albeit unnatural, smile.

"Jesus," the Defeated One says, grimacing, and looks away. "You're freaking me out, dude."

I'm still forcing a smile as I settle into the creaking swivel chair and switch on my computer. My inbox is crammed with twenty new messages from the Sycophant, all wondering where the hell I am—I reminded him about my extended weekend at least half a dozen times before I left—and requesting four sets of comps to be completed over the holidays. A rolled-up piece of paper collides with the side of my head.

"So, what's the big deal?" asks the Defeated One. "That girl with the scarf screwed your brains out last night, didn't she?"

I pick up the ball of paper and toss it in the recycling bin.

"No, New Year's resolution. Trying to keep everything positive. Not end up bitter like you."

"You're fucking with me, right?"

"Nope."

"Alrighty, then."

A moment later and Outlook pings with 1 New Message:

> From: TheDefeatedOne@theBank.com
>
> To: PostalBoy@theBank.com; Clyde@theBank.com
>
> cc: Me@theBank.com
>
> OK. Here's the deal. Mumbles just returned from his Montreal getaway with rays of sunlight bursting out of his sphincter. A New Year's resolution, apparently—he's trying to stay positive. I propose a little office pool: We each put in five bucks and pick the time when he's first gonna blow his fuse. *Price Is Right* rules: Go over and you're bust, closest time wins. I've got 11:30.

> From: Clyde@theBank.com
>
> To: TheDefeatedOne@theBank.com; PostalBoy@the Bank.com
>
> cc: Me@theBank.com
>
> Just passed the Sycophant in the corridor. He's looking mighty pissed. It's risky, but I'm going for 9:45.

From: PostalBoy@theBank.com

To: TheDefeatedOne@theBank.com; Clyde@theBank.com

cc: Me@theBank.com

9:46 (snicker, snicker)

From: Clyde@theBank.com

To: TheDefeatedOne@theBank.com; PostalBoy@the Bank.com

cc: Me@theBank.com

Postal—you fucking bastard!!!

My phone rings: the Sycophant's extension. Taking a deep breath, I tentatively pick up the receiver. Before I've even managed a New Year's greeting, I hear, "Where the hell are those comps?"

"I, uh, I wasn't—"

"*Uh, uh,*" he mocks me. "Didn't you get my e-mails? Where were you over the weekend?"

"I was in Montreal—"

"Montreal?! Who said you could go up there?"

"You did, actually—"

"And why didn't you check your BlackBerry?"

"I, uh, I left it at home by mistake. Work had slowed down before the holidays, so I didn't think—"

A sharp exhalation before he snaps at me: "Who the hell said you should think!"

I'm not losing grasp on this newfound positivity so easily. Speaking evenly, I respond, "Look, I'd really appreciate it if you stopped with the cussing. I don't think it's necessary for making your point—"

I hold the receiver away from my ear as the Sycophant proceeds to go apeshit on me. When it sounds like his voice has calmed down somewhat, I place the receiver back on my ear. He's speaking brusquely.

"This is being reported to HR immediately."

"All right."

"Do you understand the ramifications of this?"

"Yes, I do. It's fine if you want to go sit down with them."

"What?"

"I mean, I'm glad you're willing to engage in some serious dialogue about this. I really think there's something here to salvage. As long as we keep improving the ways we choose to communicate with each other—"

"What the fu—"

He's not making sense of this at all. A few seconds of this stalemate pass, going nowhere, before finally, sighing with exasperation, he says, "God almighty, just get those comps done already."

"I'll have them on your desk as soon as they're ready. You have a good day now."

After a puzzled silence the Sycophant hangs up on me.

♦

There's that saying "Smile and the whole world smiles with you," right? Perhaps it's too simplistic for the gummy Petri dish that breeds our shark-toothed Bank managers, more fitting for rosy Saturday morning *Saved by the Bell* environments than the ruthless bastards lurking just down the corridor, but every saying, no matter how facile, is inherently based on a kernel of wisdom. How else to explain the recent tangible results of my positivity?

Take this afternoon, when I've committed myself to figuring out the basic functionality of our fax machine. I feed through my seventh page and there's a clunking sound, a grumbling of success. Alas, my feeble hopes are quashed as the page is spit back out again. The LCD screen at front belittles me with its OPERA-

TIONAL MODE STANDBY and the more deviously opaque ERROR CODE 36.

Error Code 36? What happened to Error Codes 1 through 35? I'd feel less stupid about it if the Utterly Incompetent Assistant wasn't slouched at her desk, munching on some caramel corn left over from one of the Philanderer's holiday gift baskets, staring at me with obvious amusement when she's not engrossed in her game of solitaire.

"Need some help?"

The Utterly Incompetent Assistant shoves a fistful of caramel corn in her mouth and ambles over. I step aside.

"If you'd be so kind."

She spends the next ten seconds demonstrating the correct sequence of buttons. Apparently I'd been overlooking a tiny blue switch tucked away on the side. She hovers over me as I repeat the sequence, licking the excess caramel from her fingers.

"It's ridiculous," I say, chuckling wearily. "All us guys with college degrees, and none of us knows how to work the fax machine, huh?"

She shrugs.

"This model isn't the most straightforward. I've been known to have a few problems with it myself."

"Thanks again."

"No problem."

She gives me a fleeting smile before she returns to her desk. Etch this in stone, record this in the annals of history: It's the first time since I started at the Bank that the two of us have engaged in a remotely pleasant exchange of words. And stranger still: After grabbing another fistful of caramel corn, she actually gets down to completing a stack of invoices.

♦

I'm beckoned into the Philandering Managing Director's office and take a seat on one of the comfy chairs before the desk. It's staggeringly unfair that he who spends the vast majority of the workday in the backseat of his Lexus is entitled to such velour plushness, while we lowly monkeys, tethered to our desks for twenty-hour stretches at a time, have only rickety pieces of junk from IKEA.

The Philanderer gets up and shuts the door behind me. It's an ominous omen. The Philanderer never, ever closes his door, no doubt to assuage the rampant rumors circulating that he's getting up to no good with the assistants instead of producing any real work. He probably figures that as long as he keeps it contained to the parking garage, nobody will bother calling him on it.

Looking around, I'm again amazed by how much mess one man can make. Piles of pizza boxes and coffee-smeared pitch books and the flashy edibles of five-hundred-dollar gift baskets from Williams-Sonoma; all this despite the daily scrub-down by the cleaning lady with the golden caps on her teeth. The Philanderer leafs through a *Maxim* before pausing to ogle a skimpily clad Jessica Alba.

I'm struggling to remain positive while simultaneously trying to determine what trouble I've gotten myself into. Perhaps the Sycophant ratted me out after our telephone conversation the other day? Or another stern lecture for taking off the New Year's weekend? It could be just about anything. Finally, the Philanderer puts down the *Maxim* and leans back in the chair.

"Do you know why I've called you in here?"

I decide to be preemptive. "I'm sorry about leaving for Montreal when there was so much work left behind—"

The Philanderer interrupts me. "Sorry? What the hell do you have to be sorry about? We all deserve a weekend out of the office every now and again. Actually, I wanted to discuss the Nikon pitch."

Nikon. *Nikon.* I can't even remember that one. It's probably something I pulled together while half asleep at three in the morning. I flash a nervous smile, and the Philanderer nods knowingly.

And then it dawns on me: This is the moment I've been dreading since I first arrived at the Bank. My first big fuckup that got detected by a Client. Isn't Nikon a Japanese company? I probably forgot the yen-to-dollar exchange-rate conversion. Classic analyst mistake.

Predictably, the Philanderer continues:

"We didn't get the mandate—"

I brace myself for the scimitar about to swing down and lop off my head.

"—but I'd like to commend you on an excellent job. Everybody on the team was very impressed with your attention to detail."

A delayed reaction—a full minute passes before I'm able to convert my frightened expression into one of stark disbelief. The Philanderer winks at my obvious discomfort.

"I know we don't usually pay you guys enough compliments, but this time it was especially warranted."

He reaches across the desk and shakes my hand.

"Excellent job, Clyde. I'll be sure to file this with HR."

"I, uh, thanks. But it's not Cl—"

There's no point in correcting him. The switch has already turned off, the Philanderer having strayed too far over his threshold of decency and unable to trespass any further. He picks up the *Maxim* and I know that's my cue to leave.

♦

Even though she's blatantly ignoring me by this point, I'm not admitting defeat so easily:

> From: Me@theBank.com
>
> To: WomanWithTheScarf@GoodmanWeisenthal.com
>
> A somewhat belated Happy New Year—any interesting resolutions to speak of? Come on, write back, already. All right. Fine. A quick update regarding my life: Basically, everything is going really well right now (except you not writing, of course). I have no explanation for it but it's the truth. Hope you're facing something similar. One of my resolutions is to be better at balancing work & play; difficult for an investment banker but I'm really going to try. Write back.

♦

Postal Boy and Clyde are procrastinating in our office after dinner. I have a double-meat turkey six-incher from Subway again, though I'm still resisting the buttery allure of those M&M's cookies. We're ranting away on the same old subject matter—how much we hate the Sycophant, how much we hate the Prodigal Son, how everybody's stock portfolio is really in the pits despite the bullish market—and I see my healthy mental state has extended to the rest of the Gang of Four: Postal Boy is faring a lot better after a couple good nights of sleep, and Clyde is behaving himself after we saved his ass from the auction fiasco. It almost harkens back to the glory days when we first arrived at the Bank, freshly scrubbed and ruddy-cheeked, before our youthful naïveté was obliterated under the brutality of this corporate regime.

Clyde rolls up his wrapper and lobs it into the trash can.

"Hey, are we still trying to get the Prodigal Son fired?"

"Missed opportunity," the Defeated One says.

Clyde grins mischievously and says, "Not necessarily. I think we might have another shot at greatness."

"We're not going to catch them at it again. Trust me; I took a couple trips up to the boardroom and checked."

Clyde shakes his head. "No, this is something completely different."

He reaches into a pocket of his suit jacket and pulls out a clear vial.

"What's that?" Postal Boy draws near.

Clyde swats his hand away.

"Damn, Postal, this is expensive stuff. Liquid MDMA. Have any of you guys taken Ecstasy before?"

Surprisingly, Postal Boy nods. "Yeah, I took a pill once."

The Defeated One slaps his knee. "Postal wigged out on Ecstasy? Tweaking his nipples to techno music? I'd have to see it to believe it."

Postal Boy pouts, "I wasn't always like this, you know. The eye twitch, for instance; I only got it after I started working here. I'm learning to control it, though."

In demonstration of this, he speeds up the twitching to a blur, then slows it down to a light flapping motion.

The Defeated One grimaces. "Postal, that's fucking disgusting."

"Anybody else?" Clyde asks.

"Yeah, I tried it once with the girlfriend," the Defeated One admits, "but the problem is, you're all horned up but you can't get it hard. Hands down, one of the most frustrating experiences of my life."

"I feel your pain, man, though there are ways to get around that." Turning to me, he asks, "What about you?"

"What about me?"

"You ever tried the stuff?"

All right. The truth is, I've taken it once. Sophomore year of college. It was more ridiculous than anything else, really, a bunch of us stroking our forearms, strands of drool dangling from our lower lips, going *I love you, man, no, seriously, I soooo love you, man* the whole night and then refusing to acknowledge it the next morning.

"Nah, not my scene."

"Well, anyway, this liquid MDMA is much stronger than the pills you'd get on the street. It also doesn't taste like anything much. So this is the plan. We wait for the right opportunity and then slip this in the Prodigal Son's coffee, get him all fucked up before a pitch or something. Masturbating in front of a client could technically undo all the hobnobbing he's been getting up to on the squash courts, right, gentlemen?"

The Defeated One is skeptical.

"I don't know about this, Clyde. Too many external factors beyond our control. At least the video was fairly straightforward."

"Straightforward and it failed."

Clyde pauses for dramatic effect.

"Look, let's not settle into complacency just because we had one little setback. We've got to trudge ahead with this. What are we, a bunch of pussies?"

"I'm in," I reply.

The Defeated One cocks an eyebrow.

"What?" I shrug. "It's less complicated than the first plan, anyway."

The Defeated One ponders this for a few moments and finally nods augustly.

"All right, comrades. Plan number two is in effect."

♦

By the end of the week, my positivity has taken on a life of its own. It crackles from office to office, little jolts of static yanking up into precarious smiles lips that have never done anything but sneer, forcing boisterous laughter from the mucus-ridden trachea of the mummified seventy-year-old receptionist, prompting girlish squeals of delight from the frosty lair of the Ice Queen. More than that: it diffuses through the walls, crawling up the elevator shafts, until it pervades the inner sanctum of the Bank, the cedar-paneled penthouse suites of the Coldest Fish In The Pond and his executive circle of acrimonious Yes-Men.

How else do you explain this? I'm heading past the Sycophant's office, trying to steady a wobbling tower of seventy investor presentations, and I do a double-take—the whole room is starkly empty, a sterile wasteland of carpet and plaster. No computer monitor, no file folders, none of the framed pictures of his egghead son cluttering the desk. I speed-walk into our office and drop the investor presentations in a messy heap on the floor. The Defeated One swivels around with a huge grin.

"Mumbles, you are such a lucky bastard."

"What's going on?"

The Defeated One snaps his fingers. "Poof. Gone."

I slump down in my chair, dizzy with disbelief.

"You're kidding me? He got the boot?"

"Nah, you ain't that lucky, dude. He got transferred to the Biotech group. The kiss of death, really. That group of techno-dorks hasn't led a deal in two years. And they're all tucked away on the floor above us, so there'll be minimal awkward run-ins in the corridor."

"I just don't believe it."

I guess it's like winning the lottery: too overwhelming to comprehend all at once, your entire universe rearranged in the course of a few colored balls falling into their respective slots. If I concentrate really hard, I can appreciate certain isolated aspects of it—I probably won't need to get those comps done before the end of the day, for instance—but that's about it. I feel no holistic appreciation, only the occasional burst of elation bubbling up to the surface before it's drowned out again by the shock value.

I'm actually kind of miffed about something.

"It's crazy. You work with the guy for more hours than you see anybody else in this world and he doesn't even think about dropping by to tell you he's off."

"That's the way things work around here," the Defeated One says, "on a need-to-know basis. And according to the senior guys, us analysts don't need to know shit. Anyway, he's probably embarrassed about it. It's not the most prestigious of moves, I'll tell you that. And now he's a foreigner in a new group, so it'll take a couple years for him to prove himself. Meaning he's back at square one when it comes to promotions. Look, what the hell do you care? You should be ecstatic."

"I know. Still, what a sorry bastard."

There is a new emotion entering the fray. Dare I say it? A twinge of sympathy. It's loathsome, really. The Sycophant was without a doubt my archnemesis, the bane of my corporate existence. I've plotted his demise in so many grisly ways it would have curdled the blood of even the most well-adjusted inkblot psychiatrist. And yet.

I don't know. Maybe it's the Stockholm syndrome kicking in or something.

♦

I'm sitting at my computer, still in a daze, when the Philanderer sneaks up behind me. Thankfully I have a legitimate work-related spreadsheet open on my monitor.

"Clyde, I'm going to need a favor."

"Shoot."

"Listen, I left my BlackBerry behind while scrambling around today. I called a few places but only got through to a bunch of immigrants jabbering away in whatever foreign language. I'll need you to jump in a taxi and track it down."

He hands me a list. The Philanderer has had quite the busy morning judging from the potential BlackBerry hiding spots: a Starbucks way up north, a sushi joint to the east, a place scrawled as Julie's Beaver Barn in the complete opposite direction. Checking out all these places will likely result in being out of the office for at least half the day. Sounds like a sweet field trip, though this doesn't factor in the four sets of comps that still need to get churned out at some point.

I'm poring over the list, trying to map out the best itinerary, when Postal Boy sprints into our office.

"Hey," he pants, "either of you leave a BlackBerry on my desk?"

Bingo. I'm about to disclose the real owner, when the Defeated One reaches out and says, "It's mine."

Postal Boy hands it to him before adjusting his glasses and sprinting back out of the room.

"Run, Postal, run," the Defeated One cackles after him.

"What's up with the Speedy Gonzales routine?" I ask.

"He's been doing laps around the office the whole morning," the Defeated One says, tinkering with the BlackBerry. "The Ice Queen is riding him hard with some last-minute changes to a presentation."

I nod at the BlackBerry.

"What, you plan on snooping through his messages?"

"Of course not," he says, waving the idea off. "What do I care about the Philanderer's deviant porn subscriptions? It has to be returned to its rightful owner, don't you think?"

"You're going to do that?"

"No," he says, tossing me the BlackBerry. "You are. That is, after you take off the next couple hours pretending to hunt it down."

I start to shake my head, but the Defeated One frowns.

"Give me a break, Mumbles. Isn't most of your work with the Sycophant? You think he's going to swallow his pride and come down here just to check up on you?"

"I'm not so sure about this . . ."

But he's right; I have nothing to lose. Before I have time to second-guess myself, I've grabbed my coat and I'm out the door. I knock back a double shot of espresso at Starbucks before I'm standing by the curb. A taxi pulls up and I'm about to enter, when in my peripheral vision, across the courtyard, there she is—the Woman With The Scarf, smoking beside one of the bronze cow sculptures. She's dressed all KGB-like in a sleek black trench coat, a plaid Burberry scarf bunched tightly around her neck.

For a second I'm seriously considering the stress-free alternative, jumping into the taxi to avoid what's bound to be an incredibly awkward encounter, but no, she's spotted me already. She gives me a lingering gaze, and now I have no choice but to walk over and say something.

"Hey."

She greets me with a chilled ennui.

"Hello."

"I, uh, I didn't know you smoked."

The Woman With The Scarf exhales a pristine jet through closed teeth.

"Why, you have a problem with it?"

"Nah," I chuckle nervously, "I'm an ex-smoker myself."

She rolls her eyes at me.

"So, uh—"

I'm fumbling through all the junk in my pockets, a nervous

habit: keys, bank card, Twix wrapper, a tin of Altoids, something soggy.

"—why haven't you been returning my e-mails?"

"I've been busy."

"Oh. With work and stuff?"

Stubbing out her cigarette against the copper flank of one of the cows, she says, "Yeah, work and stuff. It works both ways, you know."

"I know."

"Then, why'd you ask?"

"It's just, I only, uh—"

As I try to figure out how to end that sentence, the Woman With The Scarf eyes me with unquestionable disdain.

"Look," she says, lighting up another cigarette, "maybe this is going to seem a bit out of line, but I want to be upfront about this: The reason I've been avoiding you is because I don't want to be dating a guy who's not that into me, if you want to know the truth."

"What the—"

"Let me finish," she snaps. "My last boyfriend—he was working *all the fucking time*. And while I'm fine with ambition—I mean, I'm not fooling anybody, I'm a type A myself—after a while I just couldn't take it anymore. It was driving me insane. So, bottom line is, I'm not putting up with any more half-assed relationships at this stage of my life. I just can't do it, I really can't."

"Not that into you?" I'm shaking my head in bewilderment. "What about my obsessive e-mailing? Doesn't that count for anything?"

"Two e-mails over the last week," she huffs. "Hardly obsessive. Look, I know you're working hard, and I respect it in a way, but god . . . it's like, I want somebody who can distract me from my own pathetic existence, not suck me into their own misery, you know?"

My mouth gapes open and shuts, but no words come out. There must be something in my facial expression that invokes her pity, though, because she sighs.

"I didn't mean for it to come out sounding so harsh."

"Yeah"—I struggle to keep my voice from breaking—"but you're just being honest. Speaking your mind, I guess."

She blows out a series of smoke rings, her head cocked back, before peering at me with a glimmer of remote sadness.

"This is all just really fucked up, huh?"

"What is?"

She closes her eyes, rubbing at the bridge of her nose.

"I thought I had this all worked out perfectly. I figured I'd just cut you out of my life and that would be that. But now, seeing you again . . ."

She stands there with her eyes closed, her mouth pursed tightly. I reach into my pocket and remove the soggy substance, a strip of a burrito shell from lunch. I fling it across the courtyard, wiping my fingers clean against one of the cows.

When she opens her eyes, I ask, "So, I guess this is the point in the conversation where I say my good-bye and leave you alone, right?"

"Yes. I mean, no, don't go just yet."

She takes a final puff and flicks the filter to the ground.

"I enjoyed our dinner together, I really did. You seem like a nice guy. Slightly awkward, I mean sweet; god, I don't even know how to articulate this properly. I guess what I'm trying to say is, and not doing a very good job at it, is that, well . . . I just don't know about this."

Her lips form the most wistful of smiles, but at least it's for my benefit, I think. My hands are back in my pockets, my breath visible in the cold.

"So, what are we supposed to do now?"

She shrugs. "You tell me."

"Maybe we can talk about this over coffee?"

She shakes her head reluctantly.

"What, another ten-minute coffee break and then leave it for another week? Because I told you already, I'm just not willing to accept that anymore—"

"Then how about we get out of here?"

"What are you talking about?"

"Exactly what I said. Do you really need to be at work right now?"

She blinks at me in confusion.

"My boss. She's expecting some testimony reviewed by the end of the afternoon—wait a second, are you serious about this?"

I've already clasped her hand and I'm pulling her away from the courtyard.

"What about your evil taskmasters? Won't they crucify you for disappearing on them?"

"I'm not so sure they can buy the spikes at Staples," I say with a shrug.

We speed-walk past a congregation of bike messengers, past the roasted-chestnut seller outside Han's Blue Diamond Chinese Gourmet, and I'm remembering the first time I ever played hooky. Eighth grade; I must have been about thirteen. Ditching math class to sneak under the bridge behind the bike trail, a place littered with condom wrappers and cigarette butts and the caps of Colt 45s, and smoke my very first joint with my best friend at the time, a gawky unibrowed guy named Dan Robert (the kid with two first names).

We begin exploring the relatively quiet intersections, observing how folks who aren't trapped in office towers all day while away their lives: a troop of blue-haired ladies debate the merits of Oprah's latest book club selection while draped over a Starbucks banquette; schoolchildren with ribbons in their hair cuss away like drunken sailors; a Chinese butcher strings up barbecued ducks in a sweaty window. We stop in to share a plate of noodles before slipping back into the cold, twisting and turning and laughing about random things, marveling at the minutiae in this jumbled, sprawling hodgepodge of a metropolis.

Toward the end of the afternoon we find ourselves standing before a massive snowbank. It's a miracle, this snowbank: white and powdery, with no yellow pee stains, in stark contrast to the refuse littering the rest of the street. The unmarred surface is just pleading for somebody to be pushed in. So, off she goes, though she drags me in behind her, rolling on top of me and shoving my head in it until I hurl her off my back. Eventually worn out, she turns to me, flecks of snow caught between her eyelashes.

"What are we going to do now?"

I pull her closer to me. "A hot chocolate, maybe? It's getting cold in here."

She rolls on top of me again, her lips as frozen as the iced fruits you can buy at those posh confectioners, the candies that stick to your tongue before melting into warm goo.

Pulling away, her face flushed, she says, "No, I mean, what are we going to do after this, with our lives."

Despite the spontaneous intimacy of our afternoon together, I can't help thinking it's kind of a silly question. I mean, it's the million-dollar question, the one all human beings ask themselves at least two thousand times over the course of their abbreviated lives, but it's weird she'd choose to bring it up now. Gently wiping the snow off her cheek, I refrain from defaulting to some smart-aleck remark and respond truthfully.

"I really don't know."

She eyes me skeptically, but I'm being serious; I'm not just copping out. Can anybody ever truly know what they're supposed to do with their lives? Even those kids who knew, just *knew,* they were destined to become a first-chair violinist or a veterinarian—weren't they ever plagued with doubt? Or is it what I've lately come to suspect, that you just fumble along, trying to make sense of this world, hoping that eventually things will come out right?

"Do you really think you're going to stick it out for the full two years?"

"What, this banking job?"

"Yeah."

"I think so. Maybe it's stupid, but I like following through with things. You sign a contract and you stick to it. It's the eastern European work ethic instilled in me by my grandfather or whatever."

"But what if you know you shouldn't be doing what you're doing? That it shows complete lack of integrity?"

I shake my head.

"I don't really buy into that. What is integrity? Jaunting off and saving little limbless beggar children in India? Eating organic foods? You work for any decent nonprofit and you're still dealing with the same bureaucratic bullshit."

The Woman With The Scarf slips into a contemplative quiet. When I try to kiss her, she turns her head away; I've clearly said the wrong thing. Entombed in the snowbank's muffled silence, I study her profile, trying to discern where I went astray. She closes her eyes and speaks in a voice that is barely a whisper.

"You know I'm just messing with you, right?"

Then she shoves my face in the snow again and leaps to her feet, running off in a gale of laughter as I lumber after her.

Ten

In ancient Egypt, it was believed that the god Anubis would weigh the heart of the recently deceased against the feather of Ma'at, goddess of truth and justice. If the heart weighed the same as the feather, then the deceased was granted access to the afterlife; if the heart outweighed the feather, the heart was consumed by a demon goddess, Ammut, otherwise known as the Devourer of the Dead.

A cosmic balance: Over the millennia, across civilizations, theology has been constructed around a harmony of yin and yang, some variant of a supernatural feather ensuring our species stays right side up, navigating this earth with an earnest determination. As such, the accumulation of positive energy in my own little microcosm could not last long. With one side of the scale groaning under the weight of frivolous BlackBerry excursions and Sycophantless office spaces, the forces of the universe had no choice but to impose some sort of counterbalance.

In other words: It was too much, too soon.

♦

I stroll in with my morning coffee, and my Spidey Sense goes off: Something is definitely not right. For one, the Sycophant's office is no longer empty. The present occupant, a man with a scalp struggling to retain its sparse blond curls, his pallor as pale and sickly as if he's spent the bulk of his life preserved in a jar of formaldehyde, is already hunched before the monitor, his fingers a blur as they skitter across the keyboard. Stacks of paper are piled neatly around the room, and a picture of Piccadilly Circus at sunset hangs above a collection of plaques and certificates. A seamless integration; he must have moved in over the weekend.

I tiptoe past the office without rousing his attention and switch on my computer. The Defeated One is already settled in with the *Wall Street Journal* and a brownie. He's bound to have the scoop.

"Who's the replacement?"

The Defeated One looks up from his stock quotes.

"Not sure yet. They shipped him over from England. Poached from Barclays, if I heard it right."

"A pity they found him so soon. Though he's bound to be better than the Sycophant, huh?"

"Don't jinx yourself, Mumbles," the Defeated One says, turning back to his paper.

I nod at the brownie.

"What, now you're eating chocolate first thing in the morning?"

"Piss off," he says, licking his fingers. "Leave my breakfast cake out of this."

♦

It's after lunch when my phone rings. An unfamiliar extension. A curt English accent on the other end:

"Would you mind dropping by my office?"

"Of course— "

He's already hung up on me. A minute later, I'm sitting across from the man who will eventually come to be known around these parts as the Crazy Brit. It's the eyes with their pale blue irises that give it away, of course, his gaze darting about the room before boring into you with an unflinching intensity, literally setting the hairs of your neck on end.

He could be the product of a repressed upbringing perhaps, a true man of his country. Age nine: a runtish lad staring out the window at the mossy Sussex countryside, longing to escape the home-schooling of his trio of ruler-wielding aunts. Straight out of a Roald Dahl novel these she-banshees are, hooked noses and mouths full of blackened teeth, beating him bloody senseless whenever his saintly but blissfully naive parents leave on their automobile excursions to Marks & Spencer. Age thirteen: reciting Chaucer at some formidably preppy academy before a bow-tied professor with a poorly concealed erection, distraught none of the other boys will invite him along for a hand-rolled smoke and a game of gin rummy in the boiler room (we found out later the Crazy Brit actually went to boarding school in New England, but no matter; it's far more gratifying wallowing in these gratuitous Old Empire stereotypes). Age twenty-one: resigning himself to the reality he's to be no Keats, no diplomat like Churchill, just another of those well-heeled types rushing along Bond Street with the omnipresent umbrellas, sighing with immense sorrow when they stop in for an afternoon tea of Earl Grey and watercress sandwiches.

You see, the Crazy Brit has devoted his life to i-banking—entering the industry as an analyst and working his way up from there. It's a difficult path, indeed; any sane person would finish up those two or three years and get the hell out of there, never to return. I mean, can you imagine a decade of this crap? Fuck, I'd go crazy too. While an ignorant majority would argue he is a success story—one of the youngest vice presidents at the Bank, barely over thirty and already rolling in close to half a million in comp—the Crazy Brit embodies the bitterness of his experience: a decade wasted busting his ass, not a penny left by the trio of aunts (those horrible beasts having squandered his inheritance on foul medicines and bullwhips after his kindhearted parents, naturally, plunged off a cliff in a horrible accident), while those pompous pricks from the prep academy inherited massive fortunes simply due to their minor noble pedigrees.

But back to the present. Sitting across from him, trying to avoid direct eye contact, I'm observing the Crazy Brit juggling seven things at once: blasting off an e-mail, listening to his voice messages, whipping through a file folder, buttering up a bagel, skimming the employee manual, tinkering with his CD drive, and organizing the framed pictures of a baby swathed in pink. Fifteen minutes tick by and he hasn't yet acknowledged my presence. Finally I break the silence:

"Um, how old is your daughter?"

He stops his flurry of activity, scrutinizing me from behind his thick glasses. In that frosty accent, he inquires, "Might I ask why it concerns you?"

What an asshole. He takes a bite of his bagel, records a personalized greeting for his voice mail, and flips through a new pile of paper before speaking again.

"She was born on Saturday."

"*Last* Saturday?" I ask incredulously.

He adjusts the settings of his monitor.

"Yes."

Jesus. That means the guy must have been here alphabetizing his files while his wife was pushing and shoving in the maternity ward. Talk about priorities.

"Well, then," he sighs, "where are those comps?"

I'm taken aback. "Which comps?"

His mouth clenches into a thin slit; the Crazy Brit is not pleased.

"The comps that were expected on my desk by first thing this morning."

He cracks his knuckles one by one, biting his lower lip.

"Am I to believe you have been neglecting your duties in my predecessor's absence?"

"No, not at all. It's only that I, um, was confused about the timing, what with the staffing change—"

He's clearly not buying any of this. He puts his hand up to silence me.

"I will let this slide, but no more. You will have those comps on my desk by three o'clock this afternoon."

I utter a guttural Push Back: "There's four sets of them. It's not possible—"

His entire body stiffens in the chair, and that focused stare turns my skin into gooseflesh.

"I have never come across an impossibility in this industry."

His demand is different from the maddening requests the Sycophant would drop on my plate; the Crazy Brit draws his deadlines with the weight of ten years of experience resting on his shoulders.

"Are we clear?"

"Yes," I mumble.

The Crazy Brit is unconvinced. Repeating himself, he says, "Are we clear?"

"Yes!" I nod my head vigorously.

The Crazy Brit sneers as I rise from the chair.

"Do not forget. Three o'clock."

♦

Over the next few days, the workload accelerates from moderate to heavy, then, with a final hiccup, to mind-numbing, you'd-rather-shoot-yourself-straight-through-the-gut insanity. It's not just me; the whole M&A division is shuddering under this looming crisis, namely too much work and not enough warm bodies to process it all. Even the Prodigal Son is picking up some of the slack: not sneaking off to the gym in the middle of the workday, staying an hour or two later than his normal departure time of five-thirty, and asking Postal Boy for help with basic Excel functions that every other analyst learned months ago.

My continuing encounters with our tyrant from across the pond have been anything but pleasant.

"He's a lunatic," I say, shaking my head in bewilderment.

I've just spent the last two hours trying to decipher the Crazy Brit's markup of a presentation before I finally enlisted the Defeated One's help. You'd think that in this industry, where attention to detail is crucial, where it's not uncommon for an analyst to get bitched out over inserting an extra space after a period, our senior guys would try to provide us with something more legible than chicken scratch. Instead, every page is a mess of arrows and squiggles.

I've managed to decipher most of the edits using logical deduction, but there are still a few loopy lines that could mean anything. I'd go straight to the source for clarification if the Crazy Brit didn't scare the shit out of me.

"I think he could be leaving out the vowels," the Defeated One suggests, scratching his forehead.

He swivels over with the presentation.

"There," he says, pointing to a horizontal line with only the subtlest upticks. "Doesn't that spell 'efficiency'?"

I squint at it.

"I thought that was 'structural.' "

The Defeated One scratches his forehead again and says, "Yeah, it could be that too."

"Great," I grumble.

♦

Or there is Wednesday's wild goose chase:

> From: TheCrazyBrit@theBank.com
>
> To: Me@theBank.com
>
> Please pull up press releases covering the recently announced merger of SBC and Sprint.

I begin with a Google search. A half hour later, not finding anything that is remotely related, I know something's fishy. These are two grotesquely humongous corporations we're talking about; if either CEO had passed wind, it would have been a major press event. I ask the Defeated One but he shakes his head.

"Sorry, Mumbles. Telecom has never been my forte."

I ring up our Library Department. I've trudged down there once before to return a report, so I'm not duped by the mellifluous voice of the woman on the other end asking how she may be of assistance. The Library is staffed with three female "information consultants" who look as if they've just dashed over from a prison break: high and tight haircuts, cobra tattoos crawling up their bulging calf muscles, pink-ringed eyes that dare you to fuck with them by filing your annual report on the wrong shelf. I wouldn't have a problem with any of this if it weren't for the fact that they're useless, wallowing in the depths of the value-added chain with the likes of the Toad and the Dirty Hippie Office Supply Manager. In truth, this call is merely a formality, to have an affirmative answer when the Crazy Brit asks whether I've consulted the ex-convicts downstairs.

An hour later and I've checked every news source I can think of—still nothing. I consider swinging by the Crazy Brit's office and acknowledging that I'm having difficulties, but that's the thing with these ambiguous search requests: You never want to default to the empty-handed position unless you are one hundred percent positive you haven't overlooked something. The last thing you need is a senior manager pulling up a major website, or flipping through a report, and *bingo,* there it is in all its brazen obviousness.

My phone rings. The Crazy Brit's extension. It's amazing how quickly a sequence of four numbers can be associated with such futility and despair.

"Where is that info? Come by my office immediately."

He's in the middle of dissecting a Subway sandwich, laying the tomatoes and pickles precisely on a tissue. He looks up as I enter.

"Is this task really so difficult? These are two *major* firms participating in this alliance. What sort of a nincompoop can't click on a simple corporate home page?"

He motions for me to come around behind his desk.

"Now, look here," he says, speaking to me as one would a simpleton.

He types SBC and AT&T into Google and the screen is inundated with press releases announcing their recent merger.

"But wasn't it Sprint— "

The Crazy Brit puts his hand up to silence me.

"I'm flabbergasted, truly. It was a simple request and you failed at your task. *Failed.* I will have to discuss this with Human Resources. In the meantime, I'd highly advise you to familiarize yourself with the concept of a web browser; they are quite useful for the type of work we do here."

I clench my teeth; I'm this close to snapping his brittle neck in two. The Crazy Brit isn't even paying attention, going back to his sandwich deconstruction. As I'm turning to leave, he addresses me.

"Are we clear?"

There's no point in arguing, really.

"Yes."

"Very good, then."

♦

I'm lying entwined with the Woman With The Scarf (though she's currently scarfless in only a T-shirt and sweat pants) on the couch in my living room. It's the first time I've invited her back to my place, and the standard of cleanliness could be improved: There is dirty laundry strewn everywhere, dishes piled high in the sink even with a dishwasher right beside it, and a half-eaten pizza from three weeks ago fermenting on the side table. I warned her in advance and apologized profusely as she took it all in, and so far she's been kind enough not to voice her criticism.

I stifle a yawn. I'm exhausted after the brutality of the day, barely able to keep my eyes open, but I'm trying to stay focused on an episode of *Seinfeld,* the one where they all get lost in the parking garage, so the Woman With The Scarf won't think poorly of me.

"There was this talent show at my residence hall during freshman year," I mumble. "One of those excuses to get blitzed in the middle of the week. Anyway, my roommate decides that a couple of us are going to act out an episode of *Seinfeld.* Just go up there impromptu, with no gimmicks or anything. So I'm supposed to be George— "

"Which episode?" She reaches over and strokes my cheek.

I nuzzle her neck, smelling her apricot shampoo.

"I can't remember. So, I'm George, and I have to adopt his whiny voice, but I *suck* at voices. And you know how those talent shows are, so easy to make a complete ass of yourself . . ."

I've lost my train of thought. I'm silent until she nudges me with her elbow.

"So, what happened? You blew it?"

I snap out of my stupor.

"Oh, right. Anyway, so I'm all geared up for total failure, the two shots of vodka not working at all, and then something happens. I know this sounds kind of silly, but it's almost like I *become* George. The voice, the movements—everything is dead-on. I get a standing ovation at the end of it."

"So, you're going to do the impersonation for me now?" she asks, smiling sleepily.

"Nah. It was a once-in-a-lifetime performance. I probably couldn't pull it off again if my life depended on it. But there was a point to this story. Yes, this: that no matter how old you get, you'll never stop surprising yourself."

"I already knew that," she says, yawning. "Otherwise I wouldn't be lying here with you right now."

"You evil harpy."

"Don't you know it."

I kiss her on the nose and she giggles. I'm about to kiss her again, when I spot the alarm clock rearranging its digital numbers in my peripheral vision: 2:55. Fuck; in less than four hours I need to be up all over again. It wouldn't be a big deal if I had a mindless job to wake up to—working on an assembly line or pruning some hedges or driving Miss Daisy around—but I have to be fully functioning to deal with the ticking time bomb that is the Crazy Brit.

Ah, to hell with it; I'll just have to slip another coffee or two past my quota. I'm back to nuzzling the side of her neck when she notices the alarm clock as well.

"Three already! Oh god, I've got to be up in, like, four hours."

She rolls around so she's facing away from me, pulling my arms around her waist.

"Would it be a big deal if we just went to sleep now?" she murmurs softly. "You wouldn't get the wrong idea, right?"

I'm already kissing the back of her neck.

"Shhh, don't be silly. Of course we can sleep."

I reach out and take her hand, leading her into the bedroom. Miraculously I washed my sheets only about a week ago, the first time in more than four months. I kiss her eyelids, and my hands graze her body as we assume the same position as on the couch. In less than five minutes we're both out cold.

♦

The next morning, as the market roars open, the Crazy Brit drops his worst assignment to date.

"I need you to bring up a few files from the archives. Apparently you moved some boxes recently. These are to be restored to their original location."

He has to be fucking with me. I shiver as a subconscious reflex, my body's desperate whimper.

"All of them?"

He chews on the end of a pen and sneers. "Of course all of them. How else will I know which files are required?"

"I've carefully organized everything," I plead with him. "If you tell me the specific projects, then I can gather all the related documentation—"

"Are you always this obstinate?" he says with a sigh. "I wouldn't dally; you have your work cut out for you."

You'd think he'd know better, you really would. Those ten hellish years spent in the murky depths of this industry should have enabled him to understand firsthand how an analyst can be reduced to a weeping mess by any living soul displaying even a glimmer of kindness. It's a cycle of abuse, I tell you, the Crazy Brit getting off on crushing my soul as his own was crushed many years before. I turn to leave the office and there are the notorious last words:

"Are we cl—"

I can't let him finish; it would snap the last threads that connect me to my sanity.

"Yes!"

Then I'm rushing out the door before he can blast me for my impertinence.

♦

A half hour later and I'm still overwhelmed by the ridiculousness of the Crazy Brit's request, shaking my head in disbelief as I stumble up the staircase with my third box. An hour later and I really wish that I was dead. People always say that, I know, but this time I'm not kidding. I'd love to be buried six feet under, my body caked in the cold clamminess of freshly turned earth, absolute silence except for the muffled sounds of grieving relatives. Two hours later and I've collapsed in my chair, the last box having been dredged up from the bowels of the building.

The Defeated One whistles. "Mumbles, you look like shit. I know I've said it before, but I take all those other times back. This time it's the real deal."

Somewhere in the world outside my bruised and battered body, a familiar pinging sound. Turning to my monitor, I read:

> From: TheToad@theBank.com
>
> To: Associates; Analysts; M&A Department
>
> It is with great pleasure that I announce the promotion of the Prodigal Son from analyst to associate. Please join the M&A department for a beer cart at 5pm to toast the Prodigal Son on this tremendous accomplishment.

The news hasn't yet penetrated the fogginess of my brain before Clyde and Postal Boy burst into our office.

"Do you think it's a joke?" Clyde is sputtering. "It has to be a joke, right?"

Postal Boy is looking angrier than I've ever seen him, his eye twitch a blur.

"Ridiculous. Fucking ridiculous, that's what it is."

Even the Star is shaking his head.

"Getting promoted to an associate after one year of work? That's impossible, I thought. I just don't understand it . . ."

Then the reality hits me: *"Craa-aaa-aaa-ppp."*

Clyde nods in my direction.

"What's up with him?"

"Don't ask," the Defeated One snorts.

"Anyway," Clyde says, pacing back and forth, "we have to do it this afternoon, at the beer cart."

"What?" Postal Boy asks.

"Slip that stuff into his drink. It's short notice, not as surefire as a client meeting, but it could still work. The Fish might be there; definitely the Toad."

The Defeated One rubs his hands together.

"Sowing the seeds of destruction before his ascension to corporate greatness. Clyde, I like it."

"So we're all comfortable with this?" Clyde turns to the rest of us.

Even the Star, oblivious to the intricacies of the plan but understanding there's an element of sabotage involved, bobs his head in agreement.

♦

Five o'clock is marked by the jangle of bottles directly outside our office—the notorious beer cart has arrived. It's just another of the Bank's evil tricks: They yank us up from our spreadsheets mid-keystroke, thrust a brew in our direction, and then we're expected to mingle, to shake off the mind-numbing tedium of hours of data entry (or in my case, lugging boxes around), and discuss the merits of the P/E ratio, or who made the greatest gains among the Forbes 400, all the while suppressing the bitterness that in less than an hour we'll be back at our desks, the tipsiness of those three beers not helping things at all when it comes down to seeking those extra spaces in a prospectus going out the following morning.

"All right, you ready for this?" The Defeated One turns to me.

"Yeah, let's do it."

We pull up complicated-looking spreadsheets on our monitors—no real need, given the beer cart is a sanctioned event; instinctive behavior, I guess—and exit into the throng. It's mostly analysts and associates, with Lulu Heifenschliefen presiding over the cart. I grab a Heineken and observe the Prodigal Son getting slapped on the back from all directions. He has his own entourage as well, apparently—three of the less nerdy analysts who fawn over him and laugh at everything that comes out of his mouth. It's weird: I had no idea the Prodigal Son had a posse. Then again, he's probably just as oblivious concerning our Gang of Four. Social circles upon circles upon circles in this world.

Clyde approaches from the cart. He's double-fisting it: a Rolling Rock in one hand, an Amstel Light in the other.

"Everything all set?" I ask.

Clyde holds up the Rolling Rock and grins.

"He's been drinking these since this started. I figure I'll wait until he's ready for another and then offer this one up, compliments of his especially proud peers in the M&A division."

"Perfect."

A commotion erupts from the nearby analysts, a rippling wave of excitement. I glance around for the cause: Unadulterated Sex is sashaying down the corridor toward us. She stands in the doorway and surveys the room, hugging some manila file folders to her wondrous breasts, before sashaying up to the Prodigal Son, whispering something in his ear, and cautiously—checking to ensure nobody is paying them much attention—reaching down and grazing the bulge in his pants. Then the hand is removed, so quickly it almost never happened, and she's sashaying back down the corridor.

"Goddammit," the Defeated One curses, "if this wasn't painful enough to begin with. A promotion *and* he's still screwing around with her. I swear, it seriously makes you question whether there is any justice in this world."

Clyde claps him on the shoulder.

"Take solace in what you know is coming. That's our mission, right? Dispensers of cosmic justice. The Cubicle Warriors. We should all be wearing capes for this."

The Prodigal Son makes a move toward the cart.

"It's showtime," Clyde says, winking. He strides across the room, a beaming smile on his face as he offers up his congratulations, and benevolently holds out the Rolling Rock. After a clinking of bottles, Clyde scurries back to our huddle, shoving a finger down his throat and gagging.

"All right." Clyde checks his watch. "Less than twenty minutes before the first effects."

"So what should we expect?" Postal Boy deadpans.

"I put the entire bottle in. I figured we were going all-out or bust. Trust me, gentlemen, very soon our golden boy is going to be an absolute wreck."

Suddenly I'm not sure how I feel about this. A slight remorse is creeping in.

"Guys, do you really think we should be going ahead with this?"

The Defeated One comes close to spitting out a mouthful of beer, prompting a coughing fit.

"What the fuck, Mumbles? Are you serious? Don't tell me you're turning into Postal."

Postal Boy quips back, "Hey, I'm fully behind this. Did you ever get any doubt from me? Drug the bitch, that's what I say."

From across the room, a throat is being cleared: "Ahem, ahem."

The Toad is standing beside the Prodigal Son. Their height

difference is staggering; the Toad barely comes up to the Prodigal Son's chest.

"As you are all aware," the Toad begins, "we are gathered here this afternoon to congratulate this fine young man on his excellent work ethic and a well-deserved promotion. He should stand as a fine role model for the rest of you— "

"What, slacking off and playing squash with the Fish?" Postal grunts loud enough for a few of the other analysts to turn around and frown at us.

"—to follow. Thus, will you please raise your beer and toast him on this tremendous accomplishment."

A surge of bottles is held aloft.

The Toad sputters frantically, "A beer! Won't somebody pass me a beer?"

The Prodigal Son leans down and slips him the Rolling Rock. The Toad holds the bottle up to the room, blinking once, twice.

"Oh fuck!" Postal Boy whimpers.

"*Shit shit shit shit shit,*" the Defeated One says.

The Toad takes a deep breath and belts it out with gusto: "To the Prodigal Son— "

Before he can finish his toast, Clyde lets loose a strangled bellow and bolts across the room, leaps off the ground, and tackles the Toad's pudgy frame. Picture it in slow-motion if you will: The hollow thud of two bodies connecting forcefully, a bestial groan from the Toad, the bottle flying out of his hand and flying over the crowd in a graceful trajectory before it smashes against the wall in an explosion of sparkling glass. A shuddering *oomph* as the Toad topples over, Clyde tripping forward and collapsing on top of him. Then the mass of analysts instinctively covering their mouths, the nervous stares, a shocked yelp from Lulu Heifenschliefen, and finally, conclusively, a pervasive silence.

Eleven

Clyde is given the boot the next morning. After knocking the Toad flat-out unconscious, then rolling over and splicing the Toad's palm with a shard of the broken beer bottle—the gash deep enough to require a trip to the emergency room and twenty-three stitches—he gave the greater forces at work in the HR department really no choice in the matter. He was summoned into the Toad's office first thing, beckoned in by the bandaged hand, and two minutes later he was being escorted directly to the elevators. No passing Go, no collecting $200. According to Lulu, Clyde is only the fifth analyst ever to get the pink slip, rounding off a venerable list, in chronological order:

1. *The analyst who locked himself in a bathroom stall and wouldn't come out for three days.*
2. *The analyst who took off at five every day to do a round of shopping before the stores closed. She had connections with those high up, of course, but they*

didn't hold much water after she splurged on a few pairs of five-hundred-dollar heels using the company card.

3. *The analyst who rolled out of bed one day and just stopped giving a shit: wearing T-shirts, taking two-hour lunches, and barking rabidly at the senior guys if they dared approach him with any real work. (Personally, I think this one is an urban legend of the corporate world, though Lulu insists on its veracity.)*
4. *The analyst who thought it would be a great idea to leave a giant turd on the Fish's leather chair as an April Fool's joke.*

It's the last one that gets to me the most, the guy with the turd. I mean, what sort of rational creature would have ever schemed up mixing human excrement and the Coldest Fish In The Pond, two entities as incompatible as oil and water? I can't even begin to fathom what he could have been expecting: the Fish arriving in the morning, poking at the brown mound with a gold fountain pen, scratching his chin in befuddled amusement—"By golly, how did that lump get there?"—then clutching at his sides, collapsing in a fit of hysterical giggles, tears welling up in the corners of his eyes? Though to be fair, this ingenious prank was probably hatched at four in the morning after a few weeks of intense sleep deprivation, the poor analyst going a bit loony as he slugged back cup after cup of caffeine. So, yeah, now that I'm thinking about it, I can sort of see how it could have happened.

♦

Clyde's disappearance was like an illusionist's gimmick: One minute he was sitting at his desk with his morning coffee and then—*poof!*—the next thing you know, there's the Utterly Incompetent Assistant boxing up his personal effects. The evil Toad and his HR cronies didn't even give him five minutes to exchange any final words with the rest of us.

Shortly after Clyde's anticlimactic departure, the three surviving members of our Gang of Four head down to Starbucks to regroup. Gang of Three now. It's not quite the same.

"It's surreal." I say, shaking my head sadly. "I just don't believe it."

Postal Boy nods in agreement. "It's fucked up, that's what it is. I tell you, even though Clyde was a bit, well—how do I put this gently?—*disturbed* at times, I'm really going to miss the guy."

The Defeated One has been particularly quiet throughout this morning's ordeal.

Turning to him, I ask, "What about you, man?"

The Defeated One shrugs.

"What about me? This happens all the time. Face it: Investment banking is a highly volatile industry. People come, people go. You just have to accept it and move on."

Postal Boy's left eye twitches in disgust.

"What do you mean, just move on? This is Clyde we're talking about. *Clyde.* And let's not forget, it's not as if any of us is completely blameless. We were all in on the plan, right? Shouldn't we be feeling a little guilty about this?"

The Defeated One smirks and says, "Trust me, we're all going to be paying for it too."

"What do you mean?"

"Well," the Defeated One reasons, "as I see it, I'm down for a cool twenty-five grand, both of you for fifteen. Fat chance we're ever going to see that money now."

Oh god. The painting from the auction, the one with the paddling Indians; I'd forgotten about that consequence of Clyde's firing in the mayhem of the last few hours.

"Fuck," I say.

Postal Boy looks equally downtrodden as we place our orders with the nauseatingly chipper barista, a woman who will never know the gut-wrenching conflict of losing a close colleague and fifteen thousand dollars all in the same cruel stroke of fate. But no—isn't this what I've learned during my brief tenure as an investment banker, that money only goes so far, that human relationships are infinitely more valuable than a closet full of new ties and shirts, and perhaps one of those mini i-Pods thrown in for good measure?

Fifteen thousand dollars. Oh Jesus.

I raise my cappuccino and struggle to get the words out:

"To Clyde finding his footing in the great world beyond."

The Defeated One and Postal Boy intone gravely, "To Clyde."

♦

I have less than an hour to brood and sulk before the Crazy Brit summons me into his office. He's busy dividing a stack of papers into an obsessive-compulsive's piles, peering at the edges to ensure they are all perfectly in line.

"Close the door and sit down," the Crazy Brit orders gruffly.

Before I'm even settled in the chair, he's blitzing through the rundown of a new mandate and my pen is shooting across a legal pad as I struggle to get it all down:

Biotech merger of equals. Pipeline synergies: one firm with mature cashcow acne medication and anti-something-something, the second with Fleuvo-huh(?) in first phase testing with FDA. Tax shield something something something. Combined market cap of ??? Strong backing from management and board of directors—

"This means we will be working with the Biotech team on this—"

I blurt out reflexively, "You mean the *Sycophant?*"

His thin lips purse together. "Who?"

Oh, right, he doesn't have a clue who I'm talking about.

"Never mind," I mumble.

The Crazy Brit raises an eyebrow and continues:

"This is going to be a challenging mandate. A significant amount of work needs to be completed in a relatively short time span. And I must mention, it's a very important deal to substantiate the Bank's reputation in the biotech industry. As such, I feel obliged to pose the question: Do you think this assignment will be beyond you? If so, please advise me now so I can seek a more suitable replacement . . ."

He chews on the nib of a pencil, eyeing me up and down with obvious skepticism. I'm torn between a desire to slap him silly and a pathetic need to prove my worth. I default to the latter, perhaps inspired by Clyde's recent brush with sudden unemployment:

"I, uh, I think I can manage it," I stammer.

"Good." The Crazy Brit returns to organizing his piles of paper. "Begin by putting together an information package for both companies. Are we clear?"

"Of course."

♦

The Woman With The Scarf licks the foam on her latte and reclines against a pillar. Though it's freezing out and my nose is a faucet of dribbling snot, she was craving a cigarette, so we headed to the courtyard. For some obscure reason I'm smoking as well. I take a puff and struggle to ward off a coughing fit.

"Yeah, things are still going great."

Taking a drag, she cocks her head. "You're so full of shit. Why are you lying to me?"

"I don't know. I guess it's a policy I've set for myself, keeping all work-related matters confined to the office."

She's unconvinced.

"Look, it's perfectly all right to have a lousy day. And that wasn't what was getting to me before; it was only that you weren't spending any time with me. Completely different things entirely."

Wrapping her scarf more tightly around her neck, she says, "So, now that we've established that bitching about work is well within the parameters of our relationship, what's up with you?"

Taking a sip of my coffee and trying to inconspicuously wipe the snot from the groove below my nostrils, I say, "All right, so I was just staffed on this horrible project. And then Clyde got fired this morning; he's one of the analysts I was pretty close with."

"Why, what did he do?"

"He, uh— "

It dawns on me that I don't really have an easy way of explaining this. I could take a purely clinical approach, stating the cold, hard facts—*Clyde gave our head of HR a concussion to prevent him from overdosing on extra-strength Ecstasy intended for this other analyst we all despise because he's screwing around with this super-hot assistant*—but then she'd justifiably conclude we're all a bunch of psychopaths. I mean, is that ever normal, to try to drug one of your colleagues? When we were sitting in our office, hatching the plan, it had all seemed so perfectly natural. Genius, even. Yet now, confronted with relaying our scheme to an external source of judgment, I'm not feeling all that confident about it. Maybe it's the same as that guy who left the turd on the Fish's chair; maybe in his internalized world the whole plan had made complete sense.

"He was skipping out a lot. Not showing up to work. Senior guys finally got fed up with it."

She stifles a yawn.

"A pity."

"Yeah."

"He deserved it, though, it sounds like."

"I guess so."

"Anyway"—she scoops up the remaining foam with her fingers—"what are your plans Thursday night? I was thinking I'd cook a little dinner perhaps, something hearty to warm us up: roast chicken and squash soup, maybe some asparagus. And then we could watch a movie. Play Scrabble. Or," she says, licking a dollop of foam from her pinkie, "something else entirely."

Roast chicken. *Something else entirely.* I'm getting all giddy just thinking about it.

"Sounds fantastic. What time were you thinking?"

"Eight or so?"

"Eight-thirty just to be on the safe side?"

She shakes a finger at me and we slip back inside with a quick kiss before she heads into Starbucks to pick up a round for her senior people. As the elevator ascends to the thirty-second floor, I'm still euphoric at the prospect of Thursday night, beaming cheerfully as I toss out my coffee cup and settle down at my desk. I haven't even checked my e-mail before the Defeated One sniffs at the air.

"What's that smell? Mumbles, were you out *smoking* just now?"

I sniff my shirt. Dammit. It's the curse of the lightweight smoker, I've found, that one or two cigarettes really stick to you. I contemplate making a jaunt down to the flamboyant Spanish retailer in the lobby and forking over a hundred bucks for a shirt that will inevitably be too disco-era flashy to ever wear to work again, when my phone rings.

Not now.

"Yes?"

"Drop by my office."

I hang up. Muttering the entire range of expletives I have at my disposal, I turn to the Defeated One.

"Okay. Twenty bucks if you lend me a spare shirt right now."

The Defeated One smirks. "Serves you right for smoking those cancer sticks."

"Forty bucks."

"I would, Mumbles, I really would. Problem is, all my shirts are at the dry cleaners."

He swivels back around. Good-for-nothing bastard. I turn to the Star.

"Hey, you wouldn't be able to help me out with this, would you?"

He looks up from an annual report.

"Huh?"

"You happen to have a spare shirt?"

He opens up a few of his drawers. Extending his palm and smiling apologetically, he offers, "Cuff links?"

My phone rings again. Fuck. I throw on my suit jacket, hoping the extra layer will somehow neutralize the smell, and make my way to the Crazy Brit's office. Stepping inside, I have the wind momentarily knocked out of me: Leaning against the wall, thumb-typing away on his BlackBerry, is the Sycophant. It strikes me that this is the first time we've been reunited since he made the move upstairs. We make eye contact and I smile nervously, though we both remain silent as the Crazy Brit motions for me to sit down.

"Well, then"—the Crazy Brit shuffles through his pile of perfectly aligned papers—"let's begin. I've mapped out a rough timeline of the work to be completed by the project team over the ensuing weeks."

The Crazy Brit distributes the timelines. A quick review indicates the bulk of the analysis is expected to be churned out over the next thirty-six hours. There is a catharsis that comes with the realization that the Crazy Brit's timeline is simply impossible. Even the Sycophant acknowledges this fact.

"Do you really think this is reasonable?"

The Crazy Brit glares at him, and the Sycophant visibly flinches, the three feet between them crackling with the tension of office politics.

"Yes," the Crazy Brit snaps irritably. "I do think this is perfectly reasonable."

The Sycophant shrugs and turns back to his BlackBerry. The Crazy Brit addresses me.

"You will have the comps completed by early afternoon. The precedent transactions by first thing tomorrow morning. Are we clear?"

Even the Sycophant joins me in mumbling a disheartened "Yes."

As I rise from the chair, the Crazy Brit wrinkles his nose.

"For god's sake, what is that horrible odor?"

He sniffs at the air before scowling and leaning over his desk.

"You've been *smoking*, I take it?"

"I, uh, it was a friend of mine at lunch, secondhand . . ."

The Crazy Brit curls his lip in revulsion.

"If you must feel the need to blacken your lungs, I suggest you bring a change of clothes. You will never again come in here smelling like a chimney, is that clear?"

"It wasn't— "

The Crazy Brit puts up a hand.

"I believe you now have a sufficient amount of work to do. Given your level of competency, I advise you not to waste any more time."

Affirmation of a new slippery slope: The Sycophant passes me a sympathetic stare as I make my way out of the office.

♦

The back of my chair is kicked hard.

"Mumbles, coffee break."

Without looking up from my spreadsheet, I say, "I really can't."

I brace myself for another kick. Sure enough, it lands a few seconds later, my chair pitching forward until I collide with the edge of the desk. A few paper clips topple to the floor, but otherwise my elbows minimize the impact. It's like I'm turning into Postal Boy.

Picking up the paper clips and checking my peripheral vision to ensure the Defeated One isn't gearing up for another kick, I say, "What about Postal? Can't you go bother him?"

"Not around. He snuck off to a dentist's appointment. The little fucker; you'd think he'd know better than to take off like that."

"Seriously. I haven't been to a dentist in, what, at least a year now."

"Probably for the better, dude. Your teeth have got to be rotting from all that coffee you drink."

I grunt and say, "I'd hate you if it wasn't the truth."

♦

By six o'clock I've effectively missed all of my deadlines. I just handed in the Crazy Brit's comps two hours overdue, and I'm still plugging away at the DCF model for the Sycophant. Postal Boy comes into the office, loosening his tie.

"How many cavities?" the Defeated One snorts.

Postal Boy seems a bit out of it.

"What?"

"The dentist?"

"Oh, right. Yeah, two of them in the back. The molars. They want me to schedule an appointment for next week, but no way that's happening with the Crazy Brit bringing me in on this biotech project."

I swivel around.

"You're helping out on this?"

"Looks like it."

I pump my fist in the air. Forget the implication that the Crazy Brit obviously doesn't think I'm competent enough to be the sole analyst staffed on this deal.

"What does he have you doing?"

"Looks like some precedent transactions."

"Hallelujah. Sorry, Postal, I mean, I feel your pain, but it helps to share the hurt, you know?"

"Hey, it's the least I can do," he murmurs. "You helped me out during crunch time before, remember?"

"Good point. Alrighty, back to work."

I swivel around toward my monitor. I'm finally making progress on the DCF model, when from just outside the office comes, "So, it's crazy about Clyde, huh?"

The Prodigal Son swaggers into the room and hoists himself up onto one of the filing cabinets. Postal Boy's left eye twitches frantically; the Defeated One clenches his jaw. I really can't deal with this right now, so I continue to work on the DCF model.

"It's just really fucked up," the Prodigal Son continues.

"Yeah," Postal Boy chimes in.

"Just so frickin' *weeeeeird.* Makes you wonder about it, dude."

"Wonder about what?" Postal Boy offers.

The Prodigal Son cracks his knuckles.

"Makes you think that maybe something was in that bottle, ya know what I'm saying?"

My typing is starkly out of place in the ensuing silence.

Postal Boy suggests meekly, "Perhaps somebody had it in for the Toad?"

God, won't he just shut up, already? The Prodigal Son leans back on his perch, chuckling hoarsely.

"Could very well be, dude. Could very well be. Though the

bottle was originally handed to me by none other than your pal Clyde."

The Defeated One scowls. "What are you suggesting— "

"This is what I'm thinking," the Prodigal Son says, his voice dropping a few octaves. "I think you fuckers had it in for me. Clyde couldn't have been in on it solo; he's too much of a stoner to have schemed it up all by himself."

"But, but," Postal Boy stammers, "that's ridiculous— "

"Ah, ah, ah," the Prodigal Son stops him, his face hardening. "Let me finish, bitch."

He launches himself off the filing cabinet and lands with a thud on the soles of his feet.

"So, this is the deal, you pricks. There won't be any takedowns around these parts; it'd be too hard to disguise the bruises I'm itching to pummel into your puny bodies. But let me tell you, you all better be ready."

He points to each of us in turn. It would be a goofy gesture if he didn't have the imposing size advantage. Then he shoves his hands in his pockets and swaggers out of the office. There is a prolonged silence before the Defeated One exhales sharply.

"Sheeeet."

♦

From: TheSycophant@theBank.com

To: Me@theBank.com

Where is the DCF model, already? I requested it by ten this morning. What time is it on my watch right now? Yes, that's right, 10:30. Call me with an explanation IMMEDIATELY.

From: TheCrazyBrit@theBank.com

To: Me@theBank.com

These comps are rubbish. Anerva and Pathogenix merged last August, yet you still have Anerva listed as a stand-alone company?! And what is this hogwash of Serenticum being a subsidiary of its parent? Is it too much to ask for even an iota of precision in your work?

From: TheSycophant@theBank.com

To: Me@theBank.com

10:45 . . .

From: TheCrazyBrit@theBank.com

To: Me@theBank.com

And another thing—I am sick and tired of this lousy formatting. I don't care if this is the Bank's generic template; I've attached the format from Barclays and I'd like you to adhere to it from now on.

From: TheSycophant@theBank.com

To: Me@theBank.com

11:10 . . .

From: Dad@yahoo.com

To: Me@theBank.com

Are you alive? Your mother's birthday was last week; she would have appreciated a call from her son. I've tried to tide things over but she's still very upset. I suggest you get a hold of her sooner rather than later.

From: ThePhilanderingManagingDirector@theBank.com

To: Me@theBank.com

Clyde, we need to back up a fee proposal for a Client by 4:30. Check circulars for every North American mining transaction over $500M and calculate advisory fee as percentage of equity. Thanks, bud.

From: TheCrazyBrit@theBank.com

To: Me@theBank.com

Am I to believe you are still struggling with putting those comps into the new format?!

From: TheDefeatedOne@theBank.com

To: Me@theBank.com

Mumbles, coffee break in five minutes. You have no choice in the matter.

From: Me@theBank.com

To: TheCrazyBrit@theBank.com

Piss off. Can't you see I'm dying over here?

Oh fuck. I didn't just do what I think I did.

I scramble through the Options menu, trying to figure out some way of retracting the message, but it's already too late:

From: TheCrazyBrit@theBank.com

To: Me@theBank.com

WHAT?!

Fuck fuck fuck fuck fuck fuck

Default plan: I push the keyboard out of the way and rest my head on the desk. Closing my eyes, inhaling, exhaling, I repeat the Defeated One's mantra—

nobody's going to die from this nobody's going to die from this nobody's going to die from this nobody's going to die from this nobody's going to die from this nobody's going to die from this nobody's going to die from this nobody's going to die from this

—until the words no longer have any meaning.

♦

I'm half-asleep at two in the morning, my body a lump of barely twitching flesh, but when I slip back into focus, I'm still plugging away at my spreadsheet, so I guess I'm still here. My brilliant strategy boiled down to telling the Crazy Brit the truth: The message was intended for the Defeated One, he shouldn't take any offense by it, and, besides, I'm really, really sorry. It seemed to work. I was dismissed with a frosty stare-down, ordering me back to my comps.

The Defeated One and Postal Boy return from the Most Depressing Donut Store in Downtown. I'm all but ready to burst into tears of gratitude when the Defeated One plunks an extra-large tumbler of viscous coffee and a six-pack of doughnut holes on my desk. I've wolfed down four of the holes by the time the Defeated One has crossed the room and sat back down at his desk. The caffeine and sugar race through my system, nudging me awake.

"The Prodigal Son's blowup was pretty crazy, huh?" The Defeated One kicks off his shoes.

He takes a sip of his mocha and winces.

"This coffee is terrible. That place is damn lucky they've got a monopoly on us chain-and-balls. Hey, Postal, if that fucker ever tries to mess with you, run down the corridor kicking and screaming, you hear? Three-on-one; we could definitely take him down."

"Thanks," Postal Boy mumbles between mouthfuls of doughnut.

"How are those precedent transactions coming along?" I ask.

"Pretty good. And your stuff?"

I shake my head. "It's killing me. Philanderer's 'minor' request for advisory fee percentages wiped out all my time today. Took, like, six hours to crank out."

"That sucks, man."

"Ah, well. The story of our lives, right?"

I turn back to my spreadsheet. Another half hour to get these comps done, then two hours to put through the Sycophant's changes to the DCF, then home by five, meaning I'll get three hours of sleep. It would be just another fun-filled evening at the Bank if I didn't have my dinner date with the Woman With The Scarf to think about. I can't exactly pull off the suave Don Juan bit if I conk out on her couch.

"Where's the Star?" Postal Boy asks.

"Some opera thing with his girlfriend. Said he was coming back in at three," the Defeated One snorts. "Quite the trooper, that one."

I've finished four comps before Postal Boy gets up and closes the door. He sits back down in the Star's chair.

"Guys, I have to talk to you about something."

His voice is trembling slightly. Oh please, not another breakdown. I eye him over my shoulder.

"Postal, can't we leave this until the morning? I've got all this work I still need to plow through."

Postal Boy is squirming around in discomfort, eyes downcast.

"No, I mean, I, uh, I really need to talk to you guys about this right now."

I sigh and swivel around to face him.

"All right, Postal, what's the deal?"

"I, uh, I'm not even sure how to say this—"

"Come on, Postal, I really don't have time for this. Just spit it out, already."

He takes a deep breath and does just that:

"I'm resigning tomorrow."

I swivel back around to my monitor. I continue typing, but the room stays eerily silent. Turning back to him, I say, "You're fucking with us, right?"

Postal Boy shakes his head sadly.

"All right, Postal. Very funny. But seriously, you've got to be fucking with us, right?"

He's wearing a strange conflicted expression, the same look I'd have if the situation were reversed. He's definitely serious.

"You can't do this," I spurt out. "You just can't. Not after Clyde, the Crazy Brit . . ."

I stand up, suddenly furious, my rage no doubt fueled by all the doughnut holes I consumed, and I start yelling at him:

"Over my dead body you're leaving this office without admitting this is one incredibly stupid joke!"

Peering at me, his eyes glistening, he says, "Look—"

Clenching my fists, I growl, "You stupid little shit—"

Then, from the other corner of the room:

"Leave him alone."

The Defeated One; I'd forgotten about him completely.

Whipping around, I say, "What the hell, man? You're just going to sit back and let Postal get away with this? It was the same thing with Clyde, right? You preach all this loyalty mumbo-jumbo, but you don't believe a word of it."

The Defeated One doesn't so much as flinch at this.

"Postal is making the right decision for himself."

"Bullshit! How do you know that?"

"Otherwise he wouldn't be making it."

"What the—god, to fucking hell with you too!"

I sit back down and glare at my spreadsheet. In the periphery, the Defeated One asks, "Where are you off to?"

Postal Boy's voice is still quavering.

"Procter and Gamble. Brand-management position."

"A nine-to-five, huh?"

"I guess so."

"When did you have time to interview with them?"

"Yesterday was the final round. They left a message on my cell this morning."

The Defeated One slaps his knee.

"The dentist appointment trick. I knew it!"

A lingering silence before Postal Boy drones softly at me, "I'll finish off the precedent transactions tonight. Just in case they don't want me to stay on for the two weeks."

"Just go," I mutter, my voice dripping contempt.

I know I'm not being the better man, but to hell with it; who ever said being the better man was a virtue? I hear the groan of his chair, the creaking of the door, and, finally, footsteps retreating down the corridor.

♦

As with everything at the Bank, quitting has its own hierarchy of rules. At one end of the spectrum, you have the analysts who cop out of their two or three years a bit early to go back to school. While this is a slight deviation from the natural order of things, these quitters are typically sent off amicably: a fountain pen, a mass-produced letter of recommendation, a final round of beers with folks they'll happily never see again. At the other end of the spectrum, you have those who defect to another investment bank. It's the ultimate sacrilege in the eyes of the Toad and his underlings, implying this other bank is superior to our own, a sentiment that can only lead to rumblings of ill will. These analysts are escorted directly to the elevators, but not before the Toad hints that every senior person will be "watching" them, waiting to screw them over at every future opportunity. Nevertheless, you know these courageous souls are smirking all the way down those thirty-two stories—that is, until the reality has sunk in that the other bank is no better than what they left behind. And, finally, there is the gray region in the middle for those who decide to enter industry. It's not another bank, but neither is it something so tame as academia. These resignations can go either way, depending on how much people like you. In Postal Boy's case, because he wasn't a complete bastard, they decided to keep him around for another two weeks.

Just great. On top of the Sycophant and the Crazy Brit brutalizing me to the point where I tremble every time my phone rings, there's now an awkwardness between Postal Boy and me hovering over everything like a soggy blanket. It's not that I haven't considered making the peace, I really have, but then I'll get submerged by a new wave of deadlines, and by the time I'm in the clear, I'm left feeling too drained to bother.

♦

I'm fifteen minutes late when I ring her doorbell. She opens the door a crack and says just that:

"You're fifteen minutes late."

"I'm really—"

Swinging open the door and smiling at my discomfort, she says, "I'm just messing around. I gave it a fifty-fifty probability you'd even show up in the first place. Come on in."

She's wearing a black cashmere sweater, a short black skirt, a thin silver necklace instead of the usual scarf. Everything so streamlined, so perfectly *precise*. What's amazing about it is that it's all for my benefit.

"These are for you," I say, handing her a bouquet of tired roses.

The roses are borderline passable, but it's the best I could find at the Iranian mini-mart next to Han's. Her eyes light up regardless.

"Thank you very much," she says as she gives me a peck on the lips. "Why don't you just relax on the couch and I'll find a vase for these."

While she's puttering in the kitchen, I soak in my surroundings. Her apartment is small but pleasant, and marvelously clean: gleaming hardwood floors, the big fluffy couch, a vase filled with shiny black pebbles, a framed Matisse lithograph above an orderly bookshelf holding all the *Harry Potter* novels. The aroma of fresh rosemary wafts from the kitchen. All in all, it's an environment that could only have sprung from the soothing hands of a woman.

Three doors lead off the living room. When she joins me on the couch, bringing two glasses of wine, I ask, "So, you have a roommate?"

We clink glasses and take the first sip.

"Yeah. She's a management consultant. Always traveling, so it's quite a sweet deal, really, almost like I live here alone."

"This seems like a great place," I say.

"Thanks. We call it the 'sunny shoebox.' A bit on the cramped side, but we get tons of sunlight."

We finish our wine, and the transformation is complete: Less than a half hour ago I was the quintessential stress-monkey, and now I feel a polar-opposite mellowness.

"Dinner is just about ready. You hungry yet?"

"Starved."

I help bring out the dishes from the kitchen: sweet potatoes in a maple glaze, arugula salad with toasted pecans, a golden-brown roast chicken.

"This looks incredible," I enthuse, refilling our wineglasses.

"You haven't even tasted it yet. The chicken is an old family recipe."

We clink glasses again. "Bon appétit."

I take a bite of the chicken and it's succulent perfection. I haven't had a decent home-cooked meal in what, five years now? Ever since my mom decided she was fed up with cooking for the holidays and resorted to Chinese takeout instead.

"This is delicious," I comment between mouthfuls of sweet potato.

"I'm glad you like it," she beams. "So, anyway, how was your day?"

I tell her about Postal Boy quitting on us.

"They sure are dropping like flies down at the Bank, huh?"

"Seriously. With Clyde getting fired like that, our posse has been reduced to two."

"And you're envious, of course?"

"Pardon?"

"Well, he escaped, didn't he?"

Taking a sip of wine, I reply, "Yeah, I guess so. I never really thought about it from that angle, to tell you the truth. Though I wouldn't want to be working for P and G, selling detergent or whatever."

She loads my plate up with more chicken.

"I have this theory that everybody should quit and get fired at least once in their lives. They're both important formative experiences."

"What do you mean?"

"Well, getting fired forces you to cope with instability, to realize you'll end up on both feet even if the world doesn't work out the way you want it to. And quitting; it's the ultimate in self-liberation, right? Especially because it's usually so difficult to just get up and walk away. One summer I was a waitress at an Italian restaurant. Terrible, terrible job. It was all under the table, so I didn't have to pay taxes, but the owner was this anal-retentive bastard. If we dropped a plate, we had to pay for the whole meal, and we got yelled at for not answering the phone fast enough, and all this other ridiculous crap. Then one day—I think I dropped a plate, maybe—I just snapped. I told him to fuck off and marched straight out of there in the middle of my dinner shift."

"That's great," I say with a nervous chuckle.

It's probably a harmless story, but I can't help thinking as I watch her slice a wedge of sweet potato in two, Is she chastising me for not having the balls to quit as well?

After we've finished eating and I've helped her take all the dishes into the kitchen, we settle back on the couch. Pulling her closer to me and kissing her, I taste the rosemary on her lips. We rub noses and she giggles, and we kiss again until she pulls away, her nostrils flaring slightly.

"Anything wrong?" I ask.

She shakes her head, laughing hoarsely.

"God, it's just that, I mean, I'm so unbelievably turned on right now."

I blink rapidly: Did she really just say that? She licks her lips sensuously. Yeah, she really just said that.

From this moment onward I no longer doubt there is a God, a wonderfully benevolent deity who understands the concept of divine justice, the fitting reward for languishing under the very worst of His children.

"Me too," I whisper.

She lies on top of me, and I run my hands down her back and caress her buttocks. Then she squirms her way down my body, fumbling with the zipper of my pants. She peers up at me with a playful grin before pulling down my jockey shorts.

"Are you sure you're ready for this— "

And then she's engulfed me masterfully, and it's like—fuck, to hell with analogies; how can you honestly verbalize anything so wonderful?

Perhaps too wonderful, because in less than twenty seconds, I'm whimpering, "Please . . . stop . . ."

But she doesn't stop.

"Fuck . . . please . . . *nooooo* . . ."

I yank myself out of her in the nick of time, flipping on my side and avoiding the upholstery.

"Jesus," she says, touching her lips. "That was speedy."

I'm mortified, of course.

"I'm so sorry . . ."

She grasps the sides of my head.

"It's not a big deal. Please, please don't have a hangup about this. When's the last time you had sex?"

"With myself?"

She hits me over the head with a cushion.

"I don't know, at least a couple months now."

Looking coy, she says, "So then it's completely justified. That is, as long as you have enough stamina for a second round . . ."

"I, uh, I think I can manage."

After a short recovery time we're rolling around on her bed. I nibble at her neck, and then she nibbles at my earlobe, and finally I press up close against her. I cock an eyebrow and she nods eagerly. A gentle nudge and I've slipped inside of her.

With my first ejaculation out of the way, I'm able to ride this crescendo quite skillfully. This isn't to say I'm a regular Casanova, but I can humbly state this: I'm the best I've ever been. A solid forty-five minutes later, after we've both achieved our shuddering climaxes, we drop down against the tasseled pillows and she kisses me.

"That was amazing."

"Yeah," I mumble groggily.

I stroke her hair as she rests her cheek flat against my sweaty chest. Holy shit, I really fucking needed that. It's as if everything I've put up with since I first started at the Bank, all the frustrations and disappointments and daily bouts with futility, have suddenly evaporated, leaving behind this glowing shell of holistic bliss.

"You said you had to go back to work after this, right?"

She tweaks one of my nipples and I gasp.

"What's that for?"

"For not being able to sleep over."

"I promise this weekend. Saturday night for sure—"

"I'm just playing with you," she says, tweaking my other nipple. "Tonight was really great, though."

"Yeah, definitely. You mind if I stick around a little longer? Can I set the alarm for an hour?"

She nods against my chest. I reach toward the alarm clock on the end table, scattering some papers to the floor. I lean down to pick them up, and a few of the headings permeate the dim lighting: University of Copenhagen, Columbia, Berkeley.

"Um, are you applying to grad schools?"

I can feel her breath tickling the hairs on my chest.

"Yes. For next September."

I pull myself up so I'm leaning against the headboard. Even though I know it's none of my business, I say, "And you were going to tell me about this when?"

"Huh?"

She gets into a cross-legged position on the bed, eyeing me curiously.

"I didn't think it was a big deal."

"Not a big deal? Just a minor technical detail that you're taking off in a couple months, that all of this has a ticking deadline?"

"All of what? Look, we just started seeing each other. Do I have to run my future by you for approval after only a couple of dates?"

She's absolutely right, of course. So absolutely fucking right.

And yet I've already slid off the bed and am hunting down my clothes.

"I guess I should probably get back to the office. A lot of work due first thing tomorrow morning."

She watches me rooting around under the bed for my socks, my underwear, and pulling on my pants.

"It's flattering that you're reacting this way, it really is. But I've got to tell you: I'm applying to environmental policy programs. It's what I want to do more than anything else in this world."

"That's great"—I slip on my shirt—"everybody has to follow their calling, right?"

She shrugs matter-of-factly and says, "Yeah, they do."

When I'm fully dressed she walks me to the door, reaches over, and slides back the dead bolt. There's no doubt in my head that I'm acting like a total moron, but I can't seem to get past a puerile desire to clutch at her hand and beg her not to leave me, to ask her to scrap those noble aspirations to save the world from oil spills and forest fires, to move in with me in 1.5 years, marry me in 2, and bear our children 3.5 years later.

"This whole evening, I mean, I don't want to come across too forthright or anything, but this sort of connection doesn't happen so often for me. I mean, I don't think it's ever happened to me before—"

She leans in to kiss me. A forceful kiss, leaving us both short of breath afterward.

I smile sadly and say, "Look, I know I'm being pathetic right now. I just can't help myself, I'm really sorry—"

She puts a finger to my lips.

"Don't overanalyze it. Just accept it's been a difficult day with your friend quitting like that. Give me a call tomorrow when you're feeling better about things."

"I will, I promise—"

But the door has already shut behind me, the sound of the dead bolt sliding back into place.

♦

An e-mail waiting for me back at the office:

> From: TheCrazyBrit@theBank.com
>
> To: Me@theBank.com
>
> Where are you??? I've been ringing you up and you're clearly not in. Puzzling because those final amendments to the comps were expected by 9pm—am I to believe you're shirking on your responsibilities? Call me at home immediately. If it's already the morning and you've just stumbled in, then I suggest you begin boxing up your belongings.

It's just too much. I stagger along the corridor and slip into the bathroom—empty, of course, as it's one in the morning—push open one of the stalls, and slump down on the toilet. Combined with the overhead lighting buzzing away, the gray linoleum tiles, and the roll of one-ply toilet paper that comes apart when you wipe your ass, all of the past week's events collide, producing an emotional sucker-punch: Clyde. The Crazy Brit. Postal Boy. The Woman With The Scarf.

It comes out forcefully: a wretched sob before the tears gush freely down my cheeks. It's embarrassing, kind of silly, I mean, I've never been a big crier; indeed, I can't even remember the last time I cried like this. How the fuck did I get myself into this mess? Where did my free will vanish to?

I'm never coming out of here, I'm really not; they'll have to beat down the door first. Three days as the official record by the analyst who locked himself in the bathroom is child's play compared with what I'm about to attempt. I'm not finished with my breakdown before the bathroom door opens, and somebody shuffles into the stall next to mine. I hear the Defeated One's voice.

"Mumbles, is that you?"

I suck back phlegm, struggling to keep my voice from shaking.

"Piss off. Can't you let a man take a dump in peace?"

He hadn't heard me before.

"Whatever. Just be sure to light a match when you're done. I don't want to pass out from the fumes over here."

Twelve

February, March, April: Three more pages of the Defeated One's *Pattaya Fun-Fun Girls* calendar turn over. Their passage is lethargic, agonizingly slow, so even the glossy Thai sex kittens seem to grow weary of the process, and sigh with relief when it's time for next month's replacement to fulfill her duty.

Ninety days lopped off my contract. One thousand four hundred and forty hours; it sounds weightier that way. The vast majority of the time, my eyelids feel droopy, like I've swallowed heavy sedatives, and my head feels like a barren wasteland with the iconic tumbleweed rolling past. After ten months strapped behind this desk, I can handle an analyst's official duties without suffering any serious mental strain—comps and modeling and binding and stapling—along with the rest of the degrading tasks that come with being the Crazy Brit's bitch boy. The remainder of the time, when I become more lucid, the quitting fantasies crop up in their various flavors: *the elegant disappearing act,* staying later than everybody else one evening, packing up my stuff, and leaving my keycard on the Philanderer's desk; or the short-term satisfaction of *the explosive meltdown,* waving a hole puncher around wildly to send the Utterly Incompetent Assistant cowering under her desk, and smashing computer monitors and fax machines on a maximally destructive path toward the elevators; or, finally, a *contemplation of infinity or the lack thereof,* in other words, hurling myself out the window or in front of a subway car; far-fetched, surely, but I can finally understand those folks who do decide that enough is enough and wipe their hands of this sad, bleak world.

On the subject of quitting, Postal Boy left after his two weeks expired. I'd patched things up by that point with a half-hearted shaking of hands over a late-night cup of coffee, but both of us knew it was more a social formality than anything else, and besides, shortly thereafter he moved to Chicago to start his new life as a brand manager for the launch of the dual-headed Swiffer. Postal Boy and Clyde were eventually replaced by the two Tools: Tool #1, a replica of the Star but with terrible halitosis, and Tool #2, another replica of the Star but with a serious case of acne.

Tool #2 hovers over my shoulder as I demonstrate the correct way to program a VLOOKUP statement in Excel. I've taken over as Excel Guru, Supreme Master of the Way of the Spreadsheet, since the Star came down with a nasty case of pneumonia and has been out on doctor's orders for the rest of the week, and the Defeated One left early to do damage control after a major blow-up with the girlfriend.

It's already eight o'clock, and Tool #2 still has a full twelve hours of work left. Despite the inevitability of an all-nighter, he's enthusiastically jotting his notes down, sporting the newbie's classic ensemble of a starched white shirt and Windsor-knotted tie. I'm tempted to impart to Tool #2 the True Reality, that all of his contrived efforts to impress our senior guys are utterly in vain, but decide against it. That is the sort of thing an analyst is meant to discover by himself, a futility best digested in solitude.

After Tool #2 finishes his litany of questions, I reach over and grab my coat.

Tool #2 sputters, "Where, uh, where are you going?"

"Out for a bit."

Tool #2 can't handle this at all and his eyes dart around the room in panic.

"But, uh, I have to get this stuff all done for tomorrow morning. Didn't the Crazy Brit say he needed this stuff done by, uh, tomorrow, and if I had any questions—"

Was I really this bad when I first started here? Probably worse, now that I'm thinking about it.

"Relax," I say, trying to exude calmness. "Keep plugging away at the data and I'll be back in a few hours to check everything."

"But, but . . . ," Tool #2 gasps.

I know I'm being cruel, abandoning him like this, but I'm already twenty minutes late to meet my folks for dinner halfway across town.

"Just do what you can. Go check with the Prodigal Son if you have any questions. After all, he's the associate now."

"But, but, he's, uh, never around—"

I toss on my coat and I'm already out the door.

♦

The Imperial Dragon House, a cavernous place in the belly of Chinatown, is beginning to show the wear and tear of its four decades. Gaudy paper lanterns dangle from the ceiling, plastic portly Buddhas smile from the perimeter, and there is a small pond at the front with diminutive goldfish that swish around lazily as if they're high or drunk. The cuisine—something called "Seven Treasure Fried Rice" forms a miserable lump on my plate—is no more impressive than the decor. I've identified tendrils of chicken fat and soggy carrot as two of the treasures, but I'd be hard-pressed to name the other five. Anyway, it's not the food that draws us to the Dragon every couple months; my parents met here in their early twenties, their courtship blossoming over greasy wontons, so the place is potent with nostalgic value.

Though the Dragon is almost empty, we've been crammed next to the type of family that makes you seriously question any desire to procreate. The blubbering baby immediately to my right is perhaps the best of their lot, deconstructing an eggroll and squirting plum sauce all over the tablecloth while the parents scold the other two imps sitting across from them.

I stir my gelatinous hot-and-sour soup and wince at the onset of a throbbing headache. How is it that my parents are able to tune all this out and stare at each other like gawky love-sick teenagers? My mom finally breaks off their lingering gaze and smiles sheepishly at me.

"So, you're coming to Annie's play this Wednesday night? We bought a ticket for you already."

I look up from stirring my soup.

"Huh? You know I never make social commitments during the week."

My mom shrugs. "I don't see why you can't just tell them you're leaving for a few hours. After all, this is *Annie* we're talking about."

Annie, my third cousin twice removed. I haven't yet figured out why my mom does this. Every time we get together, there's a play thrust upon me, or a graduation ceremony, or somebody falling off a swing set and landing in the hospital with a broken leg. Why is it so difficult to accept that Mondays to Thursdays are off-limits, and most weekends are doubtful as well? Why can't my mom just be the bastion of unwavering support I really need her to be right now; moreover, why won't she just envelop me in her maternal warmth and squeeze me back into the womb? I'm serious: I want to go back. Nothing to disturb me in that soft pink cocoon but the swishing sounds of bodily fluids and the muffled cooing of distant relatives.

"You know better than to ask him that," my dad chides between slurps of chow mein noodles. "He won't stand up to them. Never has and never will."

"What the hell is that supposed to mean?"

My parents share a conspiratorial glance.

"I can't believe—"

The girl at the next table over starts howling after her brother clobbers her over the head with a bottle of Kikkoman soy sauce.

"So, you don't think I stand up to them?"

My dad frowns. "What can I say? Look at the evidence."

"I'm here right now, aren't I?"

"When was the last time we saw you? Three weeks ago?"

"Five weeks," my mom corrects him. Thrusting her soup spoon in my direction, she says, "Two hours this Wednesday night—would it really kill you?"

"I know you think I can just waltz out of there, but it's not so easy—"

My dad is shaking his head.

"Heaven forbid you should leave your desk for two hours. What do you think would happen? Armageddon, right?" Throwing his hands up, he adds, "The entire free-market economy collapsing on the spot! Fortunes lost! GDPs wiped out!"

"Not to mention no more fools willing to shell out five bucks for a latte at Starbucks," my mom snorts.

I can't believe they're going on like this. Here I am on a Monday night, taking valuable time out of mentoring the Tools, and all they do is mock me for doing what every parent could only wish their children would do: roll up their sleeves, find a job, and become self-sufficient. But instead of the pity I crave (oh, this sweet, sweet pity), all I get is their unwarranted condemnation.

An explosion of porcelain beside me: The brother has pushed a platter of Moo Shu Duck off the table. The baby giggles and claps her hands as both parents lunge out of their chairs. Amid the maddening commotion, my headache reaches epic proportions until I can't deal with the racket any longer, and I whip around.

"Won't you all just shut the fuck up?"

It comes out louder than I would have liked. Substantially louder. Everything around me just freezes: the parents at the next table, my parents, the waiters in their goofy cummerbunds and matching pirate vests, the baby with a string of goo glistening out of one nostril.

Motion returns with the father clenching his hands into fists.

"You want to repeat that?"

"He didn't mean anything by it," my mom says, smiling apologetically and rotating a finger beside her head. "Tourette's, you know."

"Thanks," I mumble.

A man in a white smock, presumably the one who concocted this rice of innumerable treasures, comes storming out of the kitchen.

"No trouble. No trouble. Leave now, please."

We're ushered out of the restaurant past the pond with the drugged-up goldfish. Walking down the street and wondering how it got to be spring already—the weather is far too warm for the winter jacket I'm wearing—I sense an uncomfortable silence, until my dad speaks, shaking his head in bewilderment.

"Twenty-three and mouthing off like that to strangers. What in god's name were you thinking?"

An awful rumbling in the pit of my stomach. It's not exactly guilt; it's more a bitterness that such a precious moment beyond the clutches of the Bank has come to this. Then again, maybe it's just the fried rice.

"Look, I'm sorry. Work has been so crazy over the last few months—"

"It's always work," my dad interrupts, removing a cigar from his pocket. "Everything is always about work."

Lighting it, he continues, "You're too young to be behaving like this. You should be out there having fun, enjoying yourself. Because I'll tell you, this is the time to do it. When you start a family, everything changes."

"I know."

We approach their car, and my mom pecks me on the cheek.

"So you'll come to the play?"

"I'll try. I've just got to check—"

Slipping into the passenger seat, she says, "You know what, don't worry about it. Your uncle Bob mentioned he wanted to go. I'll pass along your ticket to him."

"I just need to double-check—"

But she's already slammed the car door shut and is frowning at me through the window.

♦

I'm summoned into the Crazy Brit's office. He's as irritable as ever, waving an Excel print-out:

"Did you put this together?"

"Yes," I say, nodding, "along with one of the new guys."

"Well, it's atrocious," he grunts. "I skimmed it over for a whopping ten seconds and I've already detected numerous inconsistencies."

It's like *Groundhog Day* with him. Every morning the two of us are trapped in this unwavering routine: me standing before his desk, him shoving a minuscule error in my face, me promising I'll be better next time.

"See, this number here is reduced to two decimal places, and this number here to three. This is unacceptable work."

He scrutinizes me from behind his thick lenses. The hairs on my neck still prickle under his gaze, but it's no more than a physical reaction; I'm too familiar with him now to feel any of the initial despair. I bring our conversation back on track, saying what is expected of me.

"I don't know how I missed that. I'm really sorry. I promise it won't happen again."

We lock eyes and it happens: Both of us sigh simultaneously. It's a Bobbsey Twins moment, a brief alignment of spirits, and we look away in mutual awkwardness.

He clears his throat and says, "You will have the table reformatted and on my desk in ten minutes."

"Of course."

Then he furrows his brow, foreseeing the looming disappointment when I turn in the table five minutes past his deadline.

"Are we clear?"

"Yeah, we're clear."

"Very good, then."

♦

From: LuluHeifenschliefen@theBank.com

To: All Employees

Just a reminder: this Saturday is the Coldest Fish In The Pond's Spring Barbecue and Pool Party. The time is 1pm until sunset. Recommended dress code is casual. Feel free to invite a guest and don't forget your swim trunks! Directions are attached.

"So you'll bring that Asian strumpet again, piglet? My heavens, she was a feisty one. We'll keep her away from the liquor cabinet, though."

"Nah, it's not happening, Lulu."

"Why not?" she huffs.

"I think once was enough."

Lulu Heifenschliefen is swathed in a giant white sheet, her feet are strapped into golden slippers, and giant hooped earrings stretch out her lobes.

The Defeated One returns from the copy room and takes one look at her.

"Lulu, what the hell is that? You're a member of the Falun Gong now?"

"*Mein Gott,* don't you recognize a toga when you see one?"

He raises an eyebrow, incredulous. "Lulu, you're wearing a *toga?* At a financial institution?"

"What?" She shakes a finger at us. "Let me tell you something, piglets, those Romans really knew what they were talking about."

"They also knew how to throw some seriously nasty orgies," the Defeated One snorts.

"Don't be cheeky, boy-chick."

"Whatever." The Defeated One swivels back around. "It's historical fact."

♦

"Mmmmm," the Woman With The Scarf purrs as my finger grazes her cheekbone.

It's well past midnight, and I've just dropped by, part of a routine we've developed over the past few months: If her roommate is traveling, then I'll go over after work, or else she'll come to me, and we'll make small talk for a bit—

"So how was work?"

"Okay, and you?"

"Uneventful."

"That's better than eventful, I guess."

"Yeah."

—mess around, and sleep until the alarm goes off at six under the pretense that one of us will get up and prepare breakfast, though our shared affection for the snooze button usually results in a mad scramble to get ready closer to seven-thirty.

So, if you really think about it, ninety-five percent of our relationship is taking place in a foggy fatigue. Not that I'm complaining or anything.

"What are you looking at?" She yawns.

I'm fixated on her profile: the gentle sloping features contrasting with her sharp jawline, and her long lashes, as thick as paintbrush bristles.

"Just you."

I lean over to kiss her eyelids. It's crazy to think this is all going to end in, what, four months from now? Five months. I listen to her soft breathing, as steady as a metronome, until she whispers, "I got my letter of acceptance from Berkeley today."

Curling my body around her, I nuzzle the back of her neck.

"That's fantastic, right? Wasn't Berkeley your first choice? Or was it Columbia?"

"Yeah, Berkeley."

She rolls away from me. I shift over to caress her shoulder, but she flinches at my touch. Weird.

"What's going on? Shouldn't you be ecstatic about this?"

She squirms around to face me and cradles her head in her arm.

"Doesn't it mean anything to you?"

"Huh? What are you talking about?"

She closes her eyes and says, "Come September, *this* upcoming September, I'll be studying on the other side of the country. Only five months from now. Isn't that important?"

She buries her face in her arm, her hair falling across the sheets like velvet. I pull myself up to a sitting position against the headboard.

"Of course it's important. But I knew about this a few months back, remember? So it's not exactly a surprise or anything."

She remains silent, her face still covered. Oh shit, I'm fucking this all up.

"Okay, I'm not really understanding this, but what choice do I have but to accept it? This is what you really want to do with your life. You said it yourself."

She looks up and groans, "But it's in *California.*"

"I know it's not the most ideal setup," I mumble, "but we can always try the long-distance thing if it comes to that, can't we?"

She rolls her eyes and says, "With your schedule? Give me a fucking break."

I'm beginning to feel a little aggravated by this attitude—I mean, what's going on here? First my parents flipped out because my work schedule interfered with some stupid play, and now this nonsense. She is the one who is deciding to leave me; it's not like I've done anything wrong. The Woman With The Scarf continues:

"I know I'm not being entirely fair. It's just . . . I wish things weren't unfolding this quickly, you know?"

She reaches out and strokes my kneecap, drawing circles with her fingertips.

"I'm not sure if you've figured this out yet, and it's strange, I tried to hold myself back over the past few months, knowing that grad school was just around the corner, knowing you'd be confined to your job here in the city, but it's like this: I care about you a lot. I mean, imagine you could jump ahead into the future, and you see yourself settled down with somebody, a nice house and a big family and everything about it just feeling so *dead-on.* And then you zip back into the present, still holding on to this vision, but you see all these peripheral factors getting in the way of things, ripping the vision apart."

Fuck, why is she telling me this now? My voice trembles, betraying my emotions. "Sometimes you can't really help these things, right? That's the way life works."

The Woman With The Scarf bites her lower lip. "Then why won't you just—"

She sighs, closing her eyes. "No, I shouldn't be asking that from you."

She covers her face with the sheet. The things that remain unsaid are left to swarm around in the darkness, keeping sleep at bay.

♦

After just a few months on the job, one of the Tools has his first meltdown. It happens on a trip back from the Most Depressing Donut Store in Downtown. Tool #2 stumbles forward and spills coffee down the front of his shirt.

"Fuuuuuuuuck!" he shrieks.

He drops his bag of doughnut holes and rubs frantically at the stain.

"Relax, man, it's only a spill," I say.

The Tool is totally overreacting; the coffee is too tepid for any scalding, and it's already the end of the workday, so none of the senior people will be around to witness it. I keep walking but stop when I realize he isn't following behind me. Turning around and seeing Tool #2 standing absolutely still, gazing forlornly at the splotch on his shirt, I retrace my steps.

"Look, it's only coffee. You can get the stain out no problem. Just take it to the dry cleaners if you're worried about it."

Tool #2 shakes his head sadly and says, "It doesn't get any better than this, does it?"

It takes me a moment to realize he's no longer talking about the shirt. When he peers at me, his eyes brimming with desolate bleakness, I figure I'll just pull something out of my ass.

"Don't worry, you get used to it. Once you start getting comfortable with Excel functions, after you've grown accustomed to the various personalities in our department . . ."

Tool #2 doesn't look too convinced as we continue our walk back to the office. Then again, neither am I.

♦

Later that evening I receive an e-mail from Mark, my college roommate who's gone off to Bulgaria with the Peace Corps. It's not the first e-mail I've received since he left; Mark has been diligent about keeping us all up-to-date on his noble quest to save the gypsies and the malnourished orphans and the marginalized farmers, toiling away to give these people the view that not all Westerners are myopic self-interested bastards, that we are not a nation of greedy capitalists itching to swoop down and usurp their natural resources and pepper their bucolic landscape with McDonald's and Wal-Mart just for shits and giggles. In other words, he is the antithesis of me.

Normally I enjoy the updates, his Marxist experiences standing in such stark contrast with my sterile days at the Bank, but as I'm reading about how he spent the past week rebuilding the collapsed roof of a village community hall and is now imploring us to send donations for a planned Internet center, I'm finding it all too earnest, too blatantly do-goody. I mean, does he seriously think he's improving anything over there? So he fixes the shingles; how long before another bad storm, and the roof collapses all over again? Better to have these megaglobalized companies enter the market—a brutal transition, perhaps, a few indigenous communities sent packing—and bring these raggedy, pathetic people up to par with the rest of the world, right?

I experience a moment of lucidity as I appreciate exactly how far I've come.

Oh god. What's happening to me?

♦

On Saturday the May weather is uncomfortably muggy as I stroll into the Fish's garden wearing a long-sleeved T-shirt, khakis, and flip-flops. Passing by a hedge, I find myself in the midst of a crowd of suits and ties and flowing dresses, the rest of the Bank employees dressed to their very ritziest. Those in my immediate vicinity eye my tackiness with a mix of curiosity and contempt.

"I thought you said this was casual," the Woman With The Scarf hisses through clenched teeth.

She's not as bad off as I am in her black sweater and floral skirt, but she's still a bit underdressed for this crowd.

"It is," I say and shrug meekly.

I wade through the throng, my face burning with embarrassment, until I reach my oasis: a suit-clad Defeated One hanging out by the bar with Tool #1, also in a suit.

"Way to go, Mumbles," the Defeated One chuckles over his beer. "Leave it to you to wear flip-flops to this thing."

"Didn't the e-mail say it was casual?"

The Defeated One takes a swig.

"There's no such thing as casual on the Street. Come on, even the Tool figured that one out."

Tool #1 bobs his head enthusiastically at this.

"Anyway," I mumble, "guys, this is my girlfriend."

The Defeated One reaches out and kisses the back of her hand.

"A pleasure. I think we've met before, actually, at Han's.

Mumbles, why don't you grab a beer for the fair lady and I'll give you both the grand tour? Wait until you check out his wine cellar."

After I've nabbed two Heinekens from the bar, we follow a manicured path toward the main house. The surrounding shrubbery is pruned to perfection, a few of the taller bushes shaped into columns supporting a canopy of vines. Jutting out from one side of the house rests a pool, seemingly carved out of the surrounding landscape.

"The other half is inside the veranda. Retractable roof, so during the summer the entire pool can be out in the open," the Defeated One explains.

I whistle. "Must have cost a fortune."

"Only the finest," the Defeated One says.

With Tool #1 and the Woman With The Scarf walking a little ahead, he whispers to me, "Dude, why'd you bring her along? Didn't you learn your lesson from the holiday party?"

I shrug. "She wanted to come—a chance to match some faces to the stories I've been laying on her."

We step through an imposing archway and enter the Fish's labyrinthine abode. Slinking past room after room, we are overwhelmed by the absurd ostentation of the decor: Napoleonic couches with gilded golden armrests, sprawling Persian carpets, sixty-inch plasma televisions, massive crystal chandeliers, a Ming vase, a reflecting pool, two grand pianos, a harp, a fully equipped gym, a room with all the contents in white, a room with all the contents in beige, a four-poster bed with each post resembling a steel girder. Hung above a blockish granite fireplace, a large painting that looks similar to the rest of Monet's water lilies series.

"It's like the love child of Versailles and Philippe Starck," the Woman With The Scarf muses in half-appreciation and half-contempt.

We're all feeling the same thing, I think: In one respect we're awed by the enormous wealth of it, the rampant materialism that must have spurred this accumulation, but at the same time, we're troubled by a tasseled pillow costing more than somebody's welfare check, that the possible Monet is more valuable than the net worth of entire African nations.

We wind our way through the house until the Defeated One ushers us into a dark room where the air is perceptibly cooler than the rest of the mansion. He flicks a light switch and we gasp: The room, shaped like a turret, is the biggest wine cellar I could ever have imagined. The bottles glint 360 degrees around us on shelves that spiral all the way up to the looming ceiling.

"Even though I've seen it before, it still gets me right here," the Defeated One says, covering his heart. "And none of these are cheap, either. You could probably hunt down thousand-dollar bottles of rare vintages somewhere in his collection."

"Jesus," I say, craning my neck.

A sound from the hallway. We hurriedly flick off the lights and rush from the room. A false alarm: It's just one of the maids feather-dusting a jewel-encrusted gong. She glances at us apathetically as we speed-walk past her.

Back in the garden, we grab a few more drinks and find a discreet niche in which to observe the crowd. Over by a bed of rosebushes, the Philandering Managing Director is chatting up the Utterly Incompetent Assistant, the latter wearing a silly broad-rimmed sunhat, her face flushed pink from too many wine coolers. Some ways behind them, the Crazy Brit stands alone, sipping a glass of brandy.

The Woman With The Scarf tugs at my elbow and says, "Come on, I didn't come here to hide away in a corner. Let's mingle for a bit."

I'm still feeling self-conscious about the flip-flops, but she's already dragging me out of our seclusion.

"Bon voyage," the Defeated One says, smirking.

Before I can resist further, she's marched straight ahead in the direction of the Crazy Brit. He scowls at our approach. I smile nervously.

"Um, hello." I extend my hand, but he's reluctant to touch it, barely shaking a few of the fingers.

"Hello," he sighs.

I introduce the Woman With The Scarf.

"My girlfriend."

He doesn't even bother making eye contact.

"A pleasure."

"So, you've been here long?"

"Too long."

"And, uh, are you having a good time?"

"Not particularly."

"Oh."

After an awkward pause, he sniffs. "An interesting choice of footwear."

"The invitation said casual," I say, blushing. "I guess I didn't interpret it correctly . . ."

I realize the Crazy Brit is barely paying attention to me, his gaze straying around the garden; he's probably hatching an escape plan.

"You will have those comps prepared for Monday morning, yes?"

"Of course."

"Funny, then, that you should be here instead of at the office, hmmm?"

"I figured a few hours wouldn't hurt—"

"Very good, then. Pip pip."

And with that he's sauntered off, crossing the garden in long, urgent strides to pay court to the Ice Queen. The Woman With The Scarf shakes her head in disbelief.

"Unbelievable! What an asshole!"

"Yeah," I say with a shrug. "That's the Crazy Brit for you."

I turn toward the Defeated One, but she's pulling me back into the throng.

"Not so fast. Let's meet a few more of these megalomaniacs."

"Why? You know they're all going to be just as terrible. Everybody molded from the same archetype."

She persists in tugging at my hand.

"You're just being uptight about the flip-flops. Come on," she pleads, "it will be enlightening for me."

"I really don't think it's a good idea."

She puffs out her lower lip. "Why'd you drag me to this, then?"

"You asked to come!" I sputter.

"Look," she says, frowning, "I don't know why you're being such a wimp about this."

And like that, something inside me just snaps. With a few bystanders looking on, I lose it right there in the garden.

"A *wimp?* What the fuck are you going on about? Standing there having a hissy fit when it's *you* that asked to come to this, *you* that's going back to grad school, *you* that's walking away from our relationship . . ."

Too late. It's out before I can stop myself. Her eyes widen in disbelief.

"Hissy fit! I can't believe you!"

"Look, I didn't mean it in exactly that context— "

"Fuck off," she snaps.

She storms across the garden and disappears behind some sculpted hedges. I consider making a pursuit but decide against it; it would probably be best if we each had a few minutes to cool down. I retreat back to the Defeated One, chugging down my beer.

"Where's that woman of yours?"

"Don't have a fucking clue."

"You sure have a way with the ladies, Mumbles."

"Tell me about it."

I head to the bar for another drink. My arrival coincides with the Coldest Fish In The Pond's, who begins pouring himself a Corona. He's clearly inebriated, swaying precariously as he munches on a hamburger.

"Hello," he slurs between mouthfuls of beef.

"Hey," I say and nod curtly.

"So kind of you to make it out this afternoon. Of course, you probably had no choice in the matter, huh?"

The Fish bursts into high-pitched laughter, wiping a glob of ketchup off his chin. I force a weak chuckle. As his laughter subsides, I glance over his shoulder and spot two solitary figures standing beside the swimming pool: the Prodigal Son and some woman with her back turned to me, probably his date. The Prodigal Son catches me staring and makes the thumbs-up sign.

I'm trying to figure out the meaning of his hand gesture, when it hits me:

The black sweater. The floral skirt.

Oh no.

My view is blocked as the Fish steps in front of me. I'm trying to peer around the sides of his head, but it's almost like he's anticipating my every movement, shuffling around so I can't get a clear vantage point. He's still slurring away, peppering me with hamburger.

"This industry is all about survival. *Survival.* The weak among you will drop like flies, one by one, after which only the strongest will remain."

"Look, I— "

"And for those final few who do make the cut," he continues, sweeping his hand over the expanse of his garden, "greatness will be yours."

He takes a final bite of his hamburger before saying, "Now, if you'll excuse me."

With the Fish gone, I have an unobstructed view of the Prodigal Son clearly putting the moves on my girlfriend. He leans down and whispers something in her ear and her shoulders shake with unabashed amusement. We make eye contact again, and he gives me another thumbs-up sign.

I'm crossing the lawn, poised and ready to do something drastic, when he places his hand on her lower back, a possessive gesture, and leads her back into the house. It's enough of a shock to stop me dead in my tracks.

Fuck.

My chest constricts; I release a guttural whimper. Aside from the anger and disbelief, I'm struck by the realization that somehow I expected our relationship to work out. A foolish indulgence in that vision of hers: a house and kids and decades of roast chicken and stupid fighting and trips to Costco and an unnerving contentment, because no two humans deserve to be so damn happy together.

And now it's all fucked up. My whole conjectured future, gone, just like that.

I'm finally in motion, sprinting hard, but no, instead of heading toward the house, I'm veering a sharp right, out through the gate, running past an endless string of glinting Mercedes hubcaps, past perfectly landscaped lawns, gasping for breath, wheezing and coughing and feeling like I'm about to collapse, but I'm still barreling ahead, spitting out great globs of phlegm, and I'm not going to stop until I'm all the way home.

Thirteen

From: PostalBoy@pg.com

To: Me@theBank.com, TheDefeatedOne@theBank.com

Hey guys!!! I'm heading back into town for a training seminar next week—any chance you both have time to sneak out for a quick lunch? I can meet you at the food court if that's easiest, though another round of Lunch Special No. 3 would be nice. Let me know!!!

The Defeated One swivels around.

"Mumbles, you interested in this?"

I slurp down the final dregs of my coffee. My two-cup-a-day resolution is officially out the window; this is my sixth jolt of caffeine and it's not even eleven yet.

"What the hell is up with those exclamation points? I don't know, man; we didn't exactly part on the best of terms."

"Aw," he smirks, "your petty hang-ups are just so darn cute

today. Come on, Mumbles, don't be such a pansy. What about next Tuesday? I'll tell him to meet us at Han's."

"I really don't think it's a good—"

"All right. One-thirty it is."

♦

The following Tuesday the three of us are squeezed into one of the cracked booths at Han's Blue Diamond Chinese Gourmet. It would almost seem like old times again if it weren't for the fact that it's not really Postal Boy sitting across the table from us; it just can't be.

For one, the eye twitch is gone. So is the bad complexion. The hair is neatly combed back. If guys didn't have such hang-ups talking about this sort of thing, I'd even go so far as saying that he's become, well, somewhat good-looking. The Entity Formerly Known As Postal Boy, dressed like a prepster in an aquamarine polo shirt, wolfs down the congealed lumps of General Tso like his life depends on it.

"I forgot how addictive this stuff is."

Even the voice is slightly off: less monotonous, more confident. In truth, the whole package is making me feel a little drab in comparison.

"So, how's the new job?" the Defeated One asks.

"It's okay," Postal Boy says. "I mean, it's a *job,* right? I'm definitely not too crazy about it when my alarm is going off in the morning. But the people are really down-to-earth, and the work is more challenging than you'd think, and I'm out of there by five-thirty every single day. Nobody ever works weekends."

"So, it must seem like Candyland, huh?"

Postal Boy grins sheepishly.

"Oh, sorry about that. I guess I was being a little insensitive."

The Defeated One waves it off.

"We're big boys. And what's it like in Chicago?"

"It's great. I found a sweet apartment that's close enough to work that I can walk, and the girlfriend lives just around the corner."

"You have a girlfriend? How'd you pull that off so quick?"

Postal Boy devours another dubious chicken morsel.

"Met her in training. She's with P and G too; a brand manager for Tide."

"You nasty *dawg,*" the Defeated One says, reaching across the table and clapping him on the shoulder. "Cubicle-cest; I definitely approve."

"Yeah, there is the convenience factor. And get this"—he leans in conspiratorially—"they've got this private bathroom upstairs, for handicapped employees or whatever, and it's equipped with a shower and everything. I tell you, it's like a brothel in there."

"Just filthy," the Defeated One guffaws.

"And what about you?" Postal Boy attempts to draw me into the conversation. "What about that chick you were screwing around with from before? The one who always wore the scarf?"

I poke at my Lunch Special No. 3, forming mounds of rice with my chopsticks.

"It's going fine," I drone monotonously.

It takes me a second to appreciate I sound exactly the way Postal Boy used to while he was still employed at the Bank.

"No, it's not," the Defeated One helps out. "The Fish had his annual barbecue last weekend. Prodigal Son, the motherfucker, put the moves on Mumbles's wench when he was distracted. Needless to say, she crumbled like all the rest of them."

"Thanks," I say, glaring at him.

"I'm sorry, man," Postal Boy says, shaking his head. "Anyway, she probably wasn't worth it, right?"

"Yeah," I mumble, "she wasn't worth it."

Settling back in the booth, I'm beginning to feel the onset of Lunch Special No. 3's various effects: heartburn, a fiery round of hiccups, a tingling in my facial extremities from all that MSG. Or maybe part of my underlying nausea can be attributed to the fact that, despite my rational side imploring me to cut my losses and move on, the Woman With The Scarf will not be exorcised from my neural pathways: Her face materializes in the reflection of my computer monitor, I can smell her perfume on my sheets, and even that damn scarf comes back to haunt me, memories of her conjured up when a woman in line at Starbucks was wearing the same thing.

Postal Boy interrupts my daze.

"I nearly forgot. You guys aren't going to believe this. I ran into Clyde yesterday, a random encounter in the drugstore next to my hotel while I was picking up some toothpaste. Apparently he's playing in a band now. I scribbled it down somewhere—"

He reaches into a pocket and pulls out a few slips of paper.

"Here we go. There's a gig on Thursday night, a tiny bar that just opened up in the Village. I was thinking about stopping by; is either of you interested?"

The Defeated One scrutinizes the address. "Clyde in a band—a long ways from banking, that's for sure. Yeah, I'm definitely in. What about you, Mumbles?"

Keeping my gaze focused on the paper plate in front of me, I say, "I don't know. I might have to finish up some precedent transactions for the Crazy Brit—"

"Mumbles, don't make me have to kick your ass."

Postal Boy pipes up, "It was just a suggestion. No pressure or anything, but if you have the time, then we could make it a night. How's the Crazy Brit, by the way? Any easing up a bit?"

Did I just detect pity in his gaze? Oh lord, now I'm getting sympathy from Postal Boy.

"No," I deadpan, "he's still a raving lunatic. It's gotten so bad I'm almost longing for the old days when I just had to deal with the Sycophant."

"The Sycophant!" Postal Boy looks puzzled. "But I thought he was your archnemesis?"

"Don't pander to him," the Defeated One orders gruffly. As he gets up from the booth, he adds, "So we're meeting for Clyde's show on Thursday?"

"It could be a lot of fun," Postal Boy says.

They both stare at me expectantly. I nod as a reflex, ignoring the Defeated One's scowl as I make my exit.

♦

From: Me@theBank.com

To: WomanWithTheScarf@GoodmanWeisenthal.com

Was it really worth it? You know you're just one of a million girls he's fucked, right? He doesn't even give a shit about you—it was all a ploy to get revenge on

Delete.

From: Me@theBank.com

To: WomanWithTheScarf@GoodmanWeisenthal.com

I just don't understand it, that's all. I thought you said you cared about this relationship, that night at your place, when you got your letter of acceptance from Berkeley

Delete.

From: Me@theBank.com

To: WomanWithTheScarf@GoodmanWeisenthal.com

I've got to ask: is this all about me not quitting my job? Because if it is

Delete.

♦

I kick the back of the Defeated One's chair.

"Let's hit Starbucks."

"Again?" he scoffs. "Didn't we just come from there? It couldn't have been more than two hours back."

"What can I say, my resolution is off and I'm craving my caffeine. It doesn't look like you're overwhelmed right now, anyway."

He is logged onto eBay, bidding up the auction for some old Batman figurines his mom found in the attic when she moved house last week.

"Lookee that," the Defeated One says. "The Joker's pulling fifty bucks already. If memory serves correct, I got that one in a Happy Meal when I was six."

"I thought you weren't allowed to bid on your own stuff."

He rolls his eyes at this.

"You set up a separate account and everything slips through."

"Come on," I plead. "Coffee time."

"Fine," he grumbles.

Waiting in line at Starbucks, I'm practically trembling with anticipation. Not for the coffee; I'm way too jittery to need any more caffeine right now. Rather, I'm furtively scanning the line, peering back across the lobby toward the elevators, hoping to catch a glimpse of Her. And then—well, I haven't really thought it through that far. I imagine there will be some sort of altercation: a bit of yelling, a bit of name-calling, whatever it takes to make her understand she's traded in a relationship with real staying power, with *substance,* for a life of meaningless one-night stands. Forty years from now she'll be standing in a pair of cheap stilettos by a bar reeking of cigarette smoke, puffing on a Virginia Slims, and hoping she'll get taken home by a burly trucker with oily chest hair and yellow-stained teeth.

"Earth to Mumbles," the Defeated One snaps in my face.

"Huh?"

"You were looking for her, weren't you?"

"No. Just a little out of it. Heh heh."

"Heh heh," the Defeated One grunts. "Dude, you're becoming a stalker. A stalking *investment banker.* On a scale of one to ten, ten being really creepy, you're frickin' off the charts."

"I swear to god I wasn't—"

"I call bullshit. Look, if you're going to get all obsessive-compulsive on her, you're on your own."

"Whatever, man."

"I'm serious"—he shakes a finger at me—"no more stalking."

"Fine," I mumble.

♦

I'm hunched before my monitor ogling the Daily Equity Raise Update—the amalgamation of porn blocked by the server that is later distributed to select analysts by one of the junior IT guys—with the safety of a complicated-looking spreadsheet just one Alt-Tab away.

"Great pictures," a voice rumbles from directly behind me.

My fingers fly to the keyboard, but the wrong hot-key combination gets pushed, so a midget performing acrobatic feats with a pylon blots out the screen. I slowly swivel around to face the Prodigal Son with his arms crossed. When his chuckling subsides, he leans in close.

"Just wanted to let you know, man, that chick of yours sure is *nasty.*" Clapping me on the shoulder, he adds, "Thanks for bringing her to that barbecue, dude."

One final pat and he's swaggering off, leaving me to mull over all the things I wanted to say and never did.

♦

Even though I have an obscene amount of work on a forestry pitch, a beauty contest with twelve investment banks competing for the same paltry mandate, on Thursday night the Defeated One coerces me into accompanying him to Clyde's gig in the Village. The bar is small and cramped, one of those single-room places that seem to sprout up like toe fungus around this neighborhood, but there's no cover charge and the beers are dirt cheap, so I'm not necessarily complaining. The crowd is predominantly hipster in their John Deere trucker hats and leather wristbands and Triple Five Soul T-shirts, strutting back and forth when they're not swaying like airy reeds to the jarring recording of a band I've never heard of. Last time I checked, though, the hipster creed had shunned John Deere trucker hats and leather wristbands; I was under the impression those accessories had already entered the realm of Urban Outfitters–cool. Regardless, the Defeated One and I are blatant pariahs of this scene, still wearing our work ensembles, as we didn't have time to go home and change.

"Fucking suits," spits out an androgynous guy dressed like Michael Jackson circa the *Thriller* years, as we make our way to the bar.

From the other side of the room, we hear a familiar voice shouting, "Hey! Guys! Over here!"

Postal Boy has a sloppy grin plastered across his face as he stumbles through the crowd, trying not to spill too much of his beer. When he reaches us, he says, "Great that you guys could come out tonight. This"—he burps—"is so fucking awesome. Who would have thought?"

With much bravado, he adds, "The Gang of Four united again!"

His face is flushed, the eye twitch back in full force. He notices me staring.

"Yeah, a lasting memento from the Bank. Whenever I drink, it comes back with a vengeance. Like I'm marked for life or something."

"Where's Clyde?" the Defeated One asks.

"Backstage, getting ready," Postal Boy says, sneezing. "His set starts up in five minutes."

Then Postal Boy lurches forward, spilling half his pint and knocking his head against the bar. I catch him under the armpit and hoist him back up again.

"Easy there, tiger."

He rubs at his forehead, slurring, "Awfully slippery down there."

Murmuring builds around us. The crowd recedes from a small space near the bathrooms, and four guys make their entrance to a polite smattering of applause and some raucous hollering from an overeager few who must be close friends or relatives. The guy with the trumpet, dressed in what seems to be a white caftan, is none other than our very own Clyde. The other three band members have adopted the garb of their audience: thrift-store jackets, natty corduroys, Puma sneakers. They spend a few moments tinkering with their instruments before jumping into the first of their set, a cover of Joy Division's "Love Will Tear Us Apart."

It's shocking: Clyde is actually pretty good. While the lead singer croons in an earnest nasal falsetto and the guitarist fiddles around with his instrument as if he's not entirely sure what it is, Clyde's precise blaring of the trumpet manages to transcend this acoustic tomfoolery. Granted, it's kind of strange mixed in with a Joy Division track, but Clyde has a keen sense of when to enter the fray and when to escape it. There's no pause as the band churns through forty more minutes of embarrassingly bad music.

A few of the hipsters in the crowd cover their ears in agony and slink noisily out of the bar. When it's finally over, Clyde packs away his trumpet and heads over to where we're standing.

"Crazy to see you guys here."

On the surface he's all chummy, shaking hands before he settles into that aloof smile. Nonetheless, I get the impression he's finding the sudden reappearance of numerous former colleagues a bit weird.

"I didn't know you could play the trumpet," I offer up, stating the perfectly obvious.

He looks back in the direction of the band packing up the rest of their equipment.

"Yeah, I started playing in music class; I think it was the sixth grade. Not Asian enough for the violin, not dumb enough for the triangle, so they handed me a trumpet. Pure middle ground."

"You're pretty good at it, though," Postal Boy says, beaming mirthfully, still basking in the feat of orchestrating our reunion.

"Thanks. Couple of buddies started jamming together and thought they could use some horn. God, that sounds dirty," he snickers. "Anyway, we haven't played together all that long now; obviously we still need more practice."

An awkward pause, before the Defeated One asks, "So, what's it like with you now? I mean, aside from the band. Are you working or anything?"

Clyde shakes his head. "Nah, I'm taking a breather."

Postal Boy, drunk off his ass, pipes up.

"But Clyde, how are you *surviving* out there? Where's the income coming from?"

Clyde glances around nervously, just long enough for all of us to remember the painting from the auction, the money he still technically owes us.

"I, uh, you know how it works. You do odd jobs here

and there. I painted an old lady's kitchen for sixty bucks last weekend."

With impeccable timing, the guitarist in Clyde's band swings by.

"Lou," he introduces himself.

A shaking of hands before he turns to Clyde.

"Dude, we're gonna have a smoke in the alley. The girl behind the bar has an eighth and she's willing to share. Bring your friends along if they're up for it."

Lou flashes us a crooked smile and heads toward the rear exit.

"You guys want to join in?" Clyde asks.

"Yeah, I'm game," Postal Boy chirps.

"What about the two of you?"

The Defeated One shakes his head and says, "The girlfriend is expecting me back home. We're still in crisis mode. Sorry, bud."

"And yourself?"

"Work," I say with a shrug. "You know how it is."

Eyes downcast, Clyde mutters, "Yeah, I know how it is."

♦

From: Me@theBank.com

To: WomanWithTheScarf@GoodmanWeisenthal.com

Why haven't you written yet? Is it because you're embarrassed about it? Ashamed, probably, and

Delete.

From: Me@theBank.com

To: WomanWithTheScarf@GoodmanWeisenthal.com

Are you still seeing him? He left early yesterday evening. Yeah, I bet that's it. Dropping by your place after work, fucking you on the same couch I once slept on

Delete.

> From: Me@theBank.com
>
> To: WomanWithTheScarf@GoodmanWeisenthal.com
>
> You don't honestly believe you're trading up, do you? Sure, he's good-looking and everything, but he's such a fucking player. Just don't come crawling back in a few weeks when he

Delete.

♦

And finally it dawns on me why I'm having such a terrible time phrasing these e-mails: It's because I don't really believe a word of them, that she made a mistake, that she's better off with me than with the Prodigal Son. Let's be brutally upfront about things: He's better-looking than I am, and since he's been promoted, he's making more cash than I do, and playing squash with the Fish puts him in the league of untouchables, meaning he won't have to cancel any of their dinner dates because a Managing Director decides to swing by with a load of comps at the last minute.

The worst thing about all of this is realizing that my youthful belief in comeuppance no longer holds up. The Prodigal Son is never going to feel the scalding shame of rejection or, worse, return home to a deathly still apartment night after night, the darkness punctuated by blinking green and red lights, the eyes of compassionless appliances mocking his loneliness, his inability to get anybody to join him for a beer when he's in desperate need of human contact. There will be none of that sitting in front of the computer jerking off to Internet porn, wondering if those pixelized breasts are all there is, if it's ever going to get any better. A decade from now and you know he'll have that nauseatingly perfect life: a super-hot wife, four football-playing sons, a retractable swimming pool, and a chauffeur to park the Bentley.

♦

The Defeated One hurls an eraser across the room. It narrowly misses my head and instead knocks over one of the computer speakers.

"You game for some teriyaki action?"

"Nah, I brought a sandwich from home."

"What type of sandwich?"

"Peanut butter and jelly."

The Defeated One snorts.

"Peanut butter and jelly? Are you in kindergarten now, Mumbles?"

"They're pretty good," I say. "Nostalgic value, right?"

"Well," he says, slipping on his jacket, "I don't know when you decided to get all PB and J on me, but I'll tell you, I don't like it one bit."

"Whatever, man."

In truth, I'm hoping to catch some fresh air over lunch, some time to make sense of things, surrounded by the bronze cows in the courtyard. It's a strange emotional vortex I've been swirling around in over the past few weeks: one minute I'm absolutely devastated by everything, the next I'm in a state of sluggish apathy. I give the Defeated One enough time to make his way into the land of food courts before I head to the elevators.

I push the button and the doors glide open. I'm grateful the elevator is empty. The speakers crank out a Muzak version of a Jewel song and the screen at front displays its useless definitions before the elevator comes to a smooth halt on floor 27. The doors slide open to reveal none other than the Woman With The Scarf rummaging around in her purse. She steps inside and the doors swoosh shut behind her before she looks up and notices me standing there.

"Oh, hell."

She quickly pushes a button. Two floors down the elevator comes to another smooth halt. She moves to exit the elevator before stopping herself.

"No, this is ridiculous."

The doors close again, and the elevator continues its descent. She stands facing away from me, as rigid as a statue, only her scarf ruffling slightly in the artificial breeze from the overhead ventilation unit. I rock back and forth on my heels, fixated on a point between her shoulder blades, and I don't really know what to make of the situation. Certainly I've longed for an isolated encounter like this, a chance to deliver the perfectly crafted barbs that would make her burn up in shame before she pleaded with me to take her back. But of course, as is always the case, when the opportunity finally presents itself, I'm left with my tongue hanging limp in my mouth like a strip of undercooked veal.

We've dinged past floor 6 when her hand slams the Stop button; the elevator shudders to an abrupt halt between floors 4 and 5.

She turns around and hisses at me, "I am so very mad at you right now."

She stands there with her fists clenched, a throbbing tic visible in the upper right of her forehead, so I'm half-expecting a *Carrie*-like meltdown: the elevator lights crunching out in a hail of glass, the distant groan of cables snapping, the elevator shaking a bit before careening down the darkened shaft.

"What, you don't have anything to say for yourself?"

"What I have to say for . . . *me?*"

It comes out meek, pathetic. I sound like a fucking mouse.

"Yes, *you!*"

She crosses the elevator in three great strides and pushes me hard in the chest, sending me toppling backward until I collide with the wall.

"I am going to have my piece. Oh yes, I am going to have it."

She reaches down and takes off a shoe, waving it right up in my face. The razor-sharp heel is dangerously close to my eyeball.

"I step inside to use the bathroom at *your* company barbecue. I'm gone for *five fucking minutes.* And then I come back outside, and wouldn't you know it, but you've just gone off and disappeared on me."

Pacing back and forth in the small compartment she takes on squeaky voices:

"Have you seen my boyfriend?—"

"No, I haven't—"

"Oh jeez, I just don't know where he's gone off to—"

"Sorry, haven't seen him—"

"But he wouldn't just leave me here—"

"Lady, I don't know what to tell you—"

She emits a strangled cry.

"And so I'm left there, all alone in the middle of suburbia, wondering what the hell happened to you."

Throwing her hands up, she continues, "Then I'm thinking there has to be a reasonable explanation. Maybe somebody in your family got hit by a car, your grandma had a brain aneurism, whatever. But, no"—her voice shakes with fury—"two weeks go by and I haven't heard *one fucking peep from you!* No phone call, not one goddamn e-mail letting me know what's going on!"

She's panting hard, still waving the heel in my face. But what is going on here? It's *her* betrayal, *her* running off with—

My thoughts are interrupted by a beeping noise and a voice warbling through the elevator speaker.

"Excuse me, but is there some type of emergency?"

"No, everything is fine," the Woman With The Scarf snaps.

"Why is the elevator stopped, then? Because otherwise there's no—"

"I said that everything is fine," she hisses.

"But ma'am," the voice continues, "it's the lunch break." In a sudden burst of authority, the voice says, "You can't just go on holding up the elevator like this!"

The Woman With The Scarf rubs at her temples, "Just give us one more minute. *Please.*"

A long pause before the speaker crackles to life again:

"All right. But any more than that and I'm checking with security."

We're left in an eerie silence. The Woman With The Scarf puts her shoe back on.

"I just don't get it, that's what's really bothering me about this. None of it makes any sense. I didn't think our fight warranted your just ditching me like that. But I guess I failed to realize what a temperamental son of a bitch you are—"

That's it for me:

"*Temperamental?* Yeah, like seeing you head off with one of my colleagues isn't enough justification for wanting nothing more to do with you? Don't you turn the tables on me again!"

She gasps, her eyes widening. "Heading off with . . . what are you talking about?"

"Fuck off," I sneer. "Don't play stupid about this. Big blond guy—remember him? Maybe it's just me, but I'd have thought it would be kind of difficult to forget the guy you fucked in the bathroom, huh?"

She stumbles backward, covering her mouth.

"You think I was . . ."

She removes her hand and purses her lips tightly.

"Let's clarify this right away: I didn't *fuck* him, if that's what you're calling it. Unless that involves both of us heading inside to relieve our bladders. *Separately.*"

I'm squinting at her, unable to process this new information.

She shakes her head in disbelief. "You've got to be joking with me. You really think I'd accompany you to one of your office functions and pick up another guy?"

Before I have time to dig myself into a deeper hole, we hear another beep and the speaker switches back on.

"All right, ma'am. Your minute is up."

"Okay." She nods to the speaker and says, "We'll be on our way."

She pushes the Lobby button and the elevator hums to life and resumes its course. She combs back a stray hair.

"Look, I know that fundamentally you're a good person. And I can kind of see where you're coming from with this. But on the other hand, well, this is all just a little too absurd. After the time we've spent together, after I've told you those things, you still think that I'd—"

"It's not like that—"

"Shhh, let me finish. It's this job of yours; I mean, it's obvious that you're not thinking clearly right now."

"Hey, that's not fair."

She puts her hand up to silence me again. "Yet I wasn't lying when I said it before, that I really do care about you."

"I do too, I mean, I had it all wrong—"

"But I guess what I'm realizing is that I just can't go on dating you while you're like this."

"While I'm like what?"

"While you're still a banker."

A pause.

"So you're asking me to quit?"

"No," she says, shaking her head sadly. "You shouldn't see

this as any sort of ultimatum. The last thing I'd want is for you to base your decisions on our relationship and then begin resenting me later."

We reach the lobby and the doors ping open. Before she steps out, she gives me a tired smile.

"In a perfect world, right?"

"Please—"

But she's already walking briskly across the lobby and disappears out the revolving doors.

Fourteen

And thus we get to the crux of the matter, the all-important question: to quit or not to quit; what's it going to be? Do I really have the balls to abandon this two-year stint halfway through? It's all I think about now, aside from the Woman With The Scarf and trivial stupid things, like whether I should wear black or gray socks to work, or what I'm going to pick up for lunch—teriyaki chicken or General Tso. I'm that flea-ridden monkey lifting his throbbing head up from the clunky typewriter, a half-finished manuscript of *War and Peace* accumulating in a messy pile beside him, staring across the rows upon rows of other typing monkeys (an infinity of them, it seems) to the only window permitted in this cavernous sweatshop, a tiny rectangle glowing eerily white against the musty darkness flooding the room. The monkey shakes the cobwebs from his head and strives to recall life beyond the window: the pungent earth smells, the wild orangutans with their splendid pink anuses, the pockmarked bananas, imperfect exteriors protecting mushy insides far more tasty than the chemical-laden torpedoes doled out at regular intervals throughout the day.

What life is this, he considers, typing away in a language he doesn't even understand until the nibs of his fingers rub raw to the bone, all to satisfy a silly rhetorical question to begin with, whether he and his brethren can really replicate all of mankind's novels (most so unreadable it's hardly worth the effort) so that some hoary academic can publish a paper about it, can clear his throat and decree pompously, *Why, yes, it can be done.*

At times it seems so agonizingly simple, just a few leaps and bounds off the shoulders of twittering typists until he's fumbling with the latch and pushing through the window. But what then? What if the world outside has changed since the halcyon days of his youth; what if things have become colder and less forgiving? He imagines landing in some scorched wasteland with nary a pock-marked banana in sight, a few days of foraging for edible twigs before a wild coyote comes hunting down a light afternoon snack. Better to stay inside, where it's safe, where even though life isn't perfect he's still surviving, being fed, hearing the reassuring buzz of millions of fingers pushing the same QWERTY configuration of keys. Best to leave these crazy notions of window-hopping to somebody else, a braver soul with nothing to lose.

The monkey droops his head in resignation and places his arthritic fingers back on the typewriter keys. A crack of the whip: It's already half past three and his daily quota of fifty pages still needs to be filled.

♦

But this time the escape fantasy is not going away. On the subway this morning, while watching a cherubic Asian girl in a pink parka giggle as she twirls around one of the poles, I think to myself, everything will be just fine. Postal Boy and Clyde are living proof of this; they're surviving decently enough, right? No sleeping in boxes on the street, no gnawing on pieces of Bubble Wrap, pretending it's a double portion of Lunch Special No. 3.

So, what is the problem, then? What's holding you back?

♦

But then, while in line at Taco Bell, I ask myself, Do you really want to be hawking dual-headed Swiffers for the rest of your life like Postal Boy? And what's going to happen to Clyde ten years down the road? Fat chance of him getting into any decent business school with such pitiful work experience, only a few months on his résumé, and no references to speak of. So, what then? Playing trumpet in dingy bars until he's far too old for that sort of thing, the next generation of hipsters holding him up as their ideal because they don't get to see the other side of his life, him quivering in fear every time another bill passes through the mail slot?

I have the same nagging feeling I used to get watching *Office Space.* It's a classic movie, sure, but look where that guy ended up before the credits: working construction. Shoveling dirt. Granted, it could be a pleasant experience for a week or two, basking in feelings of liberation from the corporate world, but what's going to happen when he's forty and he's still dirt poor, and the foreman won't stop bitching him out because he's not shoveling fast enough on account of his aching back, and the pinched discs are untreatable because health insurance has become unaffordable?

♦

I sit at my desk, drooling over six M&M's cookies (that New Year's resolution is out the window too), when the IKEA chair, weary from supporting my buttocks over the last few months, decides to call it quits. The whole frame collapses underneath me, sending me toppling to the ground.

"Fuck!"

The Defeated One starts clapping.

"Bravo, Mumbles, bravo!"

Even the Star erupts in unsympathetic cackling. I pull myself up off the floor and kick the mangled base in frustration.

♦

Wednesday is the inevitable twelfth hour for scrambling around to get out the forestry pitch I've been putting together. For some obscure reason, five of our senior guys plan on attending a beauty contest we have no chance in hell of winning, which means I have five marked-up copies of the final presentation strewn across my desk. To make matters infinitely worse, the Coldest Fish In The Pond is also joining them.

With an hour to go, the Crazy Brit appears in the doorway, checking his Rolex.

"Make sure you have twelve copies printed and bound by three. We're looking to get an early start on the road."

Three o'clock; less than twenty minutes away. Is the man off his rocker? Only one thing left to be done—old Adam Smith and his specialization of labor:

From: Me@theBank.com

To: TheDefeatedOne@theBank.com, TheStar@theBank.com, Tool#1@theBank.com, Tool#2@theBank.com

CRISIS SITUATION. Pitch going out at 3 and haven't even finalized the edits. I should be wrapped up in ten minutes, after which I'll need some help down in the copy room. 12 copies, bound, clear cover. Please let me know whether you're available.

The responses dribble in as I plow through the edits:

From: Tool#1@theBank.com

To: Me@theBank.com

Really busy right now. Hope you can find somebody else.

From: Tool#2@theBank.com

To: Me@theBank.com

Sorry, man. Too much going on at the moment.

From: TheStar@theBank.com

To: Me@theBank.com

In a crunch. Can help out after 4 if you still need it.

God fucking almighty.

I whip a pen in the Defeated One's direction. It deflects off the back of his head, prompting him to swivel around angrily.

"What the hell?"

"Dude, I really need your help."

"Tough shit. You ain't getting any sympathy by hurling pens at people, Mumbles."

"I'm not messing around," I grovel shamelessly. "I swear on my life; help me out with this and I owe you such a big one."

"How big?"

"I'll get your lunch for the next week."

He scratches his chin.

"Two weeks."

"Deal."

The Defeated One slowly rises from the chair, yawning.

"So, what do you need again?"

"Twelve color copies. Bound, clear covers. Try getting the Utterly Incompetent Assistant to help out."

Ten minutes later I've sent the final version to the printer, praying I've deciphered the Crazy Brit's squiggles correctly. I bolt toward the copy room, barreling along the corridors at breakneck speed. Fortunately the Defeated One and the Utterly Incompetent Assistant are already stationed by the binding machines. It's 2:52; we only have eight minutes.

"All right guys," I pant, rubbing my hands together. "Let's do this."

The colossal color printer hums to life and begins belching out papers. I hand them off to the Defeated One, who ensures that all the pages are in the correct order before slapping on a plastic cover. Once this is complete, he hands it over to the Utterly Incompetent Assistant for the binding. It's risky having her as our ringer, but there is no other option. And it's the most brainless of our respective brainless tasks.

With five minutes to go, our well-lubricated assembly machine has successfully bound four presentations. I breathe a sigh of relief, knowing we're going to manage this just in the nick of time. This sentiment lasts for another sixty seconds, with seven bound presentations down, when the printer halts spitting out pages.

"What the . . ."

Murphy's Law in effect, of course. I check the LCD screen for the obligatory CLEAR PAPER JAM IN TRAY 4.

"Aaargh," I groan, dropping to my knees.

Tray 1 and Tray 2 are at the front of the printer, Tray 3 is a lever at the side. But fucking hell, where is Tray 4?

"Mumbles, what's the problem?" the Defeated One calls out.

"*Mumbles?*" the Utterly Incompetent Assistant giggles.

Any other time I'd kick his ass for this, but right now I'm crawling around one side of the printer, then the other; unless it's a Houdini trapdoor, I tell you, Tray 4 does not exist.

Bolting to my feet, I snap at the Utterly Incompetent Assistant, "Can you help me out with this?"

She rolls her eyes at my wigging out. "Sure thing, *Mummmbles.*"

She drops to her knees beside me, opening up Tray 1 and Tray 2, then Tray 1 again.

"Nope, not there."

She laughs as if this is the most hilarious thing on earth. She checks the other side, opens Tray 3, and snickers, "Can't seem to find it. Sorry, *Mummmbles.*"

I'm about to go apeshit on her, when there is a clip-clop of loafers from the corridor and a gust of frigid air that breaks my skin into gooseflesh, and suddenly a flotilla of well-tailored suits bursts through the doorway: the Coldest Fish In The Pond phalanxed by a few of the Bank's biggest bigwigs: a Vice Chairman from the forestry group, two Managing Directors, and the runt of the litter, the Crazy Brit.

"Where are those presentations?" the Crazy Brit barks, checking his watch. "Did I not instruct you to have them ready by two forty-five? We're already fifteen minutes late."

I get to my feet and say, "There's been, uh, some sort of printer malfunction."

"Printer malfunction?" he snarls.

The mass of Armani shuffles around impatiently, the Coldest Fish In The Pond whipping out his BlackBerry. No doubt ten thousand bucks docked off my bonus for this; that is, if he isn't e-mailing HR with my termination already. Where did the Defeated One and the Utterly Incompetent Assistant disappear to? Of course; they're making themselves invisible at the other end of the copy room.

"Well, then," the Crazy Brit says, crossing his arms, "don't you have a printer malfunction to attend to?"

"I, uh, yeah, I'll get right on it . . ."

I'm back down on my knees, yanking and shutting the trays like a madman. Tray 4, where the fuck are you? A minute of agony later and I'm on the verge of accepting defeat, crawling into a fetal position right there in the copy room, when I spot it: a tiny 4 stenciled on the inside of Tray 2. Beside the 4, I catch a glimpse of white crushed in the printer's mechanical innards.

I'm yanking at the paper, trying to wrench it free, when the Crazy Brit just loses it.

"This is unacceptable! I told you to have the presentations ready by two forty-five. Two. Forty. Five. And what time is it now?" Checking his watch, he states, "Three-oh-five. Gentlemen, we are now officially five minutes late for our meeting."

The rest of the Suits pace the room, voicing their own agitation. Amid this commotion, the Coldest Fish In The Pond looks up from his BlackBerry with a subtle twitch of his lips. It's like in those old samurai movies: You know somebody is going to get seriously clobbered when the grand master finally starts paying attention.

Before the Fish has a chance to incapacitate me with his five-knuckle, seven-star punch, it comes in a rush of neural connections, electric spike chains whizzing about my cranium, synapses opening and shut—

A Stark Burst of Truth.

A Momentous Epiphany.

A Mindfuck of Staggering Proportion.

It goes something like this (though these epiphanies are never easily verbalized):

I'm scared to death of a five-foot-six guy with a fake tan.

And a nerd with an obnoxious accent and a receding hairline.

And four other guys I know, just *know,* are terrible specimens of humanity without their even having to open their mouths.

And it's fucking *ridiculous.*

Ridiculous that I've gotten to this point, tired and defeated and sycophantic and borderline postal, in less than twelve months, ridiculous that I'm no longer viewing myself as a creature born with free will. The free will to reject this existence, to shrug off the paranoia instilled in me by cretins like the Toad, and appreciate there is a whole other world beyond this office tower, an infinity of experiences waiting to be explored.

And it's not going to be gnawing on Bubble Wrap or shoveling dirt or signing on for another crappy job where I'm some other tyrant's spreadsheet bitch. The next step may not be perfect—there is a distinct possibility I might be spending some time at the other end of the bell curve—but there's a catharsis that comes with the knowledge that, hey, anything has to be better than this.

Because let's be frank about things: I no longer have any friends, I barely see my family, and the Woman With The Scarf just technically dumped me. It's like, day in and day out, all I want more than anything else is to fall asleep, to escape, to dream about being young, when life wasn't like this.

In short, I'm a guy with nothing to lose.

I give up trying to clear the paper jam. Rising to my feet, I wipe my ink-smeared fingers against the side of the printer. For the first time in ages my head is perfectly clear, like that flash of lucidity when you solve the last clue of a crossword puzzle.

"It's not coming out."

My voice is steady, not wavering at all. The Crazy Brit squints at me suspiciously, sensing something is awry.

"What are you talking about?"

I lock eyes with the Coldest Fish In The Pond and chuckle softly.

"Exactly what I said the first time. It's not coming out."

The Crazy Brit blinks fervently.

"What the—"

"And one more thing," I interrupt him.

This is it, I realize; I'm really going through with this.

"I'm no longer putting up with any of this bullshit. I'm done with this—"

A frosty voice breaks in.

"That is enough."

The Coldest Fish In The Pond takes two steps in my direction.

"How many presentations have you put together?"

He's caught me off guard.

"There's, uh, six. I mean, seven."

The Fish nods slowly.

"That should be acceptable."

He points to the two Managing Directors I've never met before.

"Go. We no longer require your attendance at this pitch."

One of the Managing Directors dares to protest, "But they're part of my coverage team! I play golf with the CFO twice a month—"

He is silenced by the razor-sharp glare of the Fish. He points to the door, and the two Managing Directors scamper from the room. Continuing, he asks, "Is a car waiting downstairs?"

"Yes," the Crazy Brit replies, wringing his fingers nervously.

"Good."

The copy room has an eerie stillness with the Defeated One and the Utterly Incompetent Assistant still cowering behind stacks of copier paper. The Coldest Fish In The Pond takes two steps closer, scanning me up and down with obvious contempt. My heart pounds in my chest, but I'm not backing down from this; I've already gone too far.

"Never forget," the Fish finally says, "this industry is all about one basic principle: survival."

A few seconds stretch out to an eternity before a hint of a smile creeps onto his face.

"But it's always good to have a backbone," he adds, chucking huskily.

He extends his hand and I stare at it in disbelief before slowly reaching out and shaking it firmly.

"Now"—he motions for the Crazy Brit to fetch the bound pitches—"we'll see how your work holds up with the Client."

He nods gruffly and then he's out the door. The Crazy Brit flashes me a bewildered glance before bolting after him.

Fifteen

It takes me another month to finally quit. It's actually a bit strange that the impulse should strike me now, when things are going better than they've gone in a very long time, the general mood jovial with golf season freshly upon us. But I guess it's the randomness of human nature that though the seeds were planted last month in the copy room, or even long before that, it's taken until this afternoon to burst through the ribbon at the end of this crazy detour.

The usual host of characters are packed into Boardroom 121 to discuss the next steps of the forestry mandate we won in the beauty contest: the Coldest Fish In The Pond, looking very much the part of an evil mastermind in a form-fitting black turtleneck; the Ice Queen, filing her nails under a pitch book; Tool #1, on the verge of passing out from the excitement of being staffed on his very first live deal; the rugged Client and two similarly salt-of-the-earth henchmen, eyeing us corporate types with much distrust. Across from me, the Crazy Brit scribbles his notes and peels back the wrapper of a Snickers bar with a sense of urgency. A fleck of caramel gets stuck in his front teeth; he checks to make sure the Client's attention is turned elsewhere before picking it out with a fingernail.

And then, without being fully cognizant of my own behavior, I've slunk out of the boardroom and I'm striding briskly toward the HR department. The Toad's office is an avalanche of paper waiting to happen, little piles threatening to take over every inch of counter space. The implied busyness is an illusion, of course, as a game of solitaire is reflected in the window. He startles as I rap on the door, and he picks up some loose papers and shuffles them around earnestly.

"Yes?"

"Do you have a moment?"

He eyes me as I close the door and take a seat. Then he squints knowingly, taking a sip of coffee before asking bluntly:

"Where are you going?"

"I'm not really sure."

"What do you mean, you're not sure? If you're off to another bank, then we're going to find out eventually."

"I'm not heading to another bank."

"Then which MBA program?"

"I'm not going back to school."

The Toad scratches his chin before switching gears, scowling as he leans across the desk.

"But that's just plain *stupid*. You're leaving a job where you're making great money to do *nothing*? Do you have any idea how tough the job market is right now?"

He waves a sheaf of papers right in my face.

"These are two dozen résumés I received just this week!"

Leaning back in the chair, gnawing on the eraser end of a pencil, he says, "The decision is yours, of course. But I warn you, there are hundreds of kids just itching to get their feet in the door and take your place."

The Toad is actually halfway decent at his position, honing in on your insecurities and exploiting them fully. If I wasn't so confident in my decision, I'd be crapping my pants right now. Nevertheless, I keep my voice calm and steady.

"I'm resigning. I want this to be my last day."

"Don't be a goddamn fool," the Toad snarls.

When he's accepted the fact that I'm not budging, he switches gears again, hands removed from behind his head. His tone changes ever so subtly, with a tinge of desperation now.

"Look, with the two new analysts who just started, and in light of the recent departures in your group, we really can't afford to lose somebody with M and A experience. So if it's a matter of money—"

"You can't pay me to stay."

The Toad forces a toothy grin, his voice lowering conspiratorially. "This is just between us, but I'm willing to offer you a five-thousand-dollar bonus on the spot."

I'm already rising from the chair.

"Ten thousand," he says.

"I'll be out of here by the end of the day."

"But, but," he sputters as I leave the room, "if you're not heading to a rival firm, then we require you to stay out the full two weeks—"

His voice drones on as I turn the corner and head back to the M & A department. Our office is empty: The Star is away in New Jersey on a due diligence trip, and the Defeated One is probably down on a coffee run. I begin by sweeping all the clutter on my desk into the trash can. A clean purge. No doubt if the Star ever escapes this place, he'll leave every last scrap of paper chronologically organized and color-coded. I've untacked the "Dilbert" cartoons and *Onion* articles from my message board, a small pile accumulating of the meager possessions I'll eventually take with me (my CD collection, three half-finished packs of gum, the rubber-band ball grown to the size of my fist, and a Bank paperweight), when I hear a voice from the doorway.

"Mumbles, what the hell is going on?"

The Defeated One strolls in with a Venti coffee and collapses in his chair. He swivels around to face me, wiggling his fingers together.

"Yeesssssss?"

"I . . ."

And with a cocked eyebrow, he's singlehandedly triggered my first feelings of apprehension since my departure from Boardroom 121.

"So, where are you heading off to?"

"I, uh, I'm not sure."

"Give it up, Mumbles. School, another job?"

I shrug. He leans back in the chair, chuckling.

"So, you're heading into the unknown, huh? You hate this place that much?"

I nod feebly. He stifles a yawn.

"I can't say I didn't see it coming. I'm surprised you didn't just finish off what you started in the copy room instead of sticking it out for another month."

"I'm really sorry."

"What do you have to be sorry about?"

"I mean, my ditching you like this— "

The Defeated One rolls his eyes and says, "Mumbles, that's absolute bullshit and you know it."

He rises from his chair and takes his jacket off the hook.

"Where are you going?" I ask.

"Where are *we* going. Come on, we have some final business to take care of."

I follow him into the elevator, through the lobby, and down a flight of stairs, until we're finally slumped at the bar of the Recessions Brewhouse, a dank little drinking hole tucked away in the basement of our office tower. The bartender, a jowly blond, shuffles over.

"Gentlemen?"

"Whatever you have on draft," the Defeated One says, taking out his wallet and winking at me.

What follows is a rare midafternoon boozing session, made all the more decadent with the knowledge of the soul-crushing tedium that is taking place thirty-two floors above us. Four pints in and we're comparing our battle scars under the Crazy Brit and the Sycophant. Six pints in and we're reminiscing about some of the better moments with Clyde and Postal Boy. Eight pints in and we're undisputedly shit-faced.

"Tell me again why we didn't do this when Postal left?" I slur.

"What can I say," the Defeated One says, then belches, clinking my glass. "You inspire greatness in people, Mumbles."

"And alcoholism."

We clink glasses again.

"It must be a great feeling, finally escaping this place."

"I'm not out the revolving doors just yet," I say and hiccup.

"You're on the homestretch, though."

The Defeated One orders us a fifth round. As we sip our pints thoughtfully, I ask, "Why are you sticking it out, then? I mean, you're a smart guy. Not clinically psychopathic like everybody else we work with. You could easily find something else."

"Not psychopathic? How sweet of you, Mumbles."

"Seriously, though, why haven't you tried finding something outside of the industry? Because I'll tell you, this shit is going to drive you insane."

The Defeated One nods, swigging his beer thoughtfully.

"It's fairly sadomasochistic, I'll give you that. But think of it like this: Investment banking, it's like boot camp for the corporate world. Can you imagine a regular nine-to-fiver after this? Piece of cake, right?"

We settle into a contemplative silence.

The Defeated One drains the last of his pint and says, "Anyway, don't worry about me. I'll be all right."

He slips on his jacket, wiping his mouth.

"Well, as much as I'd like to spend the rest of the afternoon drinking myself into oblivion, it's time for my return to the gallows. Are you coming back upstairs?"

"Nah. I brought all my stuff down with me."

He shakes his head in disbelief.

"So you're really out of here?"

"Yeah, I'm really out of here."

"Jesus."

"I know."

We take the stairs up to the lobby. There is an awkward moment when we're both unsure of how to bid our final farewells, eventually settling on a firm handshake followed by a quick clapping of each other's back. As he turns to the elevators, I call out:

"Wait."

I reach into a pocket and pull out the rubber-band ball, a year in the making, and toss it to him.

"Keep it."

"Aw," the Defeated One says, bouncing it in his palm, "you gave me your lucky ball. Your generosity is truly overwhelming."

"Hey, you better keep in touch."

He nods in agreement. We stand there for a bit, neither of us knowing how to prolong the conversation, before the Defeated One makes a clumsy retreat for the elevators, leaving me alone in the lobby. It's anticlimactic, I have to admit: no angels blaring their trumpets, no final movement of Wagner's *Ride of the Valkyries.* I stand there amid the chrome and the marble and the potted floral arrangements, trying to *force* the euphoria, to squeeze it out of my pores, but it's no use; there's only numbness.

Anyway, pushing through the revolving doors, stepping out into the sunlight, I'm not really all that concerned about it. I'm twenty-four, barely tainted, and things are about to change.

ten months later

Han's Blue Diamond Chinese Gourmet is a fungus of the downtown core, a grease-stained blot against the chrome landscape. Even now, when I'm crammed into a booth with the Defeated One and Postal Boy, nothing seems to have changed since we were last here over ten months ago: the crumpled Fanta cans in the corner, the dusty bottles of chili sauce lining the walls, a *Dukes of Hazzard* episode playing on the small black-and-white television above the counter. This immutable setting seems inappropriate for our first reunion since we parted ways, especially with Postal Boy transformed into a full-fledged Procter & Gamble drone:

"At the risk of sounding immodest, life is so fucking awesome right now. I just found out I'm being considered for a promotion to Brand Manager Level Four. I mean, *Level Four;* that's a full two levels above my current position. It's not the biggest pay increase, but I get to handle this sexy new dishwashing detergent launch. And that girl I mentioned before; she's moved in with me. Sweeeeet deal. We're talking steak and eggs at least twice a week for breakfast, boys. It's almost like I'm living with my mom or something," he snickers.

The Defeated One snorts, "Postal, don't force me to lean across the table and smack you goddamn silly."

He puts his hand to his heart and winces.

"Jesus, I forgot how this stuff burns when it goes down."

Postal Boy asks the Defeated One, "What about you, man? What have you been up to?"

The Defeated One gives a resounding belch before devouring another congealed lump of General Tso.

"Yeah, things are chugging along. My old lady has stopped with her whining now that I'm spending more time at home after starting up the MBA—"

"What the fuck? You're back in school already?" I ask.

I *knew* something was off with him: the healthy flush of his cheeks, his grin a little less insincere. And that means the bastard must have submitted his applications back in January, long before I left the Bank.

"There I was, stressing about quitting, worried for your sorry ass, and you had it all planned out, didn't you?" I shake a chopstick at him.

The Defeated One releases another burp.

"I was keeping it under wraps. Sorry, bud. Besides, if word got out, it would have wreaked havoc on my bonus."

"No excuses. You're still a jackass."

"And what's it like with you, Mumbles?" Postal Boy asks.

"Heh, from one cubicle to the next. Economic consulting for a small private firm. I've racked up seven months already."

"Econ consulting . . . what the fuck is that?" the Defeated One asks.

"I'm not too sure, honestly," I reply with a shrug.

"And you're doing what, specifically?"

I shrug again. “Spreadsheet bitch, part deux.”

I don’t particularly want to get into the details right now. How I was lured into consulting with the promise of billable hours, frothy cappuccinos away from my desk, and themed happy hours with imported Belgium beers and boozy assistants in the boardroom every Friday. How seven months later I’m struggling to keep my billing utilization over the bare minimum even pulling seventy-hour weeks, and Friday afternoon happy hours consist of nothing more than a few Pabst Blue Ribbons with the assistants who aren’t bogged down enough with work to chug them back. The Defeated One understands all of this without my having to verbalize it:

“Well, aren’t you just a glutton for punishment?”

“It’s in my blood, I guess. The eternal whipping boy.”

The Defeated One and Postal Boy exchange fleeting glances. I know I’m putting a damper on the intended mood of this reunion—*let us rejoice in how we’ve all moved on to bigger and better things!*—but I really can’t quell the self-pity at the moment.

“I mean, when does the cycle ever end? Is your whole life just careening from one desk to another until you’re retired in Palm Beach at age sixty-five, moping around a piss-warm swimming pool because you’ve forgotten what to do with your free time?”

The Defeated One rolls his eyes.

“Whatever, man,” I sneer. “You going back to school is just delaying the inevitable. A final stretch of freedom before you’re back to being a desk jockey.”

“On paper, yes. But I envision quite a different corporate existence from your own: a nice corner office with a door that shuts properly, a team of monkeys to do all the legwork, afternoons spent leaving little love bites on the thighs of my Scandinavian secretary. Or maybe Estonian; isn’t that where they ship them from nowadays?”

"Croatia," Postal Boy chimes in. Addressing me, he asks, "And what would you be doing otherwise, Mumbles? Sitting on your ass eating Doritos and watching *Price Is Right* reruns twenty-four/seven? Do you know how bored out of your mind you'd be? It's true what they say, that work is mankind's salvation. We're all corporate sluts at heart."

"Thanks for the sentiment, Postal."

It's a valid point, though—I have no idea how I'd be whiling away my time if I wasn't working right now. I lean back in the booth.

"Look, I'm not always this pessimistic. The consulting gig has just been especially rough recently, a few late nights, and Kate is already harping on me."

Postal Boy senses his opportunity to steer our conversation back to warmer pastures.

"She was that girl from Starbucks, right? The one with the scarf? Wasn't she supposed to head off to graduate school somewhere?"

"Yeah, she was considering Berkeley but then decided last-minute to stay in the city. She hasn't said anything outright, but I think she wanted to see if our relationship had any legs. Case in point—we moved in together last month."

"Really?" The Defeated One sticks his finger in the remains of the General Tso sauce and slurps it off with a satisfied grin. "Aw, it sounds like our very own Mumbles is in love. Isn't that just the cutest thing, like little naked mole rats rutting or somethin'."

"Piss off."

"You know you love it, dude."

Postal Boy is already scrambling out of the booth.

"Gents, sorry to break this up, but I've got to be back at my conference in five minutes. We're discussing brand-positioning strategies for the emerging markets. Sexy stuff. Get all those Indians using Tide."

"Your sexiness is killing me, Postal," the Defeated One says, frowning and sliding out behind him. "When are you next in town?"

"I'll be up over the Thanksgiving weekend."

"Should we try to meet up then?"

"Yeah, definitely."

As we leave, setting off the familiar electronic chime at Han's, the Defeated One nods gravely at me, speaking in all seriousness:

"Mumbles, the key is not to forget what it was like before. To appreciate how each cube is gradually getting better than the last. If you stick to that, you're going to be just fine."

♦

He's right, of course, though it's difficult to keep this relativity in check when I'm leaving the office at midnight for the third day in a row. The streets are desolately Gotham City–like at this hour: Steam puffs up from the open vents of the subway system, the Art Deco office lobbies are deserted, and the murky darkness is punctuated only by the odd streetlight or the faint glow of a Reuters ticker tape. I'm stopped at an intersection, waiting for the walk signal, when a tall figure approaches from my left.

"Hey, buddy."

I startle, turning my head. I'm expecting it to be one of the vagrants who patrol this neighborhood, hoping to score a few bucks from a Suit with a sudden burst of conscience, but closer inspection reveals it's none other than the Prodigal Son peering down at me, his face remarkably changed. He has the bloodshot eyes and sanguine pallor of a coke addict, a cold-sore at the side of his mouth, and a rash of pimples scattered across his forehead.

It comes out reflexively: "You look awful, man."

Don't get me wrong: Even in his zombified state, the Prodigal Son is still better-looking than I am, but the change is nonetheless a staggering one. The Prodigal Son, seemingly oblivious to his own deterioration, yawns.

"Pulled an all-nighter yesterday. I am so tired, dude. You just heading home from the office?"

"Yeah."

"What do you do now, anyway?"

"Econ consulting."

"Cool, cool," he says, nodding disinterestedly, sucking back phlegm. "And you're liking it?"

"It's all right."

"Great, man."

He horks onto the sidewalk and checks his watch in disgust.

"Fuck! Midnight already and I have to be back in the office at, like, six in the morning to prepare for a pitch. You know how it is."

"Yeah, I know the drill."

The light changes and we cross the street together in silence. I'm stealing sideways glances at his haggardness, still in a mild state of shock. At the opposite sidewalk, we quickly nod our good-byes.

"Good luck at your meeting tomorrow."

"Thanks. Have a good one, dude."

I'm still contemplating our brief encounter as I enter the plastic-plant-filled lobby of my apartment building and pass the ancient elevator with the grille door in a state of perpetual disrepair, before embarking on the four-floor climb up to our apartment. I enter the apartment, panting for breath, to a scene of domicile bliss: Kate reclined on the couch reading one of her textbooks and reaching for her mug of herbal tea. She looks up as I hang my coat in the closet.

"Hey, I made some stir-fry for dinner, with the ginger sauce that you like. There's some left in the fridge if you're still hungry."

I cross the room and kiss her forehead. She scoots over on the couch, making space for me.

"Muchas gracias," I mumble into her ear, nibbling on the lobe. "I'm really sorry I'm coming home so late again."

She closes her textbook and puts it on the side table.

"I had some studying to do, so don't worry about it. I really needed the peace and quiet."

"So, you think I'm a disruptive presence, huh?"

"Only when I want you to be," she says, grinning, pulling me down on top of her.

We're rolling around on the couch, Kate fumbling with the clasp of my belt, when suddenly I'm laughing uncontrollably, and once I've started, I just can't stop. She cocks her eyebrow in bemusement, but I have no way of explaining the images suddenly flitting before me: the Prodigal Son sprawled on his couch smoking some freebase; Postal Boy with a crooked tie, taking a bow before aisles and aisles of Swiffers; the Defeated One traipsing through a field of sunflowers, a snapshot of absolute contentment.

My laughter subsides finally, and now I'm staring at Kate hovering above me, her small mouth puckered in a half-smile, and I'm *seeing* the life we can share together: returning home from our respective offices, me loosening my tie and Kate taking off her heels, a leisurely glass of wine as we chop up vegetables for a stir-fry, some soft conversation, no pressing need to fill the quiet spaces, then sprawled out on the couch watching a *Simpsons* rerun, her breath warm against my chest.

"I just want you to know," I say, tracing her cheekbone with a finger, "that I'm so unbelievably grateful you stayed behind in the city. That you're making this all possible for me. If I could only just grasp this always, not let everything else get in the way all the time— ”

“Shhh,” she says, putting a finger to my lips. “You don’t have to verbalize any of it.”

“All right,” I say. “But just know that I— ”

“Shhh,” she says. grinning.

Then she draws my head into her lap and strokes my ears, lulling me deeper into this life we are creating.

♦

From: TheStar@theBank.com
To: Me@gmail.com, Clyde@yahoo.com,
TheDefeatedOne@wharton.edu, PostalBoy@pg.com

Hey, hope I got the e-mails correct—how are you guys doing? I know we weren't all that tight or anything, but I have to say, it's not quite the same here without you. The Tools are on the stupid side, though there's this new girl who just started up with a lot of potential. And the Prodigal Son is picking up some of the slack, but he's an Excel moron (still has the Daddy connection working for him, though). Bonuses came and went and they were better than usual. I think the Toad was getting scared with all the mice fleeing the ship and decided to juice things up a bit. And you'll be happy to hear the Sycophant got denied a promotion yet again. And get this: The Philanderer fired the Utterly Incompetent Assistant earlier this week on grounds of "gross misconduct." The rumor is that she stopped putting out. Entirely plausible. Anyway, you guys aren't going to believe it: apparently she found the CD with our xxx-mas party montage while cleaning out the Defeated One's cube (can't trace it to me, thank god). It must have been my drive—and not the CD—that was corrupt before, because she was able to extract the movie. Check out her farewell message:

»From: TheUtterlyIncompetentAssistant@theBank.com
»To: All Employees

»Some things you should know before I leave:

»- The Philanderer wears zebra print g-strings. Not
»suitable under the best of circumstances, but even worse
»with a flabby ass!!!!!
»- Those 900 numbers on his expense report are *not*

»research analyst conference calls!!!

»- Speaking of office debauchery, here's a fun little video

»for your viewing pleasure

»(www.bank.com/intranet/boardroomromp.mpg). Warning: not

»suitable for small children!!!!!

»Enjoy!!!!!!!!!

acknowledgments

A special thanks to Matt McGowan, my agent, a man of zealous faith; Helen Atsma, my editor, for an enthusiasm that rivaled my own; Kyla Epstein, Jenn Baka, and Deepa Nayak, who delivered their lashings when they were needed most; and Justin Bledin, my embryo buddy, for invaluable assistance and the title.

BACK BAY · READERS' PICK

BANK

a novel by

david bledin

Reading Group Guide

i-BANKed

FROM CUBICLE DRUDGERY TO LITERARY ENDEAVOR

The story of *Bank*'s genesis has a fitting analogy in the song "One Little Goat." This crowd-pleaser, sung at the end of a Passover Seder, is about a kid that gets eaten by a cat that gets bitten by a dog that gets hit by a stick that gets burned by fire that gets doused by water that gets drunk by an ox that gets slaughtered by a butcher who gets killed by the Angel of Death, etc., etc. "One Little Goat" is an illustration of cause and effect, proving that if you hang around baby goats too much, the Angel of Death is really going to stick it to you (be warned, you Amish types!). Likewise, *Bank* came into being through a random chain of cause and effect, beginning with a mass e-mail I sent out after six months of working at an investment bank.

It was supposed to be a cathartic experience, a chance to rant and rave and explain to my friends and family why I had seemingly disappeared off the face of the planet. The e-mail was given the brilliantly original subject header "A Day in the Life of an Investment Banker," and it was that, more or less:

11:25 a.m. Starbucks.
12:30 p.m. Finish binding 60 pitch books.
12:45 p.m. The Defeated One is skimming through the Daily M&A Activity Update. It's from the IT guy; he amalgamates all the porn blocked by the servers and sends it out to the junior employees. The Defeated One has just enough time to close a picture of two midgets doing disproportionate acrobatics with a pylon before Utterly Incompetent Assistant comes by, asking if she can help with the binding. There are two very obvious towers of pitch books beside me.
1:20 p.m. Sycophant wants two sections of the books reversed.
1:25 p.m. Utterly Incompetent Assistant gone to read the latest Shopaholic novel on her two-hour lunch break. Unbind the 60 pitch books.
1:45 p.m. Rebind the 60 pitch books.

Despite these modest intentions, sending out the e-mail triggered its own sequence of events: my friends forwarding it to their friends; the e-mail getting into the hands of Samantha Grice, a reporter at the *National Post,* who thought it would be interesting to turn it into an article on white-collar sweatshop labor; the article being published on the front page of the Arts section of that paper (including a caricature of my stick-out ears); the online version of the article being linked to by blogs around the world, aboriginal tribesmen clicking and clacking about a young i-banker's all-nighters; this click-clack chatter eventually reaching the ears of Matt McGowan at the Frances Goldin Literary Agency, who posed it to me this way:

"Dave, I can't promise you anything, and it's going to be tons of work, but hey, it could be fun to turn this e-mail of yours into a novel."

Considering that choosing a career based on actually getting paid hadn't accomplished much more than a sterile apartment, a sore wrist, and expensive dinners to stall the slow but certain death of all happiness in my life, I couldn't see the harm in putting some pro bono effort into Matt's suggestion. Plus, I had just decided to quit banking and pursue a second bout of cubicles in a less time-consuming position as an economic consultant.

If there's one thing I've learned through all of this, it's that you've got to be crazy to write a book. It's true: Something about you just can't be quite right. Otherwise, why would someone spend limitless hours typing away, grappling with syntax, fleshing out the inner psyche of Postal Boy, all for a sliver of possibility that he'd eventually get published?

But the reward, the sweet, sweet reward: finding that final resting place for your book. Seeing your name above an elegant image of an upturned finger. Knowing that your late-night typing is going to piss off a hell of a lot of people, people who you want to be pissed off. Forget Confucius: Vengeance is a wonderful thing.

Questions for Discussion — and Activities — Guaranteed to Result in the Disbanding of Your Reading Group

1. Discuss your childhood dreams and aspirations. The rest of the group should then discuss how your current career path ensures that these dreams will never, ever, be realized.

2. In *Bank,* Postal Boy has a nervous breakdown. Have you ever had a nervous breakdown? If so, were you put on medication? Distribute any antipsychotics you might have. Remember, sharing is caring.

3. At one point, Mumbles finds himself in the compromising position of having his fingers tangled in the panties of a colleague's wife. Have you ever had an affair with someone at work? Did you get an STD as a result? (This one works best if there are couples in your reading group.)

4. As bad as things get, some folks always have it worse. Select the group member whose job is so awful that you would never consider it, not even if threatened with weird Chinese torture involving stalks of bamboo and live rats.

5. Let's face it: the longer you spend in a cube, the flabbier your ass gets. Identify the group members who have put on the most pounds since college and make them finish off the bowl of Cheetos while somebody tickles their belly rolls.

6. Mumbles feels physically inadequate when he compares himself to the Prodigal Son. Divide into groups of two and determine the superiority or inferiority of each other's body parts.

7. Investment banking is an industry in which importance is directly correlated with how much money one makes. Group members should write their salaries on strips of paper and toss them into a hat. The group should then try to match each salary with each participant. The person with the highest perceived salary must go on a beer run; the person with the lowest perceived salary should be left to grapple with his or her own inner shame.